He kissed her as there was no ton

Her perfume was in hi__
dizzy. Drawing him. Irr_____. Matt pressed his lips
to her hair, lingered there, exquisite sensations
rippling through him. He pressed his lips to her brow,
then to her cold cheek. And she tilted her face so he
could find her mouth.

Blair's lips were cold but the fever burning between
them was hot. She was eager and as desperate as he.
Her chilled fingers were pressed to his cheeks. She
felt so light, so fragile…and he wanted her so badly
he trembled.

He could feel the swell of her breasts against his
chest. It felt like heaven. This was heaven. A few
minutes ago, when he'd been so afraid for her; afraid
she would never regain consciousness, he'd thought
he was in hell. Now, in his arms, he had everything
he wanted in life.

Dear Reader

Welcome to Intrigue™ and your favourite type of hero: he's handsome, he's protective and he's the kind of man you would want to be with in a dangerous situation!

In *The Runaway Bride*, professional bodyguard Jake Wilder comes face-to-face with the woman who left him at the altar a year before. But when she claims someone is trying to kill her, can he walk away and leave her in danger? Joanna Wayne's hero this month is Ray Kostner who also meets a lover from his past. Jodie Gahagen is a woman with secrets. She's being threatened by a stalker and she has never told Ray about his twin baby boys!

For those of you who have been waiting for the second in the **McCullar Brothers** series, *Whisper My Love* is as heart-stopping and suspenseful as the first book. This month, gorgeous Rio Delgado comes home only to find himself framed for a crime he didn't commit. And finally Grace Green brings us an irresistible millionaire who is *The Only Man to Trust*.

Happy Reading!

The Editors

The Only Man To Trust

GRACE GREEN

™ SILHOUETTE
INTRIGUE™

Silhouette and Colophon are registered trademarks of Harlequin Books S.A., used under licence.

First published in Great Britain 1999
Silhouette Books, Eton House, 18-24 Paradise Road,
Richmond, Surrey TW9 1SR

© Grace Green 1998

ISBN 0 373 22476 1

46-9904

Printed and bound in Spain
by Litografia Rosés S.A., Barcelona

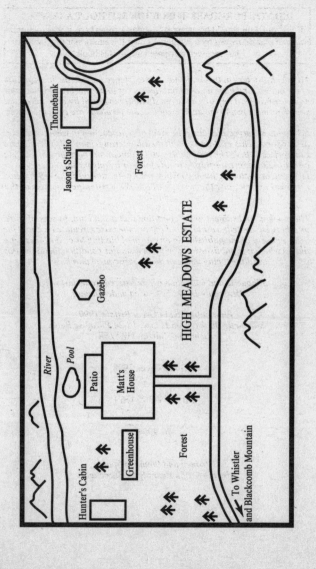

HIGH MEADOWS ESTATE

Thornebank

Jason's Studio

Forest

River

Pool

Gazebo

Patio

Matt's House

Hunter's Cabin

Greenhouse

Forest

To Whistler
and Blackcomb Mountain

For Ron Hannay

Prologue

March 15, *Vancouver Sun*

Police Call Off Search For Missing Socialite

At a news conference in Whistler, B.C. yesterday, RCMP announced they have called off their search for Meredith Straith, thirty-year-old wife of international hotelier Matt Straith. The socialite disappeared five days ago while skiing on Blackcomb Mountain. Though there is no evidence of foul play, police have not discounted that possibility.

June 18, Cougar Mountain, British Columbia

THE MAN TOUCHED the ivory-handled razor in his pocket and felt excitement burn through him like raw whiskey. With the smell of damp earth and rotting pine needles in his nostrils, he pressed his brow close to the windowpane and locked his glittering gaze on the woman inside the cabin.

She was seated on a sheepskin rug at the hearth, her arms looped around her knees, her back a graceful arc. The only light in the room came from the flickering fire—an eerie light that danced over her waist-length blond hair and outlined her frail figure.

She could have no idea she was being watched. The rage of the storm had drowned out the throb of his engine as he drove up the abandoned logging road, and the rain lashing down from the black-bellied clouds blotted out the moon.

Dragging his booted feet from the sucking mud, he moved along the path to the door. The wind howled over the rusty squeak of the knob as he turned it and moaned over the faint click as he closed it.

She didn't become aware of his presence until he was halfway across the room.

She jerked her head up suddenly, her beautiful cornflower blue eyes flashing wide with panic, a strangled scream erupting from her throat.

He smiled as she scrambled to her feet.

"It's just me," he said. "Did I startle you?"

"Yes." Her voice shook, as did the fingers she threaded through her long hair.

"But you're pleased to see me?"

"You *know* I am."

Water dripped from his jacket sleeve as he reached out and unbuttoned her silk shirt. He heard her breath hitch, but she didn't protest as he slipped the shirt off and let it fall to the floor.

She was wearing no bra. He let his gaze drift hungrily over her.

"Did you miss me?" His tone was thick.

"You *know* I did—"

"Take off your jeans."

Her pale cheeks became flushed. But she obeyed.

He put his hands on her shoulders, barely noticing the yellowing bruises on the smooth, milk-white skin.

His fingers were chilled. Her flesh was hot. Hot from the fire. He slid the cold fingers over her breasts, his fingertips lingering on the puckered nipples, teasing.

Her breath caught on a tight gasp.

"Tell me," he commanded, "that you love me."

"You *know* I do—"

He cupped her breasts aggressively. "Say it."

"I love you," she whispered.

"And want me."

"And want you…"

In a swift movement he released her breasts and swept her long hair to one side. He held the tangled bulk of it in one large hand. "I've read—" his voice had become subtly mocking, as if they shared some secret joke "—that it's not unusual for a kidnapped woman to fall in love with her captor. It's a…phenomenon. It has a name. I can't remember it." With his other hand, he dug into his jacket pocket and brought out the ivory-handled razor.

She stared at it, her eyes stark with shock. "What—"

"Hush, my darling." He flicked open the razor and pressed the flat of the ice-cold blade to the side of her throat. He unzipped his jeans, and the muscles in his arms rippled as he took her down to the floor. "I promise you, this is not going to hurt."

June 19, *Vancouver Sun*

Missing Socialite Turns Up Alive

Meredith Straith is back home today at High Meadows, the family's luxurious Whistler estate. Straith was picked up last night by RCMP after a hiker spotted her wandering along an abandoned logging road on Cougar Mountain. Straith is suf-

fering from amnesia, and so far has been unable to
assist RCMP in their ongoing investigation.

STRAITH'S HUSBAND WAS at the Whistler WhitePeak
Hotel when the news broke. On being asked by reporters if his wife's return would remove the suspicion he's
been under for the past three months, his response was
a grim, "No comment."

Chapter One

Someone is trying to kill me. I'm almost sure of it. Blair, please come to High Meadows and stay for a few days. You were always so levelheaded—you'll be able to tell if I'm just imagining things. I know we've lost touch, but there's no one else I can trust—

Blair Enderby's thoughts, as she drove her four-year-old Camry along the quiet country road, were so intensely focused on the letter tucked in her crimson leather bag that she almost missed the turnoff. The sign at the roadside seemed to loom up out of nowhere.

"Damn!" Swiftly checking her rearview mirror, Blair wrenched the steering wheel to her left. Brakes squealed, tires skidded, and her front bumper grazed the grassy bank. And then, pulse shot all to hell, she continued on her way along a narrow paved drive with evergreen forests stretching on either side and beyond, in the distance, the snowcapped peaks of the Coastal Mountains jutting raggedly into the heat-hazed summer sky.

She'd been uptight since she left Vancouver a couple of hours before. Now, as she drew ever closer to the Straith family home, her hands were white-knuckled on the steering wheel.

High Meadows.

A lovely name for a lovely house. She'd seen pictures of it in the newspapers.

But what dangers lurked there?

Meredith had always been too fanciful by far—yet within twenty-four hours of posting her desperate plea to Blair, she'd gone missing. Blair had heard about her disappearance on TV days before the letter reached her. And Meredith had remained missing for three whole months. Where had she been? How much did she remember? Was her memory spotty—or had it gone completely? Media reports hadn't been too clear in that regard. But surely she would recall having invited Blair to come for a visit and would understand why Blair hadn't been able to respond earlier. She'd come as soon as she could, and better late than never.

Blair shivered. It was going to be awkward, after their long estrangement, seeing her onetime friend again.

Seeing Matt again was going to be something else.

But Meredith had asked her for help, so how could she refuse?

Besides, the whole scenario—the letter, the disappearance, the husband under suspicion—was so intriguing she couldn't possibly turn her back on it.

She gave a short, self-derisive laugh. After all, as a freelance writer she put bread on her table by writing about people. Other people...and their private lives.

"DAMMIT, MEREDITH, you've got to see somebody!" Matt Straith fisted his hands on his hips and battled to control his rising frustration. "How long can we go on like this?"

"Oh, not again, darling!" The blond woman lounging gracefully by the heart-shaped pool made a bored moue. "You know I don't believe in shrinks. Besides, amnesia usually happens when something is so awful a person blocks it out, and the experts say it can be dangerous to try to dig up such suppressed memories." She shuddered. "I was gone for three months, Matt. Lord knows what happened to me during that time. As far as I'm concerned, this is one case where ignorance truly *is* bliss."

"You won't even see a doctor! We don't even know if you were—" He broke off, cursing under his breath, wishing he hadn't started this confrontation.

"Darling, rape isn't a four-letter word. Well, it is, actually, isn't it. But I assure you I'd know if that had happened to me. A woman would just...know. It didn't." She peeked at him from below her long blond lashes. "Is that why you've been behaving like a monk since I got home? You think I'm used goods now?"

Used goods. Yes, she was used goods...but she'd become that way long before her disappearance, only he hadn't found out until the night before she went missing. Then they'd had that unholy argument....

He avoided answering her question directly. "I just want you to get well," he said. "Once you are, we'll get our lives back in order again."

She threw off her wrap and pushed to her feet. She was still as beautiful as she'd been on their wedding day, Matt thought dispassionately, even though, sometime during the three months she'd been missing, her hair had been crudely hacked off to within an inch of her scalp. And though he no longer loved her, when he'd seen the mutilation he'd been appalled. Of all his wife's vanities, her greatest had been her hair, the silky blond tresses that had cascaded like moonlit rain down her back. *Who did that to you?* he'd demanded, fury

reverberating in his voice. She'd waved a hand weakly.
She couldn't remember—just as she couldn't remember
who had starved her until she was rake thin, just as she
couldn't remember who had inflicted the bruises on her
arms.

As soon as she'd felt up to it, Matt had summoned
stylist Alain Dumot from the beauty salon of his Whistler hotel. Within an hour, the French artiste had trans-
formed his longtime client from street urchin to sleek
sophisticate, the stark perfection of the new cut accentuating her exquisitely shaped skull. And since her return, she'd been eating reasonably well and had regained some weight. Anyone looking at her now might
think her three-month ordeal had left her virtually un-
scathed.

"Do my back, darling?" She held out a tube of Lan-
côme sunblock.

As their eyes met, Matt felt as if someone was running an ice cube slowly down his spine. Though her
cornflower blue gaze was wide, it was almost as if it
consisted of two layers, the top layer innocent as a
child's, the second layer dark with cunning. Shaken, he
took the tube from her and thought he saw the edges of
her mouth curve in a sly smile. Before he could be sure,
she'd swiveled and presented her shoulders to him. Automatically, he squeezed a large blob of lotion onto the
pale skin and with brusque movements swept the
creamy liquid over her back.

"There." He clicked the lid on again. "That's it."

She took the tube, tossed it onto the patio table.
"Darling—" her voice was husky "—I know it's difficult for you with this amnesia business, and it's not
easy for me, either. Though I don't remember much, I
just *know* that what we had together was very special."

Before he could step away, she'd raised her arms and looped them tightly around his neck. Her fingers delved into his full black hair, and her rich Oriental perfume invaded his nostrils like some potent but unwelcome drug. She arched her scantily clad body against him in a seductive way that made him grit his teeth. He was not an animal, thank God, or her blatantly erotic invitation would have been easy to accept.

He'd rather be thrown into a pit of snakes than have sex with this woman again.

FIFTY FEET AWAY, at the far end of a wide lawn skirted by dark forest, stood a gazebo. From its shadowy interior, concealed by the leaves and fragrant scarlet flowers of a recently transplanted climbing rose, someone watched. Grimly, and through fast-rising anger.

With taut fingers, the man grasped the waist-high cedar railing in front of him. The veins in his arms bulged, extended close to bursting point by the pounding pressure of his blood. Bitch! She was acting flirtatiously, provocatively—and the longer he watched, the more out-of-control he felt, but still he couldn't keep his eyes off her. It was her hair. She looked sexy as hell with it cropped that way, short as a boy's.

But she was no boy, not with those taunting blue eyes, not with that hot little body.

Jealousy surged inside him with the violence of an attacking Doberman as she arched erotically against her companion.

He hissed out an oath. Straith would have to die. He hadn't planned on killing him yet, but the way things were going...well, that changed things. He didn't want to wait any longer. The sooner the better...and to hell with the risk. He'd take his chances.

BLAIR STEPPED from the Camry and slammed the door. The sound echoed from the mountains. The air up here was as thin and clear as the finest crystal. Whistler was more than two thousand feet above sea level. The road she had followed from there had climbed most of the way, except for the final short descent that had brought her here, to High Meadows, set in a narrow valley.

The scent of roses and cut grass wafted to her on the breeze, but the pleasant fragrances did nothing to soothe her jangled nerves as she walked across the gravel forecourt to the white mansion. A balcony wrapped itself around the second story, but when Blair glanced up, sparkling windowpanes threw back sunshine, almost blinding her.

She rang the doorbell. The door was opened by a stout middle-aged woman with reddish hair.

She addressed Blair through the screen door. "Yes?"

"Hi." Blair smiled. "I've come to visit the Straiths…either Mr.…or Mrs., or both."

"Who shall I say is calling?"

"I'd like it to be a surprise."

"Wait here, please." With sturdy steps, the house-keeper walked away.

After a brief hesitation, Blair quietly opened the screen door. The soles of her sneakers made almost inaudible padding sounds on the floor as she followed the housekeeper across the foyer and through an archway into what turned out to be a dining room.

Across the way was a patio door, and just as the woman reached to open it, Blair saw them.

Meredith and Matt. She in a yellow bikini, he in a pair of navy trunks. They were locked in an embrace, their bodies melded so close it left nothing to the imagination.

Blair felt something in her heart snap, and then she felt a tearing pain. It was still there, then, the intense attraction she'd felt for him when she was eighteen. She'd hoped and she'd prayed that after ten long years it would have fizzled away and died.

The housekeeper opened the patio's screen door.

Blair saw Matt draw Meredith's hands from around his neck, then casually turn. As he did, Meredith's soft laugh filtered clearly to Blair's ears. She had heard that mocking sound thousands of times before. It took her back to their teenage years and brought goose bumps to her skin. Rubbing her prickling forearms, she watched, unable to tear her gaze away, as Meredith sauntered toward the pool, her curvy little hips wiggling in that old familiar way that had driven every teenage boy in Byng Secondary School crazy. Raising her arms gracefully, the blonde speared from a low diving board into the deep end with barely a splash to mark her entry.

Inhaling a very deep breath, Blair walked forward.

MATT'S FEELINGS of fury shocked him. He'd been about to rip his wife's arms savagely from around his neck when—thank God!—the sound of the screen door opening had put a brake on his actions. Gathering all his self-control, he'd been able to steady his response. But her softly mocking laugh had inflamed him again, almost making him lose it completely. He hadn't realized until that moment just how much he despised her.

Relaxing the tautly coiled muscles in his belly, he arranged his features in a neutral expression and turned to see the housekeeper stepping from the dining room.

"Excuse me, Mr. Straith, you have a visitor. She didn't want to give her name…"

As she spoke, someone appeared behind her. A

woman. In her late twenties, Matt guessed, and—the thought was involuntary—a looker. Dark-haired and lightly tanned, she had a lovely piquant face and huge gray eyes fringed by a mass of thick sable lashes. Her white cotton shirt and crimson walking shorts revealed an athletic figure and long, nicely shaped legs. On her feet she was wearing a pair of white sneakers, and over her shoulder was slung a crimson bag.

"It's me, Matt," she said quietly. "Blair Enderby."

"Miss," the housekeeper huffed indignantly, "I asked you to remain outside—"

"Blair?" Matt did a double take. "Good lord, this is—" He sliced a hand in an open, I-can't-believe-it gesture. "Aileen, it's all right." He kept staring at Blair as if he thought she might be a mirage and if he blinked, she'd disappear. In the end, he did glance away from her, briefly, to address the housekeeper. "Would you make us a fresh jug of iced tea, or—" he faced Blair "—would you prefer something stronger?"

"Nothing for me, thanks."

"That'll be all then, Aileen."

The housekeeper dragged the screen door shut behind her.

"She's new," Matt said, his eyes on Blair, taking her in, every detail. "The old housekeeper—Jeannie Chang—retired in April. When Meredith was…gone… she decided it would be a good time to retire. I hired Aileen a few weeks ago. So far, it seems to be working out just fine, and—" He stopped short, raked back his black hair and grinned ruefully. "I'm babbling. Not like me, is it, but you've taken me completely by surprise."

"Matt." Blair closed the space between them, put out her hands. "It's good to see you."

He took her hands in his and grasped them firmly. His green eyes were clear, his skin tanned, his wide chest sprinkled with filament-thin black hair—

Blair's heart gave a warning judder, and she dragged her gaze to his face—the face that had once filled her dreams. But it had no place there now, she warned herself, even as her wayward mind marveled anew at its incredibly beautiful structure.

"Blair—it's been ten years! Last time I saw you—"

"Was when I was bridesmaid at your wedding." She somehow kept her voice steady, though that day had been the darkest of her life. "And then we lost touch."

"It shouldn't have happened." Matt's eyes had become serious. "And I don't know how the hell it did."

Blair laughed lightly. "I was busy learning how to be a journalist, and you were busy building your empire—"

"Now out of the blue, you're here. Why, Blair?"

Blair scrambled to come up with an answer. When she'd taken Meredith's letter to the police on learning of her disappearance, the officer she'd talked to had told her to tell no one about it. So a half-truth, Blair decided, was what she would give Matt.

"I just got back from an extended trip to England, and when I discovered Meredith had turned up, but with amnesia, I wanted to offer my help. We were close friends from when we were toddlers until you and she got married. If there are any gaps in her memory from those days, I thought perhaps I could help her fill them in."

Meredith surged from the pool in a flurry of foam and lithely pulled herself onto the deck. Riffling her fingers through her cropped hair, scattering water over the pool's tiled apron, she strolled to the patio.

"Hi." She fixed her gaze on Blair as she bent and left-handedly scooped a towel from one of the lounge chairs. Patting her face dry, she said, "Who's your friend, Matt?"

Blair felt an odd prickling at her nape as she looked into Meredith's blue eyes and was met by a blank stare of nonrecognition.

"This is Blair Enderby," Matt said. "We haven't seen her since we got married, but before that, you and she used to be great friends."

For four heartbeats the slender hand patting the oval face with the yellow towel became absolutely still. Then it moved again. Matt's wife gave her skin a few quick pats on her cheeks, her brow, under her chin before tossing the towel down.

"So—" she slanted her lips in a cool smile "—sounds as if my marriage broke up our friendship. Now I wonder why that was? Were you jealous because Matt took me away from you, or were you perhaps in love with him yourself?" Her laugh had a melodious sound that was distinctly at odds with the mischief-making glint in her eyes.

Matt glowered at her. "For God's sake, Meredith—"

"Oh, darling, I'm sorry!" She grimaced. "I seem to have acquired a new habit of saying the very first thing that comes into my mind before I think it through." She tilted her head archly at Blair. "Forgive me, Blair—Matt did say Blair, didn't he?—if I've embarrassed you. I'll take myself off to my studio now and let the two of you catch up. You must have a lot of ground to cover, if you haven't seen each other for ten years. And since my own past is more or less lost to me, you and I would have nothing in common any longer." She swept up her wrap. "Where do you live?"

"Vancouver."

"You drove up this afternoon?"

"That's right."

"It's a busy road; I don't imagine you'll want to be leaving too late. Darling—" she turned to Matt "—don't forget we have to go to Jason's for dinner." There wasn't a whit of warmth in her eyes as she shifted them briefly in Blair's direction. "Goodbye. Have a safe trip back." She whirled and was gone before Blair could respond.

Blair felt a surge of resentment—resentment mingled with frustration. Idiot, she chastised herself. Why had she come here? At the very least, she should have phoned first, talked with Meredith…and perhaps saved herself this public humiliation. Taking a moment to calm herself, she walked to the edge of the patio and stood with her back to Matt, her blurred gaze settling on a cedar gazebo at the far side of the lawn, its angular lines softened by rambling roses.

She'd tried to imagine how it would be, seeing the two of them together again, but she'd never envisaged a situation as unpleasant as this. Since Meredith had no memory of the old days, for her to have suggested Blair had been in love with Matt could only have been a shot in the dark, yet to have it put into words was the last thing Blair needed. She hadn't wanted Matt to know how she'd felt about him ten years ago, and she didn't want him to know now.

"Blair—"

As he spoke, Blair thought she saw someone move in the gazebo behind the leaves of the rambling rose-bush. And she was suddenly visited by the very disturbing sensation that someone was hiding there. Skulking. Watching.

With malevolent intent.

A shiver scraped like sandpaper over her nerves. Was *this* the kind of thing that had alarmed Meredith? Alarmed her to such an extent she'd believed someone wished to kill her? Blair felt a strong urge to race over to the gazebo and investigate. But instead, she gave herself a mental shake. Meredith was the one whose mind had always soared off into flights of fancy, Blair the one who had kept her feet firmly on the ground.

And she, at least, had not changed in that regard.

Somewhere inside the house, a phone rang.

She turned. "Matt, how much does Meredith remember?"

"Nothing at all of her childhood—nothing actually until the last year or so, and even then only bits and pieces. She had no problem recognising me, but she has absolutely no recollection of the period during which she was missing or of the weeks immediately preceding her disappearance."

"Are there any clues at all as to where she was during those three months?"

"None. She just seemed to vanish off the face of the earth."

"Tell me what you know."

He shrugged. "I don't know much. She went skiing on Blackcomb with a couple of friends, and when it was time to leave, the other women couldn't find her. She'd said something earlier about having a headache, so they assumed she'd taken off on her own. But when the ski hills closed that night, her car was still in the parking lot—and one of the ski patrol members recognized it. When he checked and found out she'd never arrived home, he notified the police."

"After five days, according to the newspapers, the search was called off."

"That's right. And Meredith remembers nothing at all of—"

"Matt?" Meredith's voice came from behind them.

She was standing in the dining room, making no attempt to open the door. But even through the screen, Blair could see that her face was deathly pale—as pale as the white dress she was wearing.

Matt frowned. "What's wrong?"

"The phone rang." Meredith's tone was expressionless. "I picked it up..."

"Who was it?"

"A man. He didn't give his name, and I didn't recognize his voice—"

"What did he want?" Matt sounded impatient.

"He asked me to give you a message. He said—" her voice caught on a quiver "—he said you'd displeased him greatly by not responding to his ransom notes—"

"Ransom notes? What the hell are you talking about?"

"And now you're going to have to pay." She took in a shaky breath. "But not with money."

"Meredith, there *were* no ransom notes!"

"He's going to kill you, Matt." The screen door rattled as she pressed her hands against it and stared at him with shocked eyes. "He said he's going to kill you."

The sound of Meredith's long fingernails scratching slowly down the metal mesh screen grated on Blair's nerves. But even as she winced, she realized with a stab of horror that the other woman was crumpling, bonelessly, to the dining room's polished parquet floor.

Chapter Two

Matt wrenched the door open and stepped over his wife's inert body.

Blair stumbled to the patio door, appalled at what had transpired, and watched Matt scoop the lifeless figure up in his arms, the knife-pleated skirt of Meredith's white dress fanning down like the wings of a graceful bird.

Matt took off across the dining room with Blair just a few steps behind him. He crossed the hall and mounted the circular staircase, and Blair reached the landing just in time to see him disappear through an open doorway to the left. When she got there, he was depositing his wife on a canopied four-poster bed that dominated the room—a very feminine room, decorated in silver and blue.

Blair moved to the end of the bed as Matt drew a duvet over Meredith's slender figure. Features grimly set, he stepped back and looked at the blonde's face. At that moment, her lashes flickered and her eyelids drifted open.

Her gaze was cloudy, but it focused almost instantly when she saw Matt. Fear leaped into her eyes. And with shaking fingers, she dragged the duvet to her chin.

"Matt!" Her voice had a panicky edge. "The ransom notes…why didn't you—I don't understand. It's not as if you don't have the money—"

"For God's sake, Meredith, I told you I didn't get any ransom notes! Look, I'm going to call Dr. Axelrod—"

"No!" Meredith shoved herself up on her elbow, and her face had a frightening gray sheen to it. "I won't see him. I won't see any doctors. I thought I'd made that clear!"

Matt expelled a harsh sigh. "Then I'll get you something to drink. Hot tea with lots of sugar…that's probably what the doctor would order—"

"I'll get it, Matt," Blair offered.

Meredith jerked her head. "You're still here?"

The hostility in her voice hit Blair like a blow. Swaying, she put a steadying hand on the bedpost.

Matt must have noticed her reaction. He guided her to a wicker chair by the bedside table. "Sit down." His tone brooked no argument. "I think Meredith's not the only one who could do with a cup of strong tea."

And with that, he strode from the room.

HE HAD TO GET OUT of there before he exploded.

He went straight to the dining room and poured himself a Scotch. Tossing it back in one gulp, he felt it sear his throat, burn his gut. But it helped control the rage that had broken loose inside him when he'd seen the fear in Meredith's eyes, heard the accusation in her voice.

There were no ransom notes. At least, he'd never received any. And he couldn't imagine that a kidnapper smart enough to spirit a woman from the Blackcomb Mountain ski slopes without a trace wouldn't also be smart enough to ensure his ransom notes would reach their destination.

But Meredith had already judged and condemned him.

Dammit, how could his life have taken such a twist onto this pathway to hell! Bad enough to have found out what he had about Meredith in March. That had almost undone him. Bad enough to have had her disappear, sending him crazy with worry. Bad enough that he'd been under a cloud of suspicion during the whole three months she'd been missing.

But now, when she was safely home, he was on the kidnapper's hit list!

Abstractedly, he rolled his empty glass in his hands as he tried to figure out how the man's mind was working.

But no matter how many scenarios he came up with, they all evaporated like mist in the sun when he examined them, because everything hinged on the answer to one crucial question. Had the kidnapper set Meredith free or had she managed to escape? Meredith knew, but the information lay deep in her subconscious. And without that knowledge, Matt had nothing substantial on which to base his suppositions.

Yet it surely wasn't logical that the kidnapper would have released her. Even if he'd known at the time that Meredith was suffering from amnesia, he could never be sure she wouldn't eventually regain her memory and nail him.

But if she'd escaped, wouldn't she be the one on his hit list? Wouldn't he feel it imperative to silence her? After all, he'd held her captive for three months. Surely she must have seen him while she was imprisoned, if only when he gave her food. Or supposing he'd kept his face hidden—as he probably had while he spirited her from the mountain, using a ski mask or goggles—she had to be aware of his build, his height, his accent. In addition, she must surely have absorbed details regarding his demeanor and his habits. Dangerous details.

Yet though she'd been home for a month, the kidnapper had made no move. And now—Matt lowered his brows in a dark frown—he was the bastard's target. What could the man possibly gain by killing him? Revenge, it seemed.

But dammit, that wasn't logical either!

Nothing about the whole damned case was.

As SOON AS Matt had left to get the tea, Meredith fell back onto her pillows. She closed her eyes, making it more than obvious she had no wish to talk with Blair.

But Blair needed to talk with her. And now was her chance, now that she and Meredith were at last alone. She wanted to talk to Meredith about the letter. The letter her old friend had sent, begging her to come to High Meadows.

Yet she found herself hesitating because she'd been told not to talk about it. Told by the police.

On its arrival, she'd taken it to her local police station, since she'd thought someone ought to know about Meredith's fears. The officer on duty had faxed a copy to the Whistler detachment in charge of the case. As he was handing her back her copy, he'd said, ''Interesting that Mrs. Straith didn't seem to trust her husband. Looks bad.'' Then he'd cleared his throat and gone on briskly, ''At any rate, it would be best if you kept this to yourself. Don't show it to anybody. Don't discuss it with anybody.''

So she hadn't. But surely the officer hadn't included

Meredith in his blanket statement? Surely he hadn't meant she couldn't discuss the letter with the person who'd written it. Biting her lip, Blair mulled over the situation for a long minute, and then made her decision.

"Meredith—" she leaned forward urgently "—I need to talk to you. Before Matt comes back."

With a long-suffering sigh that said, better than any words, *Are you still here?*, the blonde opened her eyes.

"About what?" she asked indifferently.

"About the letter you sent me—"

"Letter?"

"Mmm. It was postmarked the day before you went missing, but I didn't get it until several days after your disappearance, so it was too late for me to contact you. And I've been in Europe since May and didn't know you were home until I got to Vancouver on the week-end—"

Meredith shoved herself up to a sitting position. Her pale cheeks had become oddly flushed. "You're saying I sent you a letter just the day before—"

"I felt so badly that it didn't reach me in time—"

"What did it say?"

Blair thought she heard approaching footsteps. She tilted her head and listened.

"What did it say!" Meredith's words came out in a hiss.

Startled by her vehemence, Blair took a moment to steady herself before going on. "You wrote about us not having been in touch for years, but said I'd always been levelheaded and that you wanted me to come for a visit. You asked if I'd stay for a few days. You said—"

"I said what?" Meredith demanded. "For God's sake, get to the point!"

The feverish glitter in the cornflower blue eyes sent a shaft of dismay slicing through Blair, and she found herself struck by last-minute doubts. Was she doing the right thing or was she on the point of making a mistake? Was it wise to tell Meredith that before her kidnapping she'd felt her life was in danger? Was it fair to tell her she hadn't trusted her husband enough to confide in him? But even as Blair faltered, she asked herself how she would like to be treated if she were in Meredith's position, and she knew, beyond a shadow of a doubt, that she would want to know all the facts, would feel she had a right to know them.

Casting her doubts aside, she leaned closer and touched Meredith's arm in a reassuring gesture. ''Meredith, you said in your letter to me that you believed someone was trying to—''

''Here we are,'' Matt's voice came coolly from the doorway, ''tea for two—Aileen had just made a pot. How are you feeling now, Meredith? Well, at least you're sitting up...and you have some color in your cheeks.''

Blair stiffened and drew back her hand. She'd thought she'd heard footsteps a moment ago. Had Matt been listening at the door? She hated to think that of him. But still...

He did seem distracted. After serving their tea, he started pacing the room restlessly. When Meredith said, ''Are you going to call the police to tell them about the threat on your life?'' he wheeled.

''I already phoned,'' he said tersely, ''from downstairs.''

Blair couldn't help noticing how strained his eyes were and how edgy he'd become since the kidnapper's phone call. But who could blame him for being tense?

A murder threat would send anyone's stress levels soaring. She couldn't even begin to imagine how it must feel to know someone out there wanted to kill you.

"What will the police do, Matt?" she asked.

"They can't keep a round-the-clock watch on me, nor would I want them to. As far as I'm concerned, it's business as usual. I'm not about to let some lowlife dictate how I function. It seems plain that Meredith's no longer a target, and I can look after myself."

"But shouldn't you have some kind of protection?" Blair was unable to keep the anxiety from her voice.

His mouth twisted in an ironic smile. "I prefer to take responsibility for myself rather than put my life in somebody else's hands."

Even as she admired his blunt approach, Blair felt chills ice her skin despite the warmth in the bedroom.

"What about the ransom notes?" Meredith had fixed Matt with a narrowed gaze. "Did you tell the police what the caller said about the ransom notes?"

"I didn't…and I don't intend to! I'm not about to confuse the RCMP even more than they already seem to be concerning this whole damned case by giving them some nonexistent ransom notes to chew on!"

The tension between the two was palpable…and ugly. Blair found it impossible to get a fix on how Matt and Meredith felt about each other. On her arrival, they'd been locked together in an erotic embrace. Yet since then, she'd sensed nothing between them but grating discord.

To her surprise Meredith reached a pale arm to Matt in what appeared to be a conciliatory gesture. "About Jason's party, I have an idea—"

"I'll call him—he'll give us a rain check."

"You don't understand. I *want* to go!"

''You're not going anywhere. Good lord, you were unconscious just a minute ago!''

''Let's not argue.'' Meredith set her cup and saucer firmly on the bedside table. ''We're going. And here's my idea—we bring Blair with us!''

Stunned by Meredith's volte-face, Blair tried to come up with a reason for it. Was Meredith afraid Blair would leave before revealing the contents of the letter?

''Forget it,'' Matt said. ''We'll eat here, the three of us, and we'll eat early so Blair can get home before dark. Even if you were well enough to go out—which is debatable—you know how Jason's parties drag on. They serve dinner late, and we never get home until well after midnight.''

''Then Blair must stay the night! Darling—'' Meredith's smile was rueful ''—I feel so guilty—Blair tells me I wrote her in March, before I disappeared, to invite her for a visit. Apparently I wanted to resume our old friendship, and how can we let her go again, now we have her back?''

Matt's jaw tightened, and he plowed his hands through his hair. Blair got the feeling that what he was feeling like doing was tearing it out by the roots.

Finally he turned to her and threw his hands out, palms up, in a defeated gesture. ''Okay, Blair, it's your call. Do you want to stay—or do you want to go home?''

Blair was torn. She hated being caught in the middle of their constant arguments. She found it distressing. But if Meredith needed her, then she couldn't leave.

She searched Matt's eyes and found no answer there. She turned to Meredith and was met with a pleading look.

Hiding a sigh, she switched her gaze to Matt.

"Yes," she said, sending up a silent prayer that she was making the right decision, "I'd like to stay. Actually, I was counting on Meredith's remembering she'd invited me. My weekend case is in the trunk of my car!"

MATT SHOWED BLAIR to a guest room farther along the corridor, an airy room with French doors leading to the wraparound balcony Blair had noticed on her arrival.

"Give me your car keys," he said. "I'll get your bag."

After he left, Blair unlocked the French doors and stepped outside. The sun was a blinding white ball, its heat pressing down heavily on her.

She crossed to the wrought iron railing, and as she reached it, a movement below caught her attention. She looked down and saw a gardener Dutch hoeing a rose bed. Square-shouldered and fairly tall, the man had a whipcord build, a lean, hard-boned face and flaxen hair styled in a ponytail. He was wearing jeans and work boots, and drops of sweat ran like mercury down his naked walnut-brown back.

He chose that moment to straighten and wipe his brow—and chanced to glance at the balcony.

When he saw Blair, he frowned. Their eyes locked, and she felt the same odd prickling at her nape she'd felt when she'd sensed someone spying from the gazebo. Had she been right, then? Had he been there? Was he the watcher? She wheeled away abruptly and walked into the bedroom, wishing she'd never gone outside.

She'd just pulled the doors shut when Matt arrived with her travel bag. She noticed he'd changed from his swim trunks into shorts and a sports shirt. Thank goodness.

He dumped her bag on the rack at the foot of the bed. "Admiring the view?" he asked.

"Mmm. I was looking at…the gardens." She wasn't about to tell him she'd been looking at his gardener and that the man gave her the creeps. "They're lovely."

"Hunter does a good job—Richard Hunter. Came here from Ontario a year ago—has a cottage on the grounds. His wife, Annie, is going to join him one of these days. She's trying to get her parents into a seniors' residence, but it's taking time."

Matt crossed to a side window and waved Blair over. "He built that gazebo last fall—though it's too far from the house, in my opinion, and we never use it. Meredith had wanted him to put in a flowerbed there, but in the end went along with his idea of the gazebo. He designed it himself."

Blair stood beside him—and smelled the faintest hint of alcohol on his breath. The threat on his life must have affected him more than he'd revealed, she realized with some surprise, if he'd needed a shot of whiskey to steady his nerves.

But above the smell of alcohol and the fresh-laundered smell of his shirt was Matt's own scent—musk and sweat and something spicy. Heady and disturbing, the erotic tendrils wove their way to every sensitive area in her body, tugging and teasing until she felt faint with longing.

She swallowed, hard. Determinedly forcing herself to concentrate on the view, not her reaction to Matt, she trailed her gaze from the gazebo to the forest and beyond, to where a river glinted silver in the sunshine. She didn't turn to him again until she was sure there would be no telltale evidence of her yearning clouding her gaze.

"It must be tough," she murmured, "having to choose between parents and a husband."

"Speaking of parents, how's your mother, Blair?"

His eyes were green as the forest, his hair rich and glossy, and begging to be touched. Desire broke loose again and tore through her flesh like a piercing thorn. She took a small step back, and as an added safeguard, folded her arms to keep her hands from doing anything foolish. "She's fine, and still writing. She's been in England for the past six months, doing research for her latest mystery. I spent some time with her. Just got home on the weekend. That's when I heard Meredith was back at High Meadows, and I decided to get in touch."

"She refuses to see any doctors, as you'll have gathered. And they've warned me she mustn't be pressured to try to remember what happened to her when she was away. But it might do her good to hear something of her earlier days—I'm sure that could do no harm."

"No. She had a very happy childhood. Her mother made sure of that."

"Jane passed away four years ago, not too long after she retired and moved to Calgary. Did you know?"

"Mmm, the friend she'd been living with sent Daddy a letter. Jane had always had a soft spot for him, since it was on his recommendation that Mom hired her as our housekeeper. And of course he was Jane's doctor when she was pregnant with Meredith, so there was always a special bond between them, particularly since the baby's father had already apparently opted out of the picture."

"How is he, Blair—your father?"

"Daddy has Alzheimer's, Matt. He's been in a home now for a couple of years."

Matt expressed his sympathy, and after a few silent moments, he said, "Well, I guess I'll leave you to get settled in. See you downstairs in about an hour? Do you need anything?" His smile was lopsided. "An iron for smoothing out wrinkles—or any of the other tools most females seem to find essential?"

She laughed. "No, but thanks anyway. A few wrinkles never bothered me—I'm sure I'll be fine."

Matt's smile faded. "You *are* fine, Blair. And always have been." There was a husky tightness in his voice. "In fact, it does my soul good, just looking at you."

Blair's pulse gave a wild lurch, but she gazed at him levelly, keeping her eyes totally devoid of emotion.

Matt muttered a soft oath. "I'm sorry, Blair—but I'm afraid my life has become so bizarre lately that just seeing you—so lovely and so decent and so unchanged from the way I remember you—makes me realize how offtrack it's become."

He thought she was lovely? Ten years ago she'd have been ecstatic if Matt had said such a thing to her…but now he was a married man. And strictly off-limits.

"It's a difficult time for you, Matt. For you and Meredith. I want to do anything I can to help."

"I appreciate that. We both do."

Matt ran a hand lightly down her arm, then turned toward the door.

But not before Blair had seen the haunted expression in his eyes, an expression so dark with unhappiness it made her want to weep.

THE FOYER was deserted when Blair descended the staircase an hour later, but she heard Matt's voice coming from an open doorway to the right of the foyer.

She crossed the hall, the hem of her navy palazzo

pants rustling around her ankles as she moved, the thin silk of her white camisole top brushing the tips of her breasts. Walking through the open doorway, she found herself in a large sitting room furnished in ecru.

Matt was alone, talking to someone on the phone. He looked so stunningly handsome in an icy blue shirt and navy slacks that Blair felt her breath hitch in her throat.

Noticing her, he gestured her forward. "Okay, Jason," he said into the mouthpiece, "we'll see you in a bit then."

He hung up. "Almost forgot to tell our host we'll be bringing a guest. No problem, though. The Thorne household's a very casual one."

"Thorne? You mean you're taking me to Jason Thorne's for dinner? *The* Jason Thorne?"

"You're impressed, huh?" he teased.

"Matt, the man's Canada's foremost portrait painter! Good grief, his portrait of the Queen was—"

"So you'll be angling for an interview?" He walked to a recessed bar area and said over his shoulder, "A day in the life of Jason Thorne."

"You read my syndicated column?" Surprise and delight surged through Blair.

"What'll you have? Wine? Sherry? Martini?"

"White wine. Dry. Thanks." Dismissively, Blair gave her order. "Matt—"

"Though we haven't seen each other in a long time, I've followed your career, and I tell you—" he turned, her glass in his hand "—I've been proud of you."

Blair sank onto a love seat. Praise from Matt was praise she treasured. She felt a glow in her heart. And indulging herself for once, she allowed herself to enjoy it.

Matt passed over her glass and joined her on the love seat. He held up his Scotch.

"A toast," he said, "to old friends."

Blair was echoing his toast when she heard a small sound behind her. Glancing around, she saw Meredith leaning melodramatically on the doorjamb, her eyes bright.

"Well, isn't this cozy!" Meredith's blond hair shone like a halo around her head. "Should I go out again and come back in? I wouldn't want to interrupt anything."

Blair's fingers tightened around the stem of her glass.

"For God's sake, Meredith." Matt surged to his feet. "Will you stop—"

"Darling, I was joking!" His wife glided forward, her black cat suit clinging to her sleek figure with every sinuous movement. Sapphires glittered at her ears, and as she patted Matt's arm mockingly, her sapphire ring refracted the light. "Loosen up and pour me a gin."

Matt glowered at her. "Sometimes your sense of humor eludes me." He poured his wife's drink and brought it to where she had perched on the arm of the love seat. "I tell you, I sometimes think I don't know you at all."

But as he spoke, there was no animosity in his expression—almost, Blair thought, there was a look of resignation.

And despite her firm and sincere intention to keep her emotions under lock and key where Matt was concerned, she felt them pulsing to be set free.

MATT UNLOCKED the doors of the gray Jaguar and after settling Meredith in the front seat held the back door open for Blair.

As she slipped by him with a murmured thanks, he smelled her subtle perfume and the feminine scent of her hair and her skin, and the desire that had sprung to life when she'd come into the drawing room and had been clawing at him ever since hit him again like a punch in the gut.

He shut the door briskly as she sat and wished he could as easily shut the door on his reaction to her. She was lovely. Lovely...and out of bounds.

He must have been blind, ten years ago, that he hadn't noticed how attractive she was. But at twenty-one, he'd still been very much at the mercy of his hormones, and when he'd met Meredith—blond, hot, sexy, provocative—he'd been a goner. He'd been dazzled by desire, hadn't realized that what he'd felt for her had been lust. Nothing more.

And he'd spent the last ten years living with his mistake.

He'd thought, when he'd heard she'd turned up safely, that at last he could put an end to their marriage. Instead, because of her amnesia, he was trapped. Trapped until the day came—if it ever did—when she was truly well again and he could tell her it was over.

Only an utter bastard would break it off with her now, when she was so vulnerable and unstable. And God knew what she'd already gone through, at the hands of the lunatic who'd kidnapped her. It didn't bear thinking about.

It was ironic that when she was missing, the police had believed he'd killed her. He could have confessed to them that he'd certainly *felt* like murdering her the night before she disappeared, when he'd discovered what she'd done. Felt like it, but would never have done it.

THE THORNES LIVED only a mile along the river from High Meadows, Matt told Blair as he drove, but the distance was much farther by car, along twisting side roads.

"You really ought to have some contractors in to build a road along the river's edge," Meredith said poutingly as Matt finally wheeled the Jaguar into a private driveway. "It would be so much more convenient."

"What would be the point? In the old days you used to be around here all the time, but it was like pulling teeth to get you to accept this dinner invitation."

"And I'm only here because you wouldn't stop hassling me about it!" Meredith snapped, her mood suddenly changing.

"It would have been rude to keep turning them down." Matt's tone was nonconfrontational. "They've been at High Meadows a couple of times since you've been back, but you barely spent two minutes with them."

"You can't blame me for wanting to keep to myself! When I go out, people stare at me as if I'm a freak."

"You've got to pick up your former life. Slowly, I grant you, but you have to make the effort."

"Easy for you to say!" Meredith answered viciously. "You were born with a silver spoon in your mouth and you've never had a care in the world!"

Straight ahead was a large house of cedar and glass, the forecourt crammed with cars. Matt found a parking spot and violently drove his foot on the brake.

Switching off the ignition, he wrenched himself sideways and glared at his wife.

"Are you implying that I wasn't worried about you

when you were missing?'' His voice vibrated with anger.

Meredith jerked open her door, shot out of the car, slammed the door shut behind her. And stood there, her back hostilely to the vehicle as she waited for them to join her.

Chapter Three

Jason Thorne came around the side of the house to greet them, and Blair looked curiously at the artist as he loped toward them, his wiry figure casually attired in a green cotton shirt and pleated beige pants. He had a wolfish face and deep-set eyes the same sherry brown as his shaggy beard and hair. Blair would have recognized him from his media photos, but she certainly hadn't anticipated the high-voltage intensity that charged the air around him.

"Welcome!" The artist's smile was charismatic. "Matt, Meredith, good to see you both again." He went to embrace Meredith, but when she withdrew slightly, he scooped up her hands and brushed a light kiss over her knuckles.

"Jason—" Matt guided Blair forward "—this is Blair Enderby. We knew each other years ago—I boarded with her family during my last term at college—but she's a *very* old friend of Meredith's. They more or less grew up together."

Jason clasped Blair's extended hand. "Glad you're here, Blair. Now come and meet the rest of the gang."

Stereo music was playing somewhere, and when they rounded the corner, Blair saw a sun-drenched deck crammed with people. Beyond she could see the sparkle of the river, the same river she had seen from her bedroom window. And arcing around the house, just as it did at High Meadows, was the forest.

So dark. So gloomy. So…threatening, somehow.

She controlled a shudder, and when she looked at the others, she saw Jason had drawn Meredith to one side. Whatever he was saying to her was obviously making her uncomfortable. The blonde was avoiding looking at the artist, but he kept a fast grip on her wrist as he spoke to her. Blair sensed the sharp tension jerking between the two and found herself wondering curiously what was going on.

Matt apparently had noticed nothing untoward.

"I don't see Poppy," he said casually to Blair. "Jason's wife. She must be inside—let's go look for her."

They wove their way across the crowded patio, pausing several times so Matt could introduce her to some of the other guests. After opening the sliding door into the house, he ushered her into a kitchen redolent with the tantalizing smell of spicy foods cooking. A fair-haired youth, whose good looks were spoiled by a sullen expression, lounged on a tilted chair reading a newspaper.

"Hi, Brandon," Matt said.

"Yo." The youth didn't look up, and with a shrug, Matt led Blair to a long hallway.

"Poppy's son by a previous marriage," he murmured. "Nineteen. Chip on his shoulder so big he can't carry it."

As they passed a room set up as a gym, he added wryly, "Should be able to, though, since his main interest in life is pumping iron! Hey, Poppy," he called, "where are you?"

"In here, Matt!"

Matt led Blair into a bright den, where they found Poppy Thorne sitting on a cushion on the floor, a can of beer on a low coffee table in front of her. Blair realized, with surprise, that Poppy was much older than her husband. Her freckled face was pleasant but threaded with lines, her red hair liberally streaked with gray, her figure overblown.

"Blair, come and sit down. I've been waiting to read your runes. It's a compulsory ritual, you see, on everyone's first visit to Thornebank."

"Poppy—" Matt's tone was amused "—you know I don't believe in this mumbo jumbo—will you excuse me while I get Blair a drink? What'll you have, Blair?"

"White wine," Blair said. "Thanks."

As he left, Blair perched on the low table. "I'm afraid I'm like Matt. I'm not into mumbo jumbo—"

Poppy waved her rueful words away. Lifting a small drawstring bag from the table, she held it out.

"I want you to concentrate on an aspect of your life that is causing you concern. Slip your hand inside the bag and pick a rune."

Easier to join than fight! Blair decided. She fumbled in the bag, and as she did, found her thoughts veering of their own accord to the situation at High Meadows. Though she felt a bit foolish, she tried to concentrate on the mystery—and on what part she might play in solving it.

She withdrew a rune and set it on the table.

The black glyph on the gray stone meant nothing to her.

"Oh, dear," Poppy murmured.

Blair raised her brows. "What?"

Poppy shook her head, her eyes deeply troubled.

"Don't keep me in suspense!" Blair's laugh sounded forced.

Poppy grasped Blair's hands tightly and her grave expression sent a shiver tingling down Blair's spine. "Rely on yourself, my dear," she said. "Around you are enemies, and all is not as it seems."

Blair chuckled in an attempt to lighten the atmosphere. "It's just as well I'm a skeptic, isn't it? A poor girl could have nightmares, if she really believed in—"

"Never disregard the runes." The sudden sharpness of Poppy's tone caused Blair's eyes to widen. "You alone, of course, must decide which path to take but...darkness and danger surround you. Beware of enemies. Beware of hidden depths. And most of all, beware of a woman who is not—"

Matt breezed into the den.

"So—" he cocked an amused eyebrow as he served Blair's drink "—the entrails have been scattered and read?"

Blair struggled to shake off the unsettling effect of Poppy's dark warnings, but even as she did, it occurred to her that for the second time, Matt had interrupted at a crucial point in a conversation. Had he been standing outside the door, listening? Again? Oh, she was really becoming paranoid.

But Poppy had said, *Rely on yourself, my dear. Around you are enemies.* Was Matt one of those enemies? Surely not.

Still...better safe than sorry.

"Poppy sees a bit of excitement ahead for me!" She managed to make her laugh easy. "And that's something I could use—life's been pretty dull lately."

"Well, there may be something to Poppy's mumbo jumbo after all—your bit of excitement is just around the corner. Jason's invited you to his studio to see his work in progress. Take your drink with you. Excuse us, Poppy?''

"Of course." Bracing a hand against the table, the older woman got to her feet.

Blair stood, and touched Poppy's arm. "Thanks," she said. Then grimaced. "I think."

"Come back any time—any time you need counsel."

Poppy's tone held none of the intensity that had been there earlier, and Blair chastised herself for having gotten carried away, even for a moment.

Smoke and mirrors, she told herself as she and Matt left the room. That's what it had been. She could hardly believe that she, so skeptical in matters psychic, had allowed herself to become alarmed and fearful solely from a stranger's reading danger from a glyph painted on a pebble.

The idea was laughable.

MATT GUIDED BLAIR out a side door across a springy green lawn to a narrow path in the forest.

There was room only for single file, so she followed him, pushing aside fern branches that got in her way.

They reached a small clearing above the river, and she saw Jason's studio ahead. It was a squat log building with large windows and a flat roof. When they reached the open door, Matt clanged the wrought iron knocker twice.

Jason's voice reverberated from inside. "Enter!"

"I'll see you later," Matt said to Blair.

"You're not coming in?"

"I wasn't invited—very few ever are! You must have made a good impression on the maestro." He gave her a mock salute before striding toward the forest path.

Blair watched him go, feeling a clutch of anxiety as he disappeared into the forbidding depths. Did he think of danger as he plunged among the trees where anybody could be hidden, waiting to attack?

But he'd said he could look after himself.

She had to keep that thought in mind.

She let out a sigh. It wasn't easy, though. Despite her intention to remain indifferent, she found herself worrying about him. And that old familiar ache of yearning stole up on her whenever she let her defenses down.

With a determined effort, she turned her back on the dark forest and walked through the open doorway.

The entryway was cluttered with an assortment of objects ranging from fishing rods to ski equipment, and Blair almost tripped over a huge pair of mud-caked boots. As she stepped over them and moved forward, she smelled all the scents peculiar to an artist's lair, scents strongly laced with the sweetly pungent smell of cigar smoke.

The artist was standing with his back to the windows, a crystal brandy snifter in one hand, a cheroot in the other. Blair's bright, interested gaze flicked past him to the portraits hung on the walls, portraits in the distinctive Jason Thorne style with which Blair was very familiar—the background painted in shades of gray, the subject depicted in muted colors in an impressionistic style.

Except for the eyes.

This aspect was invariably starkly portrayed in such minute detail, and with such extraordinary perception, that the eyes seized the attention of anyone studying the work.

Jason crossed to an easel facing the other way and gestured with his cigar. "Come see this," he said.

Blair walked to a spot from which she could best view the work and turned, her nerves humming with anticipation.

She stared for several spellbound moments at the beautiful nude before she spoke.

"Meredith. Before, of course. It's wonderful."

Tearing her gaze from the eyes—disturbing eyes, only half finished—she examined the rest of the portrait. The background was a moonlit meadow, the reclining figure portrayed in shades of rose and cream. The model's long, straight hair glimmered in carefully careless disarray over her breasts. One arm was stretched out in the grass above her head, the other was draped over her belly, the line of the hand enticing the viewer's eye to the juncture of the thighs, where, in a teasing game, it created a dusky shadow.

"Has Matt seen it?" she asked.

"No, it was to be a surprise. Meredith asked me to paint it for his birthday, which is only a few days away now. My model disappeared before it was finished."

"It's almost finished now…except for the eyes."

Frustratedly, Jason stubbed out his cinnamon brown cheroot on a brass ashtray set on the windowsill. "And her ladyship is unwilling to cooperate. Since she came back our old rapport is gone. I did persuade her to come along here once—Matt doesn't know that, of course— but I found that trying to read her eyes was like trying to read a book in some foreign language. She seemed so ill at ease, and put on an act so patently false I ended up shouting at her—"

He broke off, his quick anger thrumming in the air with such intensity Blair wouldn't have been surprised if his crystal brandy snifter had shattered.

"What are you going to do?" she asked.

His burst of temper subsided as quickly as it had risen. "It's the eyes," he said helplessly. "How the hell can I get a fix on her when I can't read her eyes?"

In the silence that fell between them, the beat of the stereo came, muffled, from the party.

The party.

Blair said quietly, "I shouldn't take up any more of your time. You'll be wanting to get back to your guests."

"First I want to ask if you'll do me a favor."

"If I can."

"Matt said you're a very old friend of Meredith's. That being the case, would you use your influence, if you have any, to persuade her to sit for me again? Once more should be enough—if she cooperates."

Blair realized why he'd invited her to his studio. She figured she knew the source of the tension she'd sensed between Jason and Meredith earlier. "I'll talk with her if I get the chance. But I can't make any promises. You see, I find her a bit changed, too. It seems hard to gauge her moods."

"But you'll try?"

"I'll try."

"That's all I ask."

As they walked along the forest path, Blair found heavy questions thumping around in her head.

Did Poppy know her husband had painted Matt's beautiful wife in the nude? And if so, did she mind?

Why had Meredith refused to sit again for Jason?

What intrigued Blair far more than any other question, though, was this. If the artist ever did finish the painting, how was Matt going to feel when he discovered his wife had bared all for their charismatic neighbor?

Emerging from the forest, Blair immediately spotted
Matt. He was standing with a group of people on the
patio, and when he saw her, he waved her to join them.

"The painting," Jason murmured, as she made to
move away. "Our secret, okay?"

"Our secret."

"Thanks." Jason took off toward the house.

A movement at the kitchen window caught Blair's
eye as she was about to turn away. It was Brandon. He
was standing to one side, almost hidden by the curtain
and obviously believing himself not visible. He was
staring at something...or someone. His eyes were glittering.

Blair sliced her gaze around to see what he was looking at...and she saw Meredith talking to Poppy just a
few feet from the window. Blair's breath caught in her
throat. It was Meredith the youth was staring at and—
having been there herself—she recognised the expression in his eyes.

Adoration. Teenage infatuation.

Blair tugged her intruding gaze from him and made
for Matt's group. Did Matt know, she wondered, that
Brandon had a thing for his wife? And more impor-
tantly, did Meredith know? Had she encouraged him?
The Meredith Blair had known in high school would
have done so, and taken a smug delight in adding the
youth to her list of conquests.

But perhaps she'd changed. In many other ways, she
seemed to have. Maybe she'd even tried to brush him
off.

By the time Blair reached Matt, Meredith had left
Poppy and moved to join him, too. The blond held out
her empty glass to one of the men in the small group,
a paunchy middle-aged man with a round, cheery face.

"Larry, honey," she said, "would you get me a re-fill?"

"Sure, Meredith. Gin, was it?"

"And tonic."

As Larry edged around the group, Matt stopped him.

"Blair, I'd like you to meet Larry Owen—he's a law-yer, has an office in Whistler. Larry, this is Blair Enderby, an old friend of ours. She's a freelance writer—"

"You don't have to tell me who Blair Enderby is." The lawyer grinned at her. "I read your column faith-fully, and when I'm rich and famous, m'darlin', I'd like to be featured in your private lives series."

"I'll bear that in mind!" Blair replied with a laugh, and moved back a little so the lawyer could squeeze in front of her to the bar.

She had reckoned without Matt's moving solidly be-hind her at the same time, and her move brought them into hard contact. Her back jammed against his chest. Her bottom pressed against his groin. Intimately.

Her head reeled.

Her senses spun.

As soon as Larry passed, she moved. But for three heart-hammering seconds she'd been in another world. The erotic muskiness of Matt's scent had been a pow-erful stimulant, the sexual implication of their position an unbearable excitement. For those three wild seconds, she'd been almost overwhelmed by a searing flare of desire.

And an agonizing longing to feel his arms come around her and hold her tight.

Pulses pounding, cheeks flushed, she raised her glass and drained the last of her wine. But when she chanced to glance at Meredith and saw the speculative narrowing of the other woman's eyes, she realized with a sinking feeling that the little incident had not gone unnoticed.

Damn!

She just hoped Matt hadn't noticed how his closeness had affected her.

"So tell me—" Meredith's eyes had an odd gleam as she addressed Blair "—where did you and Matt get to earlier?"

"He took me inside to meet Poppy." Blair decided to keep her visit to the studio to herself. Now wasn't the time to press Meredith about the portrait. "She read my runes!"

Meredith's laugh was supercilious. "Surely you don't waste your time on that stuff? It's a load of nonsense!"

Blair blinked. "But you used to love having your fortune told! Every year at the fair, you went straight for Madame Perilli's booth to have your palm read!"

"I did? Well, I find *that* hard to believe."

Meredith turned a shoulder to Blair, leaving her feeling royally snubbed.

So busy was she fighting a feeling of resentment at Meredith's rudeness that she barely paid any attention to the conversation going on around her until Larry returned, and she heard him say to Matt, "I believe your father bought High Meadows back in the sixties, from an eccentric politician. He was the original owner of the estate, wasn't he? Built the place for himself and his family? His name was Kingston, wasn't it?"

"Kingsley," Matt said. "Quentin Kingsley." He had scarcely touched his drink, Blair noticed. He set the glass on the patio railing. "He was apparently a very opinionated old guy, and lots of folk were turned off by his abrasive manner, but he had a huge following when he spoke out against nuclear testing and the bomb.''

''Darling.'' Meredith snagged Matt's shirtsleeve with her long-nailed fingers. ''Let's not talk about bombs— this is a party, after all!''

Matt seemed mildly surprised at the interruption, but when Blair glanced at Meredith, she was shocked at the sudden pallor of the woman's face. What was wrong?

But even as she asked herself the question, Blair found her attention caught and distracted by a small commotion by the patio doors. She turned to see what was going on and saw Jason coming toward them, an RCMP officer in tow.

A moment ago Blair had thought it must have been something Matt said that had made Meredith turn so pale, but he'd been talking about the original owner of High Meadows—nothing that could possibly have been responsible for the rapid bleaching of color from Meredith's face. She decided the blonde must have noticed the constable's approach, and that was what had upset her. Not surprising—the RCMP had probably grilled her mercilessly on her return.

Matt had his back to Jason and the officer and wasn't aware of their approach, but when Jason clamped a hand on his shoulder, he swiveled.

His brows lowered in a frown.

''Matt.'' Jason looked strained. ''This is Constable—''

''Asher. We've already met.'' Matt's gaze was direct. ''What can I do for you, Officer?''

''Mr. Straith, I'm sorry to butt in like this—I did try to catch you at home, but apparently I just missed you.''

''What's it all about?''

The babble of conversation had fallen away. Everyone was curious to know why the RCMP had crashed the party.

"I need to talk to you about your former house-keeper," the constable said.

"Jeannie Chang? But she retired back in April."

"You'll have to come to the station, Mr. Straith, and make a statement. Mrs. Chang, you see, has disappeared. And the last time anybody saw her was three months ago. In the middle of April. In your kitchen, sir, at High Meadows."

MOONLIGHT SLANTED DOWN on the gazebo, silver plating the rambling rosebushes whose leaves and blossoms had looked so vibrantly alive during the day.

Staring at them from her bedroom window, Blair shivered. They looked cold. Sterile. Dead.

Was Jeannie Chang dead?

She'd shoved that question to the farthest corner of her mind. Now it erupted, demanding to be faced. Goose bumps prickled on her bare arms, and the feeling of dread that had fallen over her after Matt had left with the constable became so heavy she could hardly bear it.

If only there had been someone she could have talked to, it might have been easier, but there had been no one. After the officer and Matt had left—Matt in his own car—everyone had studiously avoided referring to what had happened. Larry had driven Meredith and Blair to High Meadows right after dinner, and once there—to Blair's surprise, because she'd expected Meredith to collar her immediately once they were alone and ask her about the letter—the blonde had gone straight to her room.

Shortly after, Blair had gone to hers.

But she'd found it impossible to sleep. And around

midnight, she'd heard the sound of a car being driven fast—way too fast—to the house. As she'd lain tensely in bed, she'd heard the squeal of brakes followed by the loud slam of the car door, and she'd winced.

Whatever had happened to Matt, it had left him in a foul mood.

She'd itched to go down and ask how he'd fared at the police station, but she knew it wasn't her place to do so. It was his wife's place.

Instead, she'd punched her pillow, turned over and tried once again to sleep. Impossible. So here she was, at almost one in the morning, standing staring into the moonlit night.

A crashing sound from below made her jump.

She held her breath and strained to listen, but all she could hear were her heartbeats gonging against her ribs. Had someone broken in? Was the kidnapper, even as she stood there dithering, making good on his threat to kill Matt?

Fighting blind panic, she scooped up her robe, shoved her feet into her flat sandals and made for the door.

Within thirty seconds, she was downstairs, creeping along a hallway toward an open doorway from which light splashed onto the carpet.

As she drew closer, she could hear the clang of a file drawer being smashed shut, could hear Matt's savage cursing.

She reached the doorway, and with apprehension icing her spine, she stole a look around the doorjamb. The room was furnished as an office, and Matt, she saw to her intense relief, was alone. But the devastation within the four paneled walls had her gaping in utter disbelief.

The room had been ransacked.

Drawers lay open, a couple of chairs were overturned, books were piled high everywhere except in the bookcases, and strewn over every surface were papers and files and letters and folders.

"For heaven's sake." Blair raised her voice to be heard over the rattle of a file drawer being violently tugged open as she moved forward. "Matt, what on earth happened here?"

He snapped his head around, and the wild look in his eyes made her flinch. "I'm looking for something—"

"For what? I assume it's important, or you wouldn't be making this awful racket in the middle of—"

"Blair." His tone was impatient, but it was also weary. "Look, I'm sorry if I wakened you—"

"Oh, to hell with being wakened! Just tell me what's going on. If there's anything I can do to help—"

"Go back to bed. This has nothing to do with you." His harried expression took any sting out of his words.

"There's no point in my going back to bed." Blair started picking up folders, stacking papers into neat piles. "I won't sleep until you tell me what's going on."

"Stubborn as ever, Enderby." The faintest of wry smiles twisted his mouth. "And every bit as inquisitive."

"I thought someone was assaulting you!"

"And you were brave enough to come to the rescue." The look in his eyes warmed her heart. "That kind of courage deserves to be rewarded. How about a drink?"

"How about telling me what happened at the police station?" she challenged.

"Is this how you intimidate your interviewees into dishing up their most intimate secrets?" Though his eyes were still strained, they had an amused twinkle. "Okay, we'll talk…over a brandy. But we'll have it outside. I feel as if I'm suffocating in here."

"Fine. But first," Blair said firmly, "we tidy."

BY THE RIVER, the air was sweet, the walking easy. Apart from the rish-rush sound of the water and the odd crack of a twig underfoot as they strolled along the path, there was no sound to disturb the quiet.

Blair tried not to think of the dark forest looming to their right…or who could be lurking in its murky depths. Cupping her hands around her balloon glass, she took a sip of the brandy. The alcohol tingled through her veins and in a small way slackened the tension stringing her nerves.

She opened the conversation by asking Matt a question that had puzzled her.

"Why weren't the police interested in talking with Meredith? After all, as lady of the house, she'd be the one most involved in dealings with the housekeeper. She might have had some knowledge regarding Mrs. Chang's long-term plans."

"Meredith had been missing for a whole month before Jeannie Chang was last seen. And it's on record at the station that Meredith has no memory at all of the weeks before she disappeared."

"Yes, but she does have some earlier memories that—"

"Blair." Abruptly Matt stopped walking. "They're not going to bother with Meredith. The Mounties already have their man! Matt Straith is their prime suspect, and has been since the day Meredith disappeared!"

"You didn't have an alibi for that day." Blair's voice

was subdued. "It said in the newspaper reports that you'd been away on a fishing trip. On your own."

"Blair, I needed to get away—"

"I'm not asking for an explanation, Matt—"

"Meredith and I had had a hell of a fight the night before. I needed to clear my head. I drove to a lake about a hundred miles from here, spent the day there and didn't see a soul until I came home late that night and found Meredith missing."

"Do you often take off on trips like that?"

"No, dammit, I don't. There just never seems to be the time."

"I can see how that wouldn't look good." For a few minutes, they walked in silence, then Blair said, "Meredith went skiing with two friends. When they didn't meet up again, did they think she'd skied out of bounds and gotten into trouble? Perhaps fallen into a ravine?"

"At first."

"And it's the kind of thing Meredith might have done," Blair murmured. "I recall she didn't like rules, didn't like being told what to do or where to go."

Matt gulped the last of his brandy and to Blair's dismay hurled the crystal glass into the river. For a long moment he stood, with his back to her. She sensed the struggle he was having, trying to control his pent-up emotions, and her heart went out to him.

When he turned again, he said grimly, "The police still believe I was involved in the kidnapping of my own wife. God knows what they think my motivation would have been for that! And now we have another missing person. But who would have wanted to harm Jeannie Chang? She was a nice lady who kept to herself and didn't have an enemy in the world. But I was the last person reported to have been seen talking with her—

and the last person, apparently, she corresponded with before she vanished.''

''What do you mean, she *corresponded* with you?''

''The day she left she wrote me a letter.''

The moonlight cast shadows on Matt's face, accentuating the hard male strength of his bone structure in a way that caused Blair's heart to constrict painfully. How she loved him. He was everything a man should be...and more. And she had no right to feel the emotions she did. No right at all. No right to ache to touch him, no right to want to ease the lines of suffering around his eyes and his mouth.

Steeling herself to fight her unwanted attraction, she looked steadily into his eyes. ''Tell me, Matt.''

''That morning, I spoke to Mrs. Chang before I went off to the Whistler WhitePeak. I told her I'd be at the hotel all day and wouldn't be home until late. When I did get back, I found a letter in the kitchen. She apologized for leaving me in the lurch, but said she was finding it too stressful at High Meadows with Mrs. Straith missing. She wrote that she'd decided to leave— to retire, actually—and a friend had driven from Vancouver to pick her up.''

''But surely this letter will prove to the police that if something bad has happened to her, you didn't have anything to do with it?''

''I don't have the letter, Blair. I can't find it.''

Blair was visited by an image of his devastated study. ''You don't remember where you put it?''

''I could have sworn I filed it away. Dammit, I did file it away! It's gone.''

''Are you sure?''

''I'm sure.''

In the forest, somewhere quite close, an owl hooted. The sound echoed, tauntingly, from the mountains.

"Was it a handwritten note?" Blair asked.

"Yes."

"Who reported her missing, Matt?"

"Relatives. She was expected at an annual family get-together in San Francisco on the weekend. When she didn't turn up, they started making inquiries."

"How did the RCMP know you were the last to see her?"

"Before Constable Asher turned up at Thornebank, he paid a visit to High Meadows. Richard Hunter told them the last he knew of Mrs. Chang was when she'd been in the kitchen, with me. He was in charge of watering the indoor plants and he'd been in the hallway outside the kitchen when he happened to hear me tell Mrs. Chang I wouldn't be back until late. That's exactly what I told the constable—I have nothing to hide."

"Did she take all her things with her?"

"She didn't leave so much as an old pin."

Blair shuddered.

"You're cold," Matt said.

It wasn't the breeze gusting over the water that had sent ripples shivering through her body. It was the feeling someone had just stepped over her grave.

But she wasn't about to tell Matt that.

"Yes," she said, "it's a bit chilly."

"Let's go back." He put an arm around her, and she felt his warm muscled strength through the thin cotton of her robe. "If I had a jacket, I could gallantly throw it over your shoulders. Since I don't, then you'll have to make do with body warmth. How's this?" He pulled her closer, so that her head rested against his chest. "Better?"

"Mmm, much." If her voice shook, he would assume it was because she was chilled. Why would he ever think she was shaking because that was the effect his nearness had on her? "When you go to bed, will you tell Meredith what's happened?" She was aware she'd only brought Meredith's name into the conversation to set her up as a wall between them. "She may be asleep, but you ought to waken her, tell her about Mrs. Chang's letter being missing. She just might know where it is, and then you can stop worrying about it."

"I'll ask her in the morning."

"But if she's awake when you go up..."

"I won't be seeing her tonight, Blair." Matt's voice was flat. "My wife and I sleep in separate bedrooms."

They'd reached the end of the path, and as they stepped onto the lawn, Matt dropped his arm from around her shoulders. Blair immediately felt cold, alone.

Their footsteps made no sound on the grass and little sound on the patio as they crossed to the dining room door.

Matt unlocked it and paused.

"I appreciate your driving up here to offer Meredith help," he said. "And I'd like to do something in return."

"You don't have to do anything," Blair protested.

"Would you be interested in doing a feature on Matt Straith for your private lives series?"

Blair did a double take. "Would I ever! But you used to hate being in the spotlight—I remember that from when I knew you before."

"Rumors about me have been rampant since Meredith disappeared. I'd like to set the record straight, and doing it through your column will be the most painless way. And I know I can trust you. So...you'll stay on for a few days, and we can work on it? I'm going to be around most of the time except for a meeting I have to attend in Vancouver tomorrow night. So we'll start with a tour of the WhitePeak the day after—give you an idea of how I operate.''

"Sounds wonderful. Matt, I really appreciate—''

"No problem. So…get some sleep.''

"You're not coming in yet?''

"I feel restless. I'm going to go for a swim.''

Be careful.

Blair had managed, just in time, to stifle the warning words that had leaped to her tongue. Matt had already made it clear he felt perfectly able to look after himself.

She didn't want him to know how afraid she was for him.

UPSTAIRS, in the blue and silver bedroom, the sexy blonde moaned and arched her head on the pillows as the man making love to her slid his fingers over her breasts.

"Tell me,'' he growled, "that you love me.''

"You *know* I do!''

He squeezed the small twin mounds of milk-white flesh. "Say it,'' he commanded.

"I love you,'' she whispered. It was an old game. She knew her part.

"And want me.''

"And want you…''

Moonlight threaded its way through her hair, silvering it. She'd look like that, he thought, forty years from now, and if all went well, they'd still be sharing this bed. Triumphant excitement shuddered through him like an orgasm as he gloated over the utter brilliance of his plan. The perfect crime. God, he was a genius!

He moved inside her, slowly, drawing her higher, and inhaled her rich Oriental perfume as he sucked the sensitive skin below her ear. "You've forgiven me for hacking off your hair? I should have warned you from the beginning, but I knew you'd put up a fight."

"It had to be done. You terrified me, though. I thought—"

"You thought I'd flipped?" His breath tickled her ear as he laughed softly. "I knew exactly what I was doing."

"You usually do…but surely this is a risk, sneaking onto the veranda and into my room."

"No risk. He never comes to you. But I could have strangled you when I saw you playing up to him on the patio yesterday afternoon."

"It's in the plan!"

"I don't like it."

"Do you think I do?" Her lips curled contemptuously. "How much longer do I have to put up with his whining? 'When are you going to see a doctor?' If I hear that one more time… He makes me sick!"

"You said he's going to a meeting in Vancouver tomorrow night?" His breathing came harder, quicker, as he approached his climax. "Say your goodbyes to him before he leaves. Next time you see him, it'll be in the morgue."

Excitement thrilled through her, and just in time she stopped herself from raking her long fingernails over his naked back. Fresh scars would cause questions. It was something they couldn't chance. Even the smallest mistake could lead to disaster.

"What are you going to do?"

"Safer if you don't know. That way, when the police come, you can play the innocent."

"What about…her?"

"Your old friend?" His rhythm accelerated. He heard her breath catch, felt her meet every thrust with one of her own. Oh, she was hot. He couldn't get enough of her. "No problem…yet. But keep an eye on her. If she starts getting too nosy, I'll scare the hell out of her and she'll be out of here so fast you won't see her for dust."

He broke off and threw his head back. Her rasping breath, her stifled cry as she went over the edge, sent a surge of adrenaline through him.

And with an agonized groan strangled in his throat, he gave one last massive thrust, emptied his seed into her, and slumped on top of her, spent.

Chapter Four

When Blair came down for breakfast she found Meredith alone in the dining room. The blonde, dressed in a powder blue top and white shorts, had the entertainment section of the *Vancouver Sun* spread in front of her.

She greeted Blair with a cool hi, as Blair took a seat across from her.

"Good morning." Blair noticed the table was set for two. "Has Matt already eaten?"

"He's gone to the WhitePeak. He said to tell you he'd be back from the hotel around noon to have lunch with us."

The housekeeper bustled in with a silver rack of hot toast and a fresh pot of coffee. She bustled out again after Blair assured her she wanted nothing more.

"Meredith." Blair poured herself a cup of coffee. "Did Matt ask you about the letter from Mrs. Chang?"

"He did say something about a letter he claims to have had from the old dear, but I've certainly never seen such a letter. I tell you, I'm worried about him. Matt's always been an extremely organized person—if Mrs. Chang really had left him a letter he'd have been able to produce it. You've heard the expression a mind like a steel trap? In Matt's case, read a mind like a steel filing cabinet. I've been married to the man for ten years, and in all that time, he's never lost anything.'' She lifted her shoulders in a what-more-can-I-say shrug.

''You're implying that Matt's lying?''

''Blair—'' Meredith's expression was reproachful ''—I'd never accuse Matt of lying...purposely lying. All I'm saying is that he may have gotten a little...mixed up. He's been under a lot of stress lately, and you know how that can affect a person's mind.'' She put down her coffee cup, set her elbows on the table and leaned forward. ''Now tell me more about the letter I sent *you*. I find it...intriguing that you didn't want to talk about it in front of Matt.''

''That was because you'd indicated in it that I was the only one you could trust.''

''Go on.''

''You said—'' Blair had to force the words out ''—that someone wanted to...kill you.''

''You mean I knew, before I was kidnapped, that somebody was out to get me?'' Meredith blew out a sharp breath. ''Scary! What else?''

''That was it.''

''No mention of who I suspected was out to harm me?''

''No.''

Blair was puzzled by the flicker of relief she detected in the other woman's eyes. What an odd reaction! Surely, under the circumstances, Meredith should have welcomed any clue that might help police track down her kidnapper?

''So.'' Meredith sat back, looking much more relaxed than she had a minute ago. ''What are your plans for today?''

''If you're not busy perhaps we could spend some

time together. Matt thought it might be helpful to you if I were to fill you in on the old days.''

''Ah, yes.'' A cynical curl twisted Meredith's full pink lips. ''You want to tell me all about my idyllic childhood. Where do we start?''

Her attitude rasped Blair's nerves, but she answered mildly, ''At the beginning, I guess.''

''How are you going to manage that?'' It was a mocking retort. ''According to Matt, I'm a few months older than you, so you can hardly begin at the *very* beginning!''

''My father brought you into the world, Meredith, and brought your mother into our home as housekeeper. Though you didn't live with us, our two families were close…and I know as much about your beginnings as my mother does.''

''And your father? Where does he fit in? Were he and my mother involved?''

''You mean—good Lord, no!'' Blair laughed. ''But they were very fond of each other. Your father wasn't around, and Dad filled that space in your life.''

''Why was my father not around?''

''That's something I *don't* know. Your mother had been living in Ontario, and she moved to British Columbia just a few weeks before you were born. Dad delivered you at his private clinic—oh!'' Blair broke off with a frown. ''Talking of Dad…I should have made a phone call last night.''

''There's a phone over there.'' Meredith waved a hand toward a Queen Anne table set in the bay window. ''But if it's a private call, use the phone in Matt's study.''

''It's not private.'' Blair pushed her chair back. ''Excuse me.''

Using her calling card, she placed a call to the nursing home where her father was a patient.

"This is Blair Enderby," she said, when she reached the receptionist. "Alex Enderby's daughter…yes, that's right, he's in Room 12. I just want you to know where I can be reached for the next few days." She read out the phone number and added, "I'll let you know when I'm back at my home number again. Thanks."

When she turned, she noticed Meredith was looking at her with an odd glitter in her eyes.

"Your father's in the hospital?" she asked.

"He's in a Vancouver nursing home."

"What's wrong with him?"

"Dad has Alzheimer's."

A small nerve flickered above one of Meredith's eyes. "That's too bad. How…far has his illness progressed?"

"He's very frail." The unhappiness Blair always felt when she thought of her father's declining health made the room seem suddenly duller. "He had such a fine mind, it's been painful watching his gradual deterioration."

"Can you talk to him?" Meredith seemed to have become strangely tense.

"Oh, sure, but the conversation is usually one-sided. His lucid moments are rare, and becoming even rarer." Blair sighed. "Actually, now that I think of it, I can't remember when he last came out of his own little world and said anything that made any kind of sense."

"That must be really hard for you."

Blair sensed an insincerity behind the words. Yet how could she blame the other woman for that? Meredith had no recollection of ever having met Alex Enderby. How could his illness mean anything to her?

"So, Matt tells me you're staying on for a few days," Meredith said.

"You don't mind?"

"I don't mind."

Meredith's mood seemed to have mellowed, and Blair decided now would be the time to carry out Jason's request.

"Meredith, Jason showed me the painting last night. It's absolutely wonderful. He asked me to—"

"Oh, God." Irritably Meredith pushed back her chair and got to her feet. "Not again. That damned painting!"

"It would take only one more sitting."

"So he's delegated you to try to talk me into it! The nerve of that man—why can't he take no for an answer? If he's such a genius, surely he can finish the damned thing without—"

"He can't." Blair slipped her hands into the pockets of her shorts to hide the fact that they were clenched into fists. "Why don't you just pop over, sit for him and help him out?"

Meredith dragged both hands through her cropped blond hair, the gesture agitated. "I don't care about the painting! I wish I'd never asked him to do it."

"But you did ask him, and he's already put a lot of work into it. Besides, if Matt's birthday's coming up—"

"If you're going to hound me, too, you can just—"

"I'm not going to hound you." Blair kept her voice steady, though she felt like shaking the other woman. "And I won't mention it again. I will just say, though, that I find your attitude strangely out of character. The Meredith I knew would have given her eye teeth for the chance to model for an artist of Jason Thorne's caliber.

I can't believe you can have changed so much. It boggles my mind.''

Surprisingly, her quiet words seemed to have gotten through to Meredith where her aggressive arguments hadn't. The other woman's face paled a little, and Blair thought she saw her lower lip tremble.

''Oh, all right!'' she snapped resentfully. ''You win. I'll go over to Thornebank right now. I'll sit for the man one more time, but I tell you, if he raises his voice to me I'll be out of there so fast he won't have time to blink.''

''I think you're making the right decision.''

But Meredith was already halfway across the room.

And when she went out, she slammed the door so hard behind her, the china on the table rattled.

Blair moved to her chair and sat, feeling thoroughly mystified. Meredith had been adamant that she wasn't going to sit again for Jason. But in the wink of an eye, she'd changed her mind. It must have been something Blair had said.

But for the life of her, she couldn't imagine what!

Meredith had become not only a stranger to her—she had become a complete enigma.

BLAIR HAD BROUGHT her laptop computer with her to High Meadows. After breakfast, she went upstairs to fetch it, then went outside to search for a pleasant shady spot where she could sit while inputting some preliminary background notes for her Private Life of Matt Straith.

She found that spot in the gazebo.

The cedar summerhouse was hexagonal, with white-painted duckboard flooring. Built-in benches were set against three of the railings. Like everything else she'd seen at High Meadows, the gazebo was perfectly maintained, with not a scratch or bubble marring the white paint.

She set the computer on her lap and switched it on.

The private life of Matt Straith… She typed the heading and soon became engrossed in her task, listing subheadings as they came to her. House. Estate. Hotels. Family. Parents. Past.

Past.

Just by typing the word, she found herself drawn to thinking of the time when Matt had lived in the Enderby home, and thinking of those days was a mistake, because she could never do so without being reminded of the pain she'd felt when Matt told her he'd fallen in love with Meredith.

Lost in thoughts that still had the power to wound, she sighed and let her gaze drift to the duckboard flooring.

At first, she didn't notice the small shining object. But as the sunlight shifted a fraction, a thin ray slanted through the narrow space between two of the white-painted planks and danced off something bright. She leaned over to investigate. It seemed to be a piece of jewelry.

She extricated a pencil from her computer case and kneeling on the duckboard poked it between the slats. To her disappointment, it wasn't quite long enough to reach, but as she was about to draw back, she recognized the object. It was an earring of white gold and amethyst, extremely valuable—one of a pair that belonged to Meredith.

As Blair stared at it, memories slugged her heart in a series of relentless blows. The first time—and the last time—she had seen this earring had been on Meredith's wedding day, after Matt had given the set to his new bride. He'd had them designed to match her honeymoon outfit.

"Damn!" Blair sank back on her heels.

Her lips twisted in a mirthless smile. Truthfully, she wasn't sure if she was swearing because she couldn't reach the earring or because once again she was giving in to the part of her that wanted to think about the past—

Someone was watching her.

Again, that warning prickle at her nape, the same prickle she'd felt yesterday when she'd thought someone was watching her from the gazebo. The same prickle she'd felt when she'd locked eyes with Richard Hunter. The prickle crept down her spine on spider legs, making her shiver.

Bracing herself, she pushed herself to her feet, straightened her shoulders…and turned.

Richard Hunter was standing just three feet away, and from his muscled body emanated hostility…and suspicion.

"Hi!" Blair said brightly.

Stony cobalt eyes sliced from her face to the duckboard flooring. "Need some help?"

His tone was insolent, his voice gravelly, his attitude macho. Sexuality oozed from him like cheap cologne, and like an overdose of cheap cologne, it made Blair feel sick.

"Oh, I don't think so. I was just doing a few stretching exercises."

Turning from him dismissively, she busied herself with her computer but sensed he wasn't budging. Compressing her lips, she saved what she'd written and tucked the laptop into its case. And all the while she was conscious of his hard, malevolent gaze boring into her flesh.

Slinging the case over her shoulder, she swung round again.

"Oh!" She pretended surprise. "You still here?"

Dark color, angry color, flooded his tanned face.

She brushed past him and stalked toward the house.

The man gave her the creeps. She'd go back when he wasn't around and fish out the earring. Meredith must have been upset at losing it. She'd be thrilled to have it back.

"MATT." Blair looked at Matt across the patio table, over the remaining crumbs of the lemon cheesecake Aileen had served after a delicious chicken salad. "Meredith told me she doesn't recall ever having seen Mrs. Chang's letter."

Matt had come home, as promised, for lunch, but they were eating alone. Meredith hadn't returned, and when Matt had asked where she was, Blair had said vaguely that she'd driven to Thornebank to fetch something she'd left there the night before, and Matt had seemed to accept that.

But the strained expression in his eyes while they'd lunched made Blair long to comfort him, despite her determination to keep herself emotionally detached.

He was just so damned attractive! He'd lost no time in shedding the jacket of his business suit on coming home, but even with his shirtsleeves rolled back and his tie casually slackened, an aura of success and power still emanated from him, and that, along with his irresistible sexual magnetism, destroyed the barrier she'd erected around her heart.

Her defenses were down.

She was lost…and she knew it.

Thank heavens he didn't.

"I didn't expect her to. She'd have no reason to be going through my files, nor would she have been interested in doing so. Business matters are not my wife's forte."

It wasn't said in a critical manner but in a matter-of-fact way. And from what Blair remembered of Meredith, Matt's comments were right on the mark. Meredith had been a social butterfly. She'd loved people and parties and fun times, but she'd always left others to do the work. She'd considered her mere presence at any function to be sufficient contribution—and her friends had gone along with that, because with her beauty and vivacity, she'd invariably been the life and soul of the party.

But though she was just as beautiful today as she had been then, there was a bitchiness about her Blair didn't recognize—a bitchiness that grated on her nerves.

Was it a recent development? Blair had always thought that though Meredith was vain and selfish, she didn't have any malice in her. Could this nasty streak have existed always but been hidden under the surface? Matt would know.

"How was Meredith, Matt, when she came back… apart from her amnesia?"

"She'd lost a lot of weight, and her arms were bruised. Badly bruised. And the bastard had hacked off her hair. Looked as if he'd used a razor."

Blair's stomach gave an unpleasant heave. And she acknowledged silently—and guiltily—that she'd been too ready to condemn Meredith for her sour moods. Who knew what horrors she'd had to endure at the hands of her kidnapper?

"She's had it styled, though," Blair said quietly. "It suits her."

"Yeah. The bruises, though, we could do nothing about. At any rate, they've almost faded completely now. And she's been eating reasonably well, put on a bit of weight...."

"She's just as beautiful as she always was."

"Yeah, just as." Matt's tone was flat.

"Isn't it...odd that the kidnapper would drive her to such a very isolated spot to dump her?"

"He may not have dumped her. She may have escaped and found her way there on her own."

"But from where? A cabin somewhere on the mountain?"

"It's possible."

"I guess the police would have carried out a search in that general area of the mountain where she was found—"

"And the surrounding areas. As far as they were able. The forests around here are impenetrable in places."

"So of course it would be easy to miss a—"

Blair broke off as she heard the sound of someone— quite close by—whistling the melody of a hit song, "Rich Girl." Turning her head, she saw Richard Hunter come around the corner of the house. He looked as if he was off duty. He was wearing a black shirt and baggy charcoal shorts and swinging a camcorder in one hand.

He glanced toward the patio, and when he saw Matt, his face lit up and he grinned at him.

"Had a phone call from Annie last night, sir," he called. "She's finally got her folks a place in a real nice facility. She'll be here in a couple of weeks."

Matt gave him the thumbs-up sign, and the gardener,

whistling cheerfully again, sauntered off in the direction of the riverside path.

Blair felt a flash of frustration. If Matt hadn't been with her, she could have taken this opportunity to fish out the earring. But chances were Meredith hadn't confessed to him that she'd lost it. So...best if she kept her secret to herself, for the moment.

"Your gardener's into photography?" she asked.

"Took it up last year." Idly Matt watched his employee passing the gazebo. "Meredith was his favorite subject. He filmed dozens of segments of her, walking, talking, swimming, gardening, working in her studio— I expect you remember how she always loved to pose!"

Yes, she remembered. Which was why she'd been astonished that Meredith had been disinclined to pose for Jason. "Hunter was fortunate to have such a photogenic model for his first experiments. Did you see the tapes? Were they any good?"

Matt laughed, but the sound wasn't unkind. "He has a lot to learn. Too many close-ups, not enough diversity. Sure, Meredith's easy on the eye, but, well, for example, during his gardening shots, he might have zoomed in on one or two of his plants instead of focusing totally on Meredith. But he made a damned good job of filming her in her studio—he caught her fierce concentration and the almost magical way her fingers work. I did suggest he take classes, but he said he preferred to learn by his mistakes."

The gardener had walked past the gazebo without giving it a sideways glance. Blair stared after him. Had he swallowed her story about stretching exercises?

"You seem to be taken with him." Matt's amused voice broke into her thoughts. "Is he your type, Blair?"

"Lord, no!" She turned to Matt. "He's certainly *not* my type."

Matt's gaze was steady. "What *is* your type?"

An image of Andrew flashed into her head, tall, brown-eyed, brown-haired, with the body of a linebacker, the looks of a movie star and the morals—she'd found out almost too late—of a randy alley cat. "Oh, I don't have a type, per se."

"Do you mind if I ask you a personal question? Even more personal than the one I just asked?"

"Shoot," she said.

"Why have you never married?"

"I almost did, once. I was engaged…for six months. Had even booked a church for the wedding. His name is Andrew Paxton. He's a screenwriter—I met him four years ago at a writers' conference in Seattle. He knew a lot of important Hollywood people—stars, producers. He introduced me to them—dazzled the hell out of me. I thought I was in love." She shrugged. "And I thought he was, too."

"What happened?"

"I guess I was the flavor of the month—the month we met, that is. We were well into our sixth month before I discovered Andrew Paxton was a man who liked variety." Blair's smile was derisive.

Matt's eyes held a gleam of compassion. "I'm sorry," he said. "But only if you are."

"It hurt at the time. I'm over it now. And I did learn that it's better to be alone than to be involved with the wrong person. I just wish I'd known earlier what I know now—it takes time, a whole lot of time, to get to know a person. Truly, truly know a person."

"Yes." Matt's voice had an edge of weariness. "It's all too easy to be dazzled by glamorous packaging."

Blair had the oddest feeling he was referring not to her situation, but to his own. Could it be that he had regretted marrying Meredith? But if so, why were they still together? Were they trapped in a love-hate relationship?

"Some of the best days of my life," he went on, "were those I spent with you and your folks. I'll always have a great appreciation for having been allowed to experience again what it was like to be part of a loving family. I didn't have much of a home life after my mother died. Dad was so grief-stricken he closed a large part of himself off from me. I don't think he knew how to handle his pain, or me, so he sent me off to boarding school."

"How old were you, Matt? And how did you handle that huge change in your life? It must have been traumatic for a small boy. Not only had you lost your mother, you had to adjust to having an emotionally distant father, which was in its own way just as devastating a loss. Do you think these things have affected you in later life?"

Matt's laugh was dry. "Want to borrow a pen and a pad of paper?"

For a moment, Blair didn't understand what he was getting at. When she realised he had misinterpreted her compassion and caring, had translated it into something that could be measured in dollars and cents, she felt a stab of anger. "When I'm interviewing you for my article on your private life—" her voice had become cool "—you'll know it!"

She stood and spun away from him toward the door. She heard his quick, heavy tread behind her and had barely taken five steps when his hand clapped down on her shoulder. A firm hand. And a hand with a powerful grip from which she had little hope of freeing herself. She froze, refusing to do anything as undignified as struggling.

He turned her around and looked at her.

"Well, well," he said softly. "Temper, temper!"

Sensation. On all sides, Blair was bombarded by sensation. She stifled a moan as she inhaled the musky smell of him, stiffened as electricity surged from his fingertips to sizzle through her. Her skin hummed, her nerves quivered, and deep inside resonated a shivering excitement as pleasurable as it was disturbing.

She swayed.

"Blair?" He frowned. "Are you all right?"

She got a grip on herself and slipped from his grasp.

"I'm sorry." She pulled trembling fingers through her hair. "I overreacted. It just…upset me that you didn't understand where I was coming from."

"And where was that?"

Their eyes locked, and sexual tension snapped into place between them with an unexpectedness that sucked the breath from her lungs. Matt felt it, too…or felt something. She saw his pupils dilate, heard his swift intake of air.

He grasped her shoulders again, this time so savagely she gasped. His clouded gaze dropped to her parted lips. He lowered his head. He was going to kiss her. She knew it. She tasted his breath, sweet as wine—

The sound of a door slamming in the house shattered the moment, and with a harsh mutter, Matt released her.

Neither of them spoke. The only sound she could hear was Matt's rapid breathing and her own. And the blood pulsing with unseen violence against her eardrums.

Her head was averted, but she felt Matt's gaze on

her. He must know she'd been his for the taking. And he had wanted her, too. Wanted her the way a man wants a woman. And she sensed that it had shaken him to the core.

Things would never be the same between them again, she realized with a feeling of despair. She already felt an awkwardness in the air—a new tension, a new reserve.

She cleared her throat, yet when she spoke, her voice still came out huskily. ''Now that we've finished our lunch, will you show me Meredith's studio? Poppy was telling me that for the past few years she's been selling her pottery to galleries as far afield as San Francisco and she's made quite a name for herself. I'd love to see her work.''

''Sure.'' Matt's tone was strained. ''No problem.''

THE STUDIO was on the main floor, at the far end of a long hallway.

It was a corner room with two windowed walls. That much Blair could see as Matt opened the door. But instead of standing aside to let her by, he stopped short, and her view was impeded by his back and his wide shoulders.

''Good God!'' His exclamation was uttered in a tone of mingled incredulity and horror. ''What the devil—''

Blair had almost walked into him when he stopped. Now, as he stepped forward, she discovered the reason for his shock. Every shelf and table was bare. The floor was littered with smashed pottery.

''Matt.'' Blair's voice was weak. ''Who could have done this?''

Fury emanated from him in pulsing waves. ''God

knows,'' he said hoarsely, ''but believe me, I intend to
find out!''

He scooped up a section of broken pottery from a
pile at his feet. ''This is from a piece Meredith finished
in February. She was so proud of it—said she thought
it was the best thing she'd ever done.'' He swore viciously under his breath. ''When I find out who did this,
I'll—''

''It was a piece of crap.''

They both turned sharply as Meredith's voice came
from the doorway. Blair's mind reeled in bewilderment,
and she imagined Matt must be feeling just as confused.

The blonde walked forward, her cornflower blue eyes
smug, a triumphant smile twisting her mouth.

''Darling,'' she said to Matt, ''don't upset yourself—
you won't have to go charging off in all directions to
defend my honor. You see, I smashed all those pieces
myself!''

Chapter Five

From Horstman Hut at the top of the Seventh Heaven ski run on Blackcomb Mountain, the view of the Black Tusk was awesome.

But as Blair alighted from the chairlift with Matt and Meredith, she was in no mood to appreciate the splendor of the raw jutting peak. Meredith's wildly unpredictable mood swings had thrown her for a loop.

The blonde had followed her bold declaration that she'd destroyed her own work with another equally startling announcement. Her visit to Thornebank had done her a power of good, she said, and she was ready to try to unearth some of her buried memories.

"Let's go to Blackcomb where the mystery started!" Her gurgling laugh had suggested she thought the trip might be fun. "Who knows, I might see something that'll trigger a memory."

So here they were, wandering aimlessly from the chairlift amid a crowd of tourists, looking for…what?

Meredith tucked an arm through Blair's.

"It's beautiful up here, isn't it?" she said. "One thing I do remember is that I had a standing date with Jan and Chantal—my best friends—on a Thursday, and we'd spend the day and evening on the slopes. Just the three of us."

"Richard Hunter joined you on one occasion," Matt said.

"He did?" Meredith wrinkled her nose at him.

"He wanted to film you skiing. It turned out to be one of his better attempts—vivid and colorful. You were wearing a new ski outfit, a silver and fuchsia affair you picked up when we were at the Alps WhitePeak in December."

"The same suit," Meredith said thoughtfully, "that I was wearing the day I disappeared."

"You remember that?" Blair asked.

"No, but I've read all the old newspaper reports." Meredith unhooked her arm from Blair's. "I shouldn't have had all that coffee at Thornebank.... I need to go to the washroom. Meet you over there at the lookout point."

She set off toward the hut, her bottom wiggling in its distinctive sexy way. Blair noticed several heads turn to follow her progress. With her blond hair cropped so short and her royal blue shirt tucked into the waistband of her perky taupe shorts, she was certainly an eyecatching sight.

But as Blair turned her attention to Matt, she found his gaze wasn't on his wife but on her.

"This can't be much fun for you," he said. "You should have stayed at High Meadows—lounged by the pool...."

"Matt, I'm as keen to solve this mystery as you are." They started walking in the direction of the lookout point. "Tell me, where was Meredith last seen on the mountain?"

"She met Jan and Chantal in the parking lot in the

morning, and they came up here in the chairlift together.''

"They didn't travel in the same car, then?''

"Jan and Chantal did—they share a condo in the village. Meredith came in her own car, a red Lexus. She split off not long after they arrived—'' he gestured toward the hut ''—I think she went to the washroom. The slopes were very busy, and somehow they never caught up with her again.''

"What was the weather like that day?''

"It had been bitterly cold all week, but there was a warming trend and snow was forecast for that evening. It started around seven, and by the time the hill closed for the night, there was a raging blizzard, which of course hampered the search and rescue teams when they were called out.''

They had reached a wooden fence. They took up a stance together, leaning against the rough cedar railing. All around them was the chatter of voices—American, Japanese, European—and in the crisp air was the scent of summer.

"You must notice a big change in Meredith,'' Matt said.

"I have to admit I see changes in her that I shouldn't have expected, even given the ten-year time lapse.''

"Such as?''

"Such as the change in her attitude to her work. The Meredith I knew would never have acted so destructively. The Meredith I knew didn't destroy. She created. If she wasn't painting she was working with clay, or illustrating her journals, or doing silver work, or making stained-glass windows, or—'' Blair broke off with a helpless gesture. "And on and on and on. An artist first, and last.''

"You know, Blair, I sometimes wonder...."

"What?" Blair prompted, as his voice trailed away.

"Oh, forget it. The idea's stupid."

"Let me be the judge."

He shrugged. "I find myself wondering—what if someone brainwashed her during the time she was missing?"

"I don't think that's stupid. It would explain her new attitudes, but it doesn't make any sense, does it? Why on earth would anyone want to brainwash her?"

"I told you it was a stupid idea."

"No, wait, I've just had a thought. You're a very wealthy man—what if someone had come up with a plan, a devious plan, to get their hands on your fortune? Good Lord—" a chill skated across her skin "—they might even—"

It was her turn to stop abruptly.

"What?"

"Nothing. It was a ridiculous thought."

With an edge of mocking to his tone, Matt said, "Let me be the judge."

"Oh, it's too wild, but what if someone did have a plan, one that involved getting at you through Meredith. She'd never cooperate willingly so they'd have to brainwash her first, or rather, hypnotize her." Blair felt a surge of excitement. "You know, it's not impossible."

"Yes, Blair, I know." There was a hint of amusement in his tone. "And I also remember how you loved reading your mother's mystery novels, and the more outlandish the plot, the more you relished it."

If nothing else had come out of this trip up Blackcomb, Blair thought with a faint lift of her spirits, at least their shared worry about Meredith had gotten rid of the awkwardness that had fallen between them earlier. Like herself, Matt had put the sexually explosive incident behind him. That was obvious by the expression in his eyes. It was warm and friendly, but nothing else.

"Let's not lose sight of the fact that you were the one who suggested the possibility of brainwashing!" Laughter lurked in her voice.

"Okay, let's scrub the idea. It's bizarre. But it's no more bizarre than the kidnapper's insisting he'd sent ransom notes when there were none."

Blair glanced around to see if Meredith was coming back, and her casual gaze almost missed the other woman. In fact, she had to look twice to make sure it really was Meredith approaching. She was sporting a taupe sunhat and must have tucked her blue shirt into her bag, revealing the taupe tank top she'd been wearing under it. She was all in taupe, and Blair realized this was why she hadn't spotted her. She'd been looking for the blue jacket and blond hair.

"Here's Meredith," she murmured.

Matt turned.

Meredith walked toward them, her face shadowed by the brim of her hat. When she reached them, she smiled.

"I'm ready," she said. "Shall we take a walk? I can't wait to find out if I'm going to have a sudden burst of memory. It's really quite exciting, isn't it!"

EXCITING IT WAS NOT.

Despite Meredith's apparent enthusiasm, a stroll down the Ridge Walk, with its view of Whistler Valley below and the Overlord Glacier across the way, stimulated not even the tiniest memory cell in her brain.

She seemed subdued as they descended in the chair-lift, and on their return to High Meadows immediately excused herself, saying the sun had given her a headache.

"Or maybe not the sun," she added rather wearily as they crossed the foyer. "Perhaps I did get a knock on the head during the time I was missing, Matt, as you've often suggested. And perhaps that's the reason I can't remember anything. I guess I should have listened to you and not been so damned stubborn." She put a hand on his arm and looked into his face. "I'm ready to see that doctor, darling. I'll make an appointment for some time next week."

Blair could tell by the change in Matt's expression that this was very good news, indeed.

"Thank God for that," he said. "And you're doing the right thing, Meredith. John Gillam's an excellent man."

John Gillam, Blair knew, was the head neurosurgeon at Lions Gate Hospital in North Vancouver, and Blair silently agreed with Matt. If Meredith put herself in his care, she would be in excellent hands, indeed.

She felt a sudden surge of intense compassion for the other woman. Not affection—she doubted she'd ever feel that again for her—but compassion.

"Can I send Aileen up with something?" Matt went on.

"No thanks, darling," Meredith said over her shoulder as she made for the stairs. "Tell Aileen I'm not to be disturbed. If I can sleep for a while, that may help."

As she disappeared upstairs, Blair turned to Matt.

"Shall I go and look for Aileen?"

"Would you? I need to go to my office and check for messages. You'll find her in the kitchen, I would imagine, preparing dinner."

AILEEN WAS STANDING at a long harvest table, slicing carrots. After Blair had delivered Meredith's message and was about to leave, the housekeeper said, "And are you enjoying your stay here, Miss Enderby?"

"Yes, I am. It's such a lovely house."

"And quiet. Though maybe that'll change, once Mrs. Straith gets better and starts having her friends around again like in the old days. Rita, the girl that comes up to help me once a week with the heavy work, has told me all about the fancy parties Mrs. Straith used to have."

"She always did like parties. But it would mean a lot more work for you."

"Oh, Rita would help out. She always did. She's a pretty wee thing," the housekeeper went on, "and Mrs. Straith apparently took a fancy to her—liked to have her around when she was getting dressed for her parties. Rita would lay her outfit on the bed for her, set out her jewelry and her shoes and such like. Then afterward, at dinner, Rita would do the waitressing, because Mrs. Chang preferred to stay in the kitchen. Richard Hunter did the bartending."

"That must have made a nice break in his routine. Variety, as they say, is the spice of life."

"That's as may be." Aileen's eyes sparked. "But the man is married, and even though his wife's in Ontario, that's no excuse for the way he is with other women!"

Blair raised her brows.

"The man's totally obsessed with Mrs. Straith." Aileen kept her voice low. "Rita told me all about it. She likes a good time, does Rita, and when Richard Hunter started work here, she told me he really came on to her. She flirted with him a bit—she knew he was married so she never let him get very far. Thing is, Rita came to realize he was only using her to find out things about Mrs. Straith.''

Blair frowned. ''What kind of things?''

''He wanted to know what was her favorite perfume, what TV programs she liked to watch, her favorite foods, her favorite drinks, what she listened to on her CD player. But then one day he asked Rita to tell her what kind of undies Mrs. Straith wore, and Rita told him to get lost. And that was the end of that.''

''Did Rita tell anybody?''

''She said she did think of telling Mrs. Straith, but she felt it wasn't her place. Besides, she used to see the two of them together, and Mrs. Straith seemed to like him. He's into photography, and she loves having her picture taken. Used to,'' the housekeeper corrected herself. ''Since she came back, Mrs. Straith doesn't have any time for him. Barely speaks a word to him unless she has to.'' She cleared her throat. ''I was wondering if you think I ought to say something. Well, of course not to Mrs. Straith—we've been warned not to upset her—but to Mr. Straith.''

''I'll think about it,'' Blair said cautiously. ''It's a tricky situation, and not the sort of thing I'd want to rush into without considering everything that's involved.''

''I feel better already, just by talking with you. Lightens the load, I always think, to share it.''

Sure, Blair thought wryly, *it lightens your load. Unfortunately, it only adds to mine!*

But she would give the matter some serious thought.

If the gardener was obsessed by Meredith and had, in the past, been encouraged by her but was now getting the brush-off, he wouldn't like it.

He wouldn't like it one little bit.

And Richard Hunter did not seem to be the kind of man who would take kindly to rejection.

THE GARDENER, Blair discovered over dinner, had driven into Whistler for the evening.

"He's gone to see that new movie *Rich Girl*," Matt said. "Have you seen it, Blair?"

"No, but I hear it's very good."

"Your cup of tea." Matt grinned. "Murder, mystery, mayhem."

But Blair's thoughts had drifted at a tangent as she realized that with the gardener's absence, she might with luck have an opportunity to retrieve the earring.

That opportunity came when Matt excused himself right after dinner, saying that he was going upstairs to check on Meredith, who had had her meal sent up to her room.

Blair wasted no time in making her move.

She borrowed a pair of tongs from the kitchen and in two minutes flat was outside and on her way to the gazebo.

But when she got there, she saw, with a feeling of dismay, that a sign was set against the entrance. Wet paint—Keep out.

The smell of the paint drifted to her on the breeze, and the duckboard glistened with its fresh white coat.

Blair felt a hard slap of anger. The floor had been in perfect shape. Richard Hunter had painted it to keep her out. It was the only possible explanation.

Fighting to contain her outrage, she moved around the gazebo until she was right behind the spot on the bench where she'd been sitting when she saw the piece of jewelry sparkling. She hoisted herself onto the railing and swung herself onto the bench. She crouched there, a hand clutching the railing for balance, and leaned forward as far as she could.

She focused her gaze on the slats between the white planks, and as she did, her heart did an erratic and jarring quickstep.

It was unbelievable, yet it was a fact.

The earring was gone.

"DID YOU ALWAYS want to work in the hotel business?" Blair set her small black tape recorder on the coffee table between herself and Matt. "You don't mind, by the way, if I record our conversation?"

"No problem."

Matt had come downstairs as she entered the house after her trip to the gazebo. He'd changed into a casual shirt and shorts. He told her Meredith was feeling better and would be coming down shortly. Then he'd suggested they begin the interview for her article.

"We'll talk in the drawing room," he'd suggested.

So here they were, sitting across from each other with an oval rosewood coffee table between them.

"Did I always want to be a hotelier? Well, I always wanted to be in the hospitality business from the time I was in high school. I used to work part-time in hotels not only to make myself money, but to gain experience."

"You've built up a chain of exceptionally fine hotels. What's the secret of your success?"

"A little money—the cash my father left me—a little luck, plus a lot of faith in myself. And vision. Take the Whistler WhitePeak. It was badly run-down—I bought it when nobody else wanted it. And for a song. Of course Whistler in those days didn't have the high profile it has now."

"How many WhitePeak Internationals are there?"

"Ten. And run by nine general managers."

"Nine? Why not ten?"

"I oversee the whole operation from the Whistler WhitePeak. It's my special baby."

Blair knew that if she hadn't had the tape recorder playing, if she'd been depending on herself to take notes, she'd have ended up with a pad of empty pages. Her attention kept drifting, her gaze flitting wistfully from the tiny scar just below his left eye to the dark sweep of hair over his brow to the enticing fullness of his lower lip and back to the eyes, steady, serious, today taking on the blue-green of his cotton-knit shirt.

"Tell me about it, Matt. About your vision for it when you took over."

He talked at length about those early days, but as he did, she became slowly aware that his eyes, those beautiful, dark-fringed green eyes, were beginning to darken with awareness as he looked at her.

She ran a nervous hand over her hair and felt her stomach flutter as he got to his feet. He looked, she thought in panic, like a man with a mission. Her pulse leaped, but she remained where she was.

"So—" her voice was squeaky "—the WhitePeak was your first success. What made you decide to open a hotel in Europe next? Why not another here in North America?"

"That's enough for now." Matt leaned over the table as if to switch off the tape recorder, but before he could, the door opened, and he straightened.

Meredith came in.

"Ah, here you are," she said.

"Perfect timing," Matt said, and Blair was sure that only she detected the faint thread of frustration in his tone. "We were just finishing. I've got to catch up on some paperwork."

"Pour us a drink, darling?" Meredith sank down on the sofa Matt had vacated. "What would you like, Blair?"

A double brandy! "Nothing for me, thanks."

"Sure? I'll have my usual, darling."

Meredith was wearing a lounging robe of pastel blue silk, and Blair thought she'd never looked more beautiful. She reminded Blair of Jane Grigor. Meredith's mother had also been beautiful, but modest and reserved, unlike her vivacious outgoing daughter. As Blair's thoughts went to the past, she decided this would be as good a time as any to talk to Meredith about the old days.

She waited till Matt had gone out and then said, "Mom and I were so sorry to hear that your mother had died. Do you remember anything at all of her?"

"Not a blessed thing! But I'm sure," she added tersely, "you're going to fill me in on all the details!"

Blair was taken aback by Meredith's brusqueness, but she managed to keep that hidden. "Those were very happy days."

"Oh, yes, Matt assured me that what you would have to tell me would be all sunshine and flowers. Lucky me, having an idyllic childhood and a mother who spoiled me rotten!"

Her words had a distinctly sarcastic edge, and Blair couldn't let it pass. "Your mother was a warm and compassionate woman, Meredith. You were her whole life. You were her only child. You were her sun, her moon."

"And, I'm sure, her stars! It sounds like the perfect functional family unit—"

"How can you be so cold? Up until the day you married Matt, she denied you nothing!" Blair's temper suddenly flared. "Even your wedding dress—the one you desperately wanted—cost far more than she could afford, but that didn't satisfy you, you had to have the honeymoon outfit of your dreams, too, amethyst blue silk! It cost the earth, but she didn't mind. Nothing was too good for you."

"And Matt took up where she left off."

"He did," Blair said grimly. "Exactly where she left off! He bought you gorgeous amethyst and gold earrings to go with that dress. And by the way, I found one of those earrings this morning." She hadn't meant to tell Meredith like this, while they were spatting with each other. But now that she'd started, she went on. "It was in the gazebo, under the duckboards. Did you even know you'd lost it? Do you even remember those earrings?" At the thought, Blair felt a rush of shame, and her anger faded. Good grief, here she was, railing at Meredith, when Matt's wife probably didn't remember anything at all about the dress—or the outrageously expensive matching earrings.

But to her surprise, Meredith said, "Yes, I remember the earrings. And I also remember losing one last fall. You say you found it in the gazebo? May I have it?"

Blair explained what had happened in the gazebo, telling Meredith about the gardener having seen her poking around. She also told her about his having painted the slats of the duckboard, presumably to keep her out. She suggested he might have helped himself to the earring.

"You're accusing him of stealing?"

"Well, has he returned the earring to you?"

Meredith surged to her feet and glared at Blair. "You

have no right to accuse Richard Hunter without any proof.''

''But—''

''In any case, after I lost it I had the other one made into a ring, so now it's of no consequence.'' Her eyes had become shuttered. ''Have you mentioned the earring to Matt?''

Blair got to her feet. ''Look, I only wanted to help. No, I haven't told Matt—I thought perhaps you might not have told him you'd lost the earring in the first place.''

''Of course I told him! He said not to worry, and I shouldn't get myself in a state.''

''Excuse me, Mrs. Straith.''

At the sound of the voice coming from behind, both Blair and Meredith turned.

Speak of the devil, Blair thought as she saw Richard Hunter standing in the doorway. Armed with a large watering can, he must have come to attend to the room's many plants.

''Go right ahead.'' Meredith waved him in.

Her cheeks, Blair noticed, had become flushed. Was she wondering if the gardener had overheard Blair's accusations? Was she embarrassed for him? Hunter barely looked at the blonde. His arrogant gaze was fixed on Blair.

Biting back a challenging ''What's *your* problem?'' she said to Meredith, ''I'm going to change and have a swim.''

''Right.'' Meredith's tone was slightly higher than usual, as if her nerves were charged. ''I may join you.''

The gardener stood his ground as Blair made for the door, and gritting her teeth, she detoured around him. His cocky attitude and rudeness had made her want to slap him, but somehow she managed to control herself, though her hand itched to leave its prints on his hard-boned face.

It wasn't until she was in the bathroom a few minutes later, slipping on her bikini, that she remembered she'd left her tape recorder in the drawing room.

She muttered a soft damn and then grimaced as she remembered she'd also omitted to switch the recorder off after she and Matt had finished talking. Following their conversation would be her altercation with Meredith about her mother and the gardener and the missing earring.

She made a mental note to edit those segments before she and Matt had their next interview.

Chapter Six

That night, Blair's sleep was disturbed by ugly dreams.

Through them swaggered Richard Hunter, his hair drawn back to reveal a gold and amethyst earring on his earlobe and on his face a mocking leer as he watched Blair flee from the gazebo leaving a trail of white-paint footprints behind.

Jason, too, found his way into her nightmares. With the muscles of his compact body bulging, he seduced a reluctant Meredith in the monochrome meadow of his painting. At the moment of his climax, lightning zig-zagged over the sky, revealing his psychic wife, her hair witch-dark, her eyes as black as the cat on her broom-stick. Watching from behind a tree was her son...

And in his eyes was murder.

Blair's muffled screams woke her.

She lay, panting heavily, sweat gluing her nightie to her body. Fragments of the nightmare flashed in her mind like a series of horrifying slides. She dug her fists into her eyes to try to block out the gardener's mocking leer, the artist's assault, Poppy's witchy appearance.

And Brandon.

She shuddered. It had all seemed so real. It had all been so frightening.

Gradually, her breathing became less agitated, and the distressing images began to fade. Fumbling, she pushed aside the covers, got up and crossed to the window.

It wasn't yet seven, but the sun was shining, holding out the promise of another lovely day. The garden was deserted, as was the pool. Its waters sparkled a tantalizing invitation—an invitation she decided to accept.

A swim would surely wash away the last vestiges of her dark nightmare.

She met no one as she made her way downstairs, barefooted and in her emerald bikini, a towel slung around her neck.

There was no one in the dining room as she crossed it to get to the patio. But she found the patio door unlocked, and when she stepped outside, she saw Matt.

He was unwinding a canvas awning over the patio area. He was wearing black trunks, but they were dry.

He hadn't heard her, the creak of the winding mechanism having drowned out the noise of the screen door opening.

"Good morning, Matt," Blair said, raising her voice.

He turned sharply, and as his glance flicked over her, his expression tightened. But when his gaze met hers, it was steady.

"Morning, Blair." His smile was friendly, nothing more.

But for just a second, Blair's traitorous heart betrayed her, tormenting her with a fleeting sample of what life would be like married to Matt. She would come down in the morning, after having spent the night in his arms. They would swim together, breakfast together, and between them—always—would be warmth and a love that surpassed anything they had ever known before.

"I thought I'd have a swim." She kept her tone light. "Great minds…"

Smiling, she dropped her towel on one of the cushioned chaises, and they walked together toward the shallow end of the pool. The heat was already intense, and Blair enjoyed the feeling of the sun's rays on her back. She sat on the edge, dipped a toe in. The water was cool.

"You do more than just look before you leap, I see!"

"I like to know what I'm getting into." She squinted as she looked at him challengingly. "Is that so bad?"

"Too much caution," he retorted, "can be boring."

He leaped into the pool and hauled her in beside him.

"Beast!" she spluttered. He shoved her under, and when she came up her hair was plastered to her head and her face. She swept it back to find that Matt was laughing at her. She chuckled, and then plunged away from him.

They swam laps for about half an hour. Blair was the first to stroke her way to the side. Hanging onto the lip above the water level, she leaned breathlessly back.

Matt, with a strong crawl stroke, joined her.

"That was great," she said, closing her eyes and offering her face to the sun. "If there was one thing I missed when Mom sold the house, it was our fabulous pool and those early morning swims."

"When did she sell?"

"When Dad moved into the home."

"So where does she live now?"

"She bought a condo in Kitsilano."

"And you, Blair?"

"I have an apartment in a newish building in Vancouver—it overlooks Stanley Park. Wonderful view."

She opened her eyes and looked at him. Her move

had obviously been unexpected. He was looking at her, and the expression in his eyes almost stopped her heart.

The easy friendliness had gone, as had the open smile. His gaze was clouded with passion, passion so intimate she trembled as if he'd drawn his hand over her flesh. Her eyes widened, and their gazes locked so tightly she couldn't have looked away had her life depended on it.

Her throat muscles constricted, making it difficult to breathe. Her breasts felt tight, the peaks tingly. She felt her cheeks flush, knew he would see it.

"God—" Matt's voice was husky "—you're beautiful."

"Matt." Blair's protesting gesture was weak. "Don't."

He closed his eyes and dropped his head back...and it was her turn to look on him unseen. His wet hair clung to his skull, his jaw was darkly stubbled, his lips were parted slightly...and she ached to touch them with her own. She gazed at his closed eyes, at the long black lashes brushing his skin.

HE SENSED that she was looking at him.

He opened his eyes, and his heart took a flying leap as he saw her misty, yearning gaze. It was like waking up from an empty dream and finding a miracle unfolding in front of him, but even as a strangled murmur came from his throat, her cheeks became scarlet and she dropped her gaze.

Guiltily.

Damn. Regret tore through him. He ached to draw her into his arms, tell her it was all right, but he was in no position to say such a thing. He was married. And though he had told Meredith, the night before she disappeared, that he was going to divorce her, she had no memory of that night or anything that was said. And until her mind stabilized, he couldn't bring up the subject again.

"Blair." His voice had an unfamiliar roughness. "I'm sorry. I shouldn't have—"

"It's all right." She raised her eyes and bravely met his. "I was just as much at fault."

"We've always liked each other, and now—" he succeeded in sprinkling his words with just the right amount of wry humor "—with hot sun and half-naked bodies thrown into the mix, it's only natural that we'd...feel something. But we both have more sense than to think it's more than just a momentary thing...a product of affection and proximity. We're both adult enough to understand that and not let it spoil the relationship we do have. Friends, Blair?"

He saw her throat muscles give a faint convulsive movement.

"Friends," she said.

"Good. How about a cup of coffee to seal the bargain?"

"Sounds great!"

Her tone was upbeat, but he was sure the airiness was faked. As faked as his own had been.

He hoisted himself out of the pool, then held out a hand to help her up. But as he clasped her fragile-boned wrist, his emotions started roiling again.

The feelings erupting in his heart were like none he'd ever experienced. They threatened to knock the knees from under him, threatened to make the honor and integrity he lived by mere words, to be swept aside like dross.

He dropped her wrist the moment she was upright on

the deck and crossed the patio to open the screen door for her.

With a murmured thanks she stepped past him.

For a dangerous moment, he was tempted to sweep her into his arms and claim her soft lips in a fierce and possessive kiss. Ah, to hold that sweet body close to his, to feel her naked flesh humming against his own. To take her and bury himself in her...

But he knew that such a move would drive her from High Meadows and out of his life forever.

A life that had been hell since he'd discovered how Meredith had betrayed him.

And now would be worse than hell, knowing there truly was a paradise on earth but a paradise that—for him at least—was forbidden.

MATT LEFT for the WhitePeak after they'd eaten breakfast.

Since Meredith still hadn't appeared, Blair decided to go up to her room and work on her article.

She sat in a chair by the bedroom window, switched on her laptop and called up the Straith file only to see, flashing on the screen, the message, No File of This Name.

Of course there's a file of that name, she thought, grumbling, and called up the file manager.

But there was no file listed with the name Straith. Nor was there any backup file.

Blair stared blankly at the list of available files.

Had she deleted the Straith file by mistake? It was possible, of course, but the program she used had built-in safeguards to preclude that kind of carelessness. That the backup file was also deleted suggested someone had tampered with her computer.

But who?

And why?

There had been nothing there of any importance. She hadn't transcribed any of the taped conversation she and Matt had had the day before.

Should she discuss the matter with Matt? Surely he had enough worries, without adding to them.

Still, he ought to be made aware something strange was going on. She'd bring it up when he came back from the hotel.

In the meantime, she'd go downstairs, fetch her tape recorder and start editing her interview with Matt.

She was closing her bedroom door behind her when she heard someone run lightly up the stairs, and as she walked toward the landing Meredith appeared.

"I was looking for you!" the blonde chirped. "Poppy just phoned to invite us to Thornebank for coffee. I accepted for you, but I'm dashing into the village for a manicure appointment. Walk along by the river, much quicker than taking your car, and it's a glorious day. You'll probably get to see Jason's painting. It's finished."

With a careless wave of her hand, she was gone, leaving Blair feeling quite breathless.

And also leaving her to make her mind up whether to walk to Thornebank along the riverside path or drive.

But Meredith was right. It was a glorious day.

And she could do with the exercise.

BLAIR HAD ALMOST REACHED Thornebank when the first bullet whistled past her ear.

She'd been strolling along, enjoying the swish of the water and the summer scents drifting from the wild-flowers on the riverbank. Hands slipped into the hip pockets of her jeans, she was humming the tune from *Rich Girl* when she heard what sounded like a car backfiring.

At the same time, something—an insect?—flew past her so closely it lifted a strand of her hair.

She halted. Frowned. Put a hand to her head. Her mind had become blank. Surely that hadn't been a gunshot?

Heart pounding, her breathing quick and shallow, she stared into the forest where the sound had come from.

She saw nothing.

She swallowed, tried to steady her breathing. There was nobody there. She was crazy to think what she'd heard had been a gunshot. It must have been a car backfiring.

The second shot made her scream.

As the sound echoed from the mountains, she took to her heels and dashed hell-for-leather along the path toward Thornebank. She didn't consider going back to High Meadows. She knew she must be closer to the Thorne place. *It can't be far now,* she prayed as she raced on. It must be just around the corner....

It was.

Breath coming in swift, rasping shudders, she made for the patio door at the back. Her feet hit the wooden deck with enough sound to waken the dead. When she reached the door, she found to her profound relief that it wasn't locked. She wasted no time in knocking. She crashed the door open, hurled herself inside, slammed it shut again.

She leaned against the wall, feeling as if her heart and lungs were going to explode.

It was only when she started to calm down that she realized no one could have heard her come in despite the noise she'd made, because someone was playing a stereo. And just as her breathing settled down to close to normal, the music stopped, followed by absolute silence.

Into the silence, quaveringly, she rose her voice.

"Poppy!"

A nearby door opened, and Brandon appeared.

"You're looking for Mom? She's in the shower. Hang on, I'll tell her you're here."

He disappeared into the house, and after a time that seemed to Blair to be endlessly long, he reappeared. Poppy hurried behind him, her head turbanned in a towel, her feet in mules, her voluptuous body clothed in a loose cotton robe.

"Blair, dear," she said warmly, holding her hands out in greeting. "How nice to see you. And I love surprises! But if I'd known you were going to pay me a visit this morning, I'd have— What's wrong, dear, you look so white— Brandon, quick, catch her—she's going to faint."

When Blair came to, she was lying on something soft and comfortable.

It seemed to be a long sofa in a room that was bright with sunshine. And after she'd blinked a couple of times to clear the fuzziness from her gaze, she found she wasn't alone. Poppy was leaning over her. The other woman's face was drawn, her eyes filled with concern, and when she addressed Blair, that concern was echoed in her voice.

"Well, thank heavens! You gave me the fright of my life. I've never seen anyone pass out before."

Blair shakily pushed herself up on her elbow. "It was

really weird…like a black curtain slipping down in front of my eyes, and then I had a hazy sensation of falling.''

''You did start to keel over, dear, but fortunately Brandon caught you before you hit the ground.'' Poppy straightened and reached up to adjust her turban towel. ''Brandon called Matt—he's on his way. Luckily he was at the hotel riding stables just a couple of miles from here—''

''But Matt's so busy! There's no need—''

''He won't be too busy to come and check up on you! Now, let me get you something to drink and then you must rest until he comes. Coffee?''

''Thanks, Poppy.'' Blair ran her tongue over her parched lips. ''I could really use a cup of coffee.''

''I'll put on a fresh pot. You just take it easy. I'll be back in a few minutes.''

As Poppy went out, Blair slumped and closed her eyes. Somebody had shot at her. But who? And why?

She must have drifted off for goodness knows how long. The sound of Poppy's voice startled her.

''Sit up, dear, here's your coffee.''

She'd brought two mugs on a tray. She set them down on the low coffee table. ''Sugar? Cream?''

For a few minutes, they sat in silence drinking their coffee. Poppy was obviously waiting for Blair to speak.

Finally, Blair reached over and put down her mug. Lying back, she wove a shaky hand through her hair.

''Poppy, I'm a bit confused. I gathered from what you said earlier that you weren't expecting me.''

''Don't give it a second thought, honey. When you were here the other evening didn't I tell you to pop by any time? I'm delighted to see you, and if I gave you any other impression, it was only because I was disappointed I was in the shower when you arrived.''

"It's not that. You see, I only came along be-cause—"

She broke off as she heard the sound of heavy foot-steps pounding fast along the hallway. A second later, Matt strode into the room. Dressed in a business suit, with his features grimly set and his eyes hard as steel, he emanated such an aura of tension that Blair shrank back.

He came to a halt in front of her, his jacket pushed back, his hands on his hips. Aggressively he leaned over her.

"What the hell happened?" he snapped, his angry breath hitting her face. "Are you all right now?"

"Matt!" Poppy's tone was outraged. "What way is that to talk to someone who's recovering from a fainting spell!"

Matt inhaled a deep breath and rubbed a hand—frus-tratedly, Blair thought—over his nape. He straightened.

"Sorry, Blair." Gruffness roughened his words. "You can't blame me for being worried, though. People don't faint for no reason. So…what's wrong?"

"I was walking along the riverside path," Blair said, surprised that she was managing to sound so calm, "when someone shot at me."

She heard Poppy's incredulous gasp, saw stark shock in Matt's eyes. He interrupted in a harsh voice, "My God, Blair—"

"Twice. Someone shot at me from the forest twice. If Brandon hadn't had his stereo playing, Poppy, you'd probably have heard the shots. Or maybe not, since you were in the shower. The first bullet was so close it skimmed my hair." She bit her lip, hard, to keep it from trembling.

A phone sat on the table beside Blair's coffee mug.

Almost before she'd finished speaking, Matt had it in his hand. Seconds later, with his eyes never leaving hers, he was talking to a police officer.

As soon as he'd replaced the receiver, Poppy said, "Someone's going to come over?"

"Damned right." He scowled at Blair. "They're on their way."

Blair found herself scowling at him. If she hadn't known better, she'd have thought he was blaming her for the whole incident.

Poppy must have sensed the tension sparking between them.

"Matt," she said, "would you like a mug of—"

Blair jumped when a sharp crack sounded from outside.

Poppy put a hand on her shoulder. "It's all right, honey, that's just Brandon." She crossed to the window and pushed it open. "Brand, will you cut that out?"

Blair blew out a shaky breath. She felt Matt's eyes on her. "It's okay," she reassured him. "I'm fine. Just a bit nervy."

Poppy turned to the room.

"I wish that boy would get a job. He's driving me crazy—he's got a dozen tin cans hanging from a tree branch and he spends hours on end throwing stones at them." She rolled her eyes. "Kids! Who'd have 'em? So, Matt, how's about that coffee now? And if you're feeling up to it, Blair, we'll go out and have it on the deck. At least you can have some sunshine while we wait for the Mounties."

TWO RCMP OFFICERS came, listened and took statements.

After Blair had described exactly where she was

when the shots were fired and from which direction the shots had come, the constables left to search the area. When they returned, it was to report they had found no evidence to support Blair's story.

"But of course," the first officer said, "there's no way we could search the whole area."

"And it's highly likely," the second officer added, "that if those *were* shots you heard, the bullets were strays from a hunter's gun. This time of year, accidents do happen. There'll always be the irresponsible idiot who doesn't make sure he's shooting at what he wants to shoot at before he fires. If you plan on doing any more wandering around close to the forest, Miss Enderby, it might be a good idea to wear orange as a precaution."

After the Mounties left, the atmosphere was strained.

"I've never had any problems with hunters before," Matt said. "How about you, Poppy?"

"No, none."

Matt turned his gaze to Blair. "Where were you going when you heard the shots?"

"I was on my way here, Matt. Poppy phoned High Meadows an hour or so ago and invited me to come over for coffee—"

"Blair!" Poppy's eyes widened. "What are you saying? I hadn't talked to you today until you turned up here and Brandon came to fetch me!"

"Well, no, we hadn't talked," Blair said, confused, "but Meredith passed on your message. She said you'd called to invite us for coffee, but since she had an appointment in the village, she said I should just walk over alone—"

"I didn't call High Meadows this morning." Poppy's big bosom heaved with distress. "I didn't talk with you,

Blair, or with Meredith! I swear I didn't make any call. Matt, you do believe me, don't you?''

"I believe you, Poppy. Perhaps Jason made the call and forgot to tell you he'd invited Meredith and Blair to come over. You know how absentminded he can be.''

"Jason's not here." Poppy's voice shook. "He drove down to Vancouver last night—I don't expect him home until early afternoon. Matt…what's going on?''

"I don't know, but I sure as hell plan to find out. The next step is to talk with Meredith.''

"It must be some kind of a mistake," Blair said, trying to sound upbeat. "Perhaps Aileen passed a message on to Meredith, and just got the name wrong.''

"That might be it!'' Poppy said, eagerly latching on to a possible solution.

"And,'' Blair went on, "the police were probably right about the shots I heard. Shots from the gun of some idiot hunter.'' She essayed a careless shrug. "Stray bullets. That's all they were.''

"I hope you're right,'' Poppy said quietly.

"So do I.'' Matt rammed his hands into his pockets. "Because the alternative scenario is too damned alarming.''

"The alternative scenario?'' A prickle of fear danced down Blair's spine. "You mean, if it wasn't a careless error…it would mean someone deliberately shot at me?''

"But why?'' Poppy asked. "Why would anyone want to hurt you, Blair?''

Blair shook her head, unwilling to speak in case her voice cracked.

"Let's hope we get some answers from Meredith,'' Matt said. "If you'll excuse us, Poppy, we'll get back to High Meadows. She should be home from the village by now. But I don't want to talk with her on the phone. This problem is one that needs to be discussed in person.''

Blair's stomach muscles had gnarled into a hard knot.

If Aileen hadn't been the one to take the call, then it must have been taken by Meredith.

And what reason could she possibly have had for lying?

Chapter Seven

"Somebody phoned!" Meredith's cornflower blue eyes were wide with a blend of injured innocence and dismay. "And she *sounded* like Poppy, and she *said* she was Poppy...why in heaven's name shouldn't I have believed it *was* Poppy!"

The three of them were standing in the High Meadows greenhouse, where Blair and Matt had found Meredith plucking figs and laying them in a flat basket. She'd greeted them with an airy smile, a smile that had faded as Matt filled her in on what had happened and asked about the phone call.

Yes, she'd taken the call herself, but she exploded in outrage at Matt's thinly veiled suggestion that she might have been involved in some kind of deceit.

Blair searched Matt's face to gauge his reaction to his wife's response—which in Blair's ears had certainly rung true—and saw he looked every bit as frustrated as she was. They'd hoped Meredith could solve the mystery. Her response had muddied the waters.

"The plot thickens!" Blair's bright tone gave no hint of the sickening churning in her stomach. "Oh, Mom would love this. Let's see...unsuspecting guest is lured along lonely riverside path so villain can take potshots at her, only he's so incompetent he merely succeeds in terrifying the hell out of her, and—''

"Stop it, Blair!" Matt looked as if he wanted to shake her until her teeth rattled. "This is serious."

"Indeed it is!" Meredith interjected with a delicate shudder. "Don't forget we were both invited to Thornebank, Blair, and if I'd canceled my appointment and gone with you, this story might have a different ending."

"This story hasn't come to its ending yet!" Matt snapped. "I'm going to contact the police again, have them come around, ask you some questions—it's possible the call you took was from the kidnapper. The police will want you to describe the call. Accent, distinctive phrase, timbre, and so on. Are you up to it?"

"Of course." Meredith tugged a fig from the nearest tree, and with her small white teeth bit into the succulent flesh. She went on, speaking around the tiny morsel in her mouth, "All I can tell them, darling, is what I've been telling them—and you—all along. The truth."

THE MOUNTIES talked with Meredith for half an hour, took a statement, had her sign it and drove off again in their blue and white Caprice.

"No," she told Matt and Blair after they'd gone, "I couldn't come up with one thing that might have helped."

Meredith's tone had been indifferent, almost careless, as she spoke, and Blair saw Matt was having a hard time keeping his temper under control. Fortunately, the housekeeper came into the room then to announce lunch, and the meal created a much-needed diversion.

AFTER THEY'D EATEN, Meredith excused herself, saying she was going upstairs for a nap.

As soon as she'd left, Matt said to Blair, "I want to talk to you. Let's go to my office."

He could see the frown pulling her brows together and the wariness in her eyes. The urge to fold her in his arms and hold her close, keep her safe, was so strong that harnessing it called for all the self-control he possessed.

He cupped her elbow impersonally and ushered her to his office. Her scent—something sweet, a mixture of vanilla and violets—drifted to him as they walked and made him weak at the knees. He dropped his hand the moment they were inside the room. And then turned to shut the door firmly before saying, "Blair, I want you to go back to Vancouver."

"No." Challenge rang in her voice. "I'm staying."

He'd expected a protest; he hadn't expected defiance.

He bit back an oath and went on as if he hadn't heard her. "I have to go to Vancouver this evening for a meeting. You'll drive with me, in my car, because I don't want you going down that road on your own. I'll have a chauffeur follow with your Camry." His features were grimly set. "Blair, I want you out of here."

"Because I was shot at this morning? But that was just an accident. You heard what the police said—it was more than likely a hunter. He probably mistook me for a moose!"

"Yeah, right," Matt said heavily, "some moose."

"Look, you don't have to worry about me. Really. I can take care of myself. Or—" her tone had taken on a taunting edge "—is this just a subtle way for you to renege on your offer to let me do a feature article on you?"

"You know damned well it's not. Regarding that, we can have an interview on the way to Vancouver, and if we don't cover everything, we can talk on the phone any time."

"I'm staying." Blair tilted her chin like a stubborn child determined not to be thwarted. "I truly don't think I'm in any danger—why should anyone want to harm me?"

"Jeannie Chang has disappeared. Who would have wanted to harm her? Meredith was missing for three months. Who would have wanted to harm her?"

"I'm not involved, Matt. I've just come on the scene. I'm just a bystander."

He wondered if she believed that. She'd seemed shaky earlier, when she'd talked about some villain taking potshots at her. Was she trying to fool him now? Or was she fooling herself? Was she truly convinced the gunshots had been fired by a careless hunter? That might have been a feasible explanation had it not been for the mysterious phone call purporting to be from Poppy. Together, the two incidents took on an ominous aspect.

But he couldn't force Blair to leave. He remembered only too well how impossible it had always been to get her to change her mind once it was made up.

"All right." He shrugged in graceful defeat. "You stay. But for God's sake, be careful. We don't know what we're dealing with here...or who. But one thing we do know. The man is cunning as a fox."

MATT LEFT, and Blair decided to go to her room and lie down for ten minutes.

But she dozed off, and when she awoke, it was almost four.

Deciding to take her laptop to the patio and input some information about Matt from his student days, she changed into her bikini and went downstairs.

She found Meredith lounging on the patio, immersed in a glossy movie magazine with a picture of Brad Pitt on the cover. She glanced up, and when she saw Blair take a seat in the shade and click open the computer, she grimaced.

"I have a confession to make," she said, pouting her full pink lips. "I went to your room to look for you yesterday, and you weren't there...but I saw your computer. I was curious. I switched it on and pressed a few buttons—all sorts of stuff flashed on the screen and then disappeared. I hope I didn't wreck anything?"

Incredible how the woman could lie! No way could she have deleted the Straith file and its backup by accident. But she wasn't about to give Meredith the satisfaction of knowing how much she resented her prying.

"Nothing important. But I'd appreciate if you don't touch my laptop again. It isn't a toy. It's a work tool."

"Sorry." But even as Meredith apologized, she was flipping the pages of her magazine.

Blair snapped the laptop shut and slid it under her chair. She rose and made for the pool, wondering furiously why this woman could so easily get under her skin. If she hadn't moved away, she knew, she might have smashed the computer over Meredith's cropped blond head!

She swam lengths until she was exhausted and her rage had subsided. She had just climbed from the pool and grabbed her towel when she heard the patio doors open.

Her heartbeat tottered drunkenly when she saw Matt come out. He was in his business suit, and his eyes were faded with fatigue and more strained than she'd ever seen them.

He glanced at Meredith, who seemed to be asleep, then crossed to join Blair beside the pool.

"Hi," he said, "how's it going?"

"I'm fine, but you look bushed. Why don't you have a swim? It'll help ease some of your tension."

His gaze skimmed over her, and she was suddenly terribly aware of her wet bikini top with its silky fabric clinging revealingly to her breasts. As his gaze lingered, she felt the peaks tighten.

She swallowed, her mouth parched. Quickly, she rubbed the terry towel over her hair, and then with a deliberately casual movement, looped the towel around her neck, making sure the ends concealed her breasts.

"Yeah—" Matt cleared his throat "—sounds like a good idea." But he didn't move.

"Did you get much done this afternoon?"

"I've been organizing a horseback riding camp over by the River of Goldendreams and I had to make several calls. There's a lot more than skiing available in the Whistler area now, and at the WhitePeak we try to offer everything from hiking to biking, white-water rafting to kayaking, paragliding, tennis, and of course golf—I played the Nicklaus North course the other day…"

Blair noticed that his eyes had become less strained as he talked, and it came back to her that he'd always loved golfing. She jumped at the chance to take his mind off work and other worries.

"We should have a game together sometime," she said.

"Do you golf? When did you take it up?"

"Andrew taught me. He played well." Blair added dryly, "He did everything well."

"Except caring for you."

Matt's quiet words changed the mood, charged the air. Blair felt tension tingle through her, felt it pull her toward him and knew, by the dilation of Matt's pupils, the pulse hammering at his temple, that he felt it, too.

"I think," she said, her voice taut with contained emotion, "you'd better go for that swim."

"A cold shower might be more appropriate!"

Meredith had risen from her lounge chair, though neither of them had been aware of it, or of her soft-footed approach, but her voice, threaded with sarcasm, was another matter.

Blair inhaled a deep breath and turned. She sensed the quick stiffening of Matt's body.

Lord knew what might have happened next had the silence and the tension not been abruptly shattered by the roar of a powerful vehicle hurtling up the drive. As brakes squealed, Matt said wearily to Meredith, "Sounds like Chantal's MG. I'm going to follow your advice and have a shower. I'm in no mood for a hen party."

The rough way he dragged the screen door shut behind him was a blatant sign of his rattled emotions.

"Oh, damn!" Meredith screwed up her nose sulkily. "I've been avoiding her like the Black Death. She'll expect me to be the way I was, and I'm not. I won't ever be, until my memory comes back! I'm going to hide in the greenhouse. You'll have to cover for me, Blair. Tell her I'm not home."

Ignoring Blair's protests, Meredith slipped out of sight behind a high hedge. Blair heard the quick patter of her feet on the cement as she made her way along a paved path that led around the back.

"Well, great!" she murmured, turning toward the patio doors to wait for the visitor. "Now what?"

Chantal O'Keefe turned out to be a very attractive redhead. She must have been driving with the roof of her MG down, Blair decided. The wind had wrought havoc on the tangled copper curls spilling over her shoulders, but it had also brought a flush to her skin and a sparkle to her eyes.

After Aileen had introduced Blair as an old friend of Meredith's, Blair relayed Meredith's message. If Chantal was disappointed to find her friend unavailable, she showed no sign of it.

"Would you be a dear," she said to the housekeeper, who was hovering, "and bring me a tall glass of iced lemonade? And how about you, Blair?"

"Lemonade for me, too, thanks."

After Aileen came with their drinks, Chantal said, "Let's go over to the gazebo. It'll be cooler."

As they walked across the lawn, she went on in a low tone, "I know Meredith's at home. When I arrived, the housekeeper told me she was out on the patio—she's played this trick on me several times since she came back. Matt says she's avoiding me because she feels we're strangers now, but I feel I ought to persevere, not desert her... Though her attitude does make it hard not to give up."

The Wet Paint sign was still there, but Chantal stooped and ran a testing fingertip over the white boards.

"Bone dry!" she announced, and blithely stepped inside.

Blair cast a wary glance around, but the gardener was nowhere in sight. She felt a wave of relief. The man gave her the willies. She followed Chantal and took a seat across from her on one of the cushioned benches.

Chantal was wearing a cinnamon silk dress, and the skirt rippled as she stretched her long, shapely legs in front of her. Frowning, she toyed with her topaz necklace. "Aileen said you and Meredith were old friends. Funny, I don't recall Meredith ever mentioning you."

"Old as in long-ago," Blair murmured. "We lost touch after she married." In case Chantal wanted to follow up on that, she went on quickly, "I came up here to see if there was anything I could do to help. Matt hoped that talking with me might be a safe way to jog Meredith's memory."

"And has it?"

"I haven't had much chance to talk with her yet. She seems...evasive."

"Exactly. Jan and I—we're worried about her." Chantal placed her glass on the railing. "The reason I suggested coming to the gazebo was I wanted to make sure Meredith wouldn't be able to hear what we were saying."

Blair waited, feeling tense.

"That morning on Blackcomb—the day she disappeared—she was very jumpy when we met up. Not like herself at all. When Jan asked if there was anything wrong, at first she wouldn't say, but after we prodded, she told us—very reluctantly—that she and Matt had had a huge fight the night before."

"I read about that in the newspapers. Apparently they were overheard by the housekeeper and the gardener."

"But nobody overheard what went on between them afterward." Chantal's features tightened. "When she was getting ready for bed, she told us, Matt suddenly spun out of control. Snapped. Lost it. He hit her—"

"No!" Blair's denial was fierce. "Matt would never—"

"Let me finish. While she was telling us about it, we were standing outside the hut. It was a fairly mild day, but Meredith was all bundled up. She had her wool hat pulled over her brow, her scarf pulled up covering half her face, and she was wearing wraparound shades. She said—" and Chantal shuddered "—that Matt had given her a black eye!"

Even as Blair's mind reeled, she felt every cell in her body reject that statement. "Did she show you?"

"She wouldn't take off her dark glasses."

Blair surged to her feet, blood pounding furiously in her ears as she stared at the redhead. "If she'd had a black eye, she'd have shown it to you!"

Chantal got to her feet, too. "Yes."

"There, then!"

"Exactly. So the sixty-four-thousand-dollar question is, Why would she lie?"

Blair had been all set to continue her vehement defense of Matt, but when she heard the genuine puzzlement in the other woman's tone, she realized Chantal put no more credence in Meredith's tale than Blair did.

"Then you believe she lied?"

"Meredith wasn't herself that day—both Jan and I thought so. She was strained and sort of closed off from us. It's hard to describe—it was the weirdest thing. You couldn't really put your finger on it. She was there with us, but she seemed like a robot going through the motions. Jan and I talked about it—about how off she seemed. It was almost as if she'd been hypnotized. I tell you, her behavior had us spooked!" Chantal's eyes had a derisive glint. "Bizarre, huh? Perhaps Jan and I were the ones who needed our heads examined."

Blair didn't tell her she and Matt had discussed that same possibility and dismissed it.

Perhaps that dismissal had been premature.

"Look, I'm sorry to have unloaded that on you," Chantal said, retrieving her glass," but it might help you, if you're trying to help her. God, I hope so."

After Chantal had driven off in her MG, Blair found her mind kept returning to what the redhead had said about Meredith's strange behavior on the morning of her disappearance.

Was it possible that Meredith had been in some kind of trance? And was she still in that trance after all these months?

Oh, it did seem too bizarre to be true!

But at least she was willing to consult a doctor, which was a positive step, especially if the neurosurgeon could persuade her to see a psychiatrist. Such an expert would surely help her unlock the dark doors in her mind and let her memories burst free.

Had Meredith kept her promise to set up an appointment with the neurosurgeon?

Blair decided to go to the greenhouse and ask her.

The greenhouse was large, at the southwest corner of the house, and the sun blinked back from the sparkling glass panes as Blair walked up the path to it.

She stepped inside and had just closed the door behind her when she spotted Meredith.

The blonde was not alone.

Richard Hunter was with her.

They were standing at the end of a narrow walkway between tables sagging with trays of exquisite orchids. And they were engrossed in conversation. Even if they hadn't been twenty feet away, Blair couldn't have heard their words, because music was thumping into the hot, moist air. The beat drowned out every other sound, which meant that the couple so intent on one another didn't hear Blair either.

Meredith was looking at the gardener. He was doing the talking, and as he spoke, he gestured with the nasty-looking curved knife in his hand. The hard muscles of his arms bunched with every abrupt movement. The blade of the knife glinted like an arc of white ice.

Blair shivered. The man had a mean look on his face, and though she imagined the knife was for cutting the grapes that hung from the vines trailing above, she could just as easily picture him using it to slice somebody's throat.

Oh, now she was being melodramatic! Yet there was something about this man that disturbed her. He was more than unpleasant. Was evil too strong a word?

Whatever, she certainly didn't want to talk with Meredith while he was around. But as she made a move, she saw something that froze her in her tracks.

Meredith, with a lazy cat smile, took a small step forward and cupped the gardener's crotch in her hand.

Blair's shocked gasp was—thank heaven—drowned out by the thumping music. Catching her breath, she lost no time in opening the door and slipping outside. After closing the glass-paned door behind her, she stole a swift glance back to check whether they'd noticed her, and with a heady feeling of relief saw they hadn't. Hunter had his back to the door, and Meredith was hidden from view.

Sick. Meredith was sick.

Blair said the word over and over to herself as she hurried along the path toward the house. *Sick, sick, sick.*

Or, as Chantal and Matt had suggested, brainwashed.

Brainwashed so she was doing things she would never ordinarily have done.

Meredith Grigor had been an inveterate social snob. Though she had delighted in her power to attract men of any and every background, she had always been extremely finicky about the class of male she'd get involved with.

Richard Hunter would never have had a hope in hell of getting to first base with her.

But this latest incident showed Blair yet another way in which her old friend had changed.

Aileen had said the gardener was obsessed with Meredith. The obsession, it seemed, was not one-sided.

THE STILLNESS that had been in the air all day should have served as a warning that a thunderstorm was on the way.

But Blair had been too distracted to take much notice, and when the first rumbles rolled across the heavens early that evening, just a couple of minutes after Matt had left the house for his trip to Vancouver, they took her by surprise. She got up and crossed to the window. Already drops of rain were splattering against the windowpanes.

Through the blurred glass, she saw that Matt hadn't left yet. His antique silver Jaguar was still in the forecourt. She wondered what was up as she saw him get out and stride, his briefcase over his head, to the house.

She turned to Meredith, who was pacing the room with a restless air, a glass of wine in her hand. She looked paler than usual. And even more uptight. What could be wrong?

''Matt's coming in again,'' Blair remarked.

Meredith stopped her pacing. ''What?''

"Matt, he's—"

The front door slammed. Moments later, Matt swept in. He threw down his briefcase.

"Meeting's canceled." He sounded pleased. "I got a call just now on my cell phone—the storm hit Vancouver a couple of hours ago, gale force winds, flooding downtown, power cuts all over the place. So ladies—" he rubbed his hands together briskly "—dinner at the WhitePeak?"

"You're not going to Vancouver?" Meredith's voice had a peculiar squeaky sound. "But..."

"But what?" Matt looked at her impatiently. "I told you, the meeting's canceled. These guys are going to come up to Whistler tomorrow morning instead, and we'll have our meeting at the WhitePeak. Tonight I'm inviting you and Blair out for dinner—it'll give me a chance to show Blair the hotel. Okay?"

"That sounds wonderful," Blair began, only to be interrupted by Meredith.

"Blair and I will eat here as planned. Aileen will have cooked us a nice meal—"

"It'll keep. Now get yourselves in gear. How about we leave in fifteen minutes or so?"

"Count me out," Meredith snapped. "I have a headache. Why don't you go by yourself! Blair will keep me company."

Blair felt a jolt of shock when she saw Meredith's face. It was ashen. If she had a headache, it was a dilly.

"Go by myself?" Matt said. "You've got to be kidding. We'll all stay home. Maybe we can eat out tomorrow night—"

"No!" Meredith's eyes had a feverish glitter. "You and Blair must go, then. Tonight. I don't mind staying here by myself. I'll go to my room, have Aileen bring up my dinner. Then I'll take an aspirin and try to sleep.''

Meredith's swift reversal made Blair dizzy. ''Tomorrow night,'' she said, ''is fine with me. If you're feeling better, we can all go.''

''I don't want to go tomorrow night, either.'' Meredith's lips curved in a peevish grimace. ''I hate eating out. People stare.''

''In that case,'' Matt said, ''Blair and I will go on our own. Okay, Blair?''

Blair hesitated.

''Oh, go,'' Meredith snapped. ''You won't have any company here. I'm going to bed.''

Blair sensed Matt's intense green gaze on her. She felt a quiver of something shiver through her. Dinner alone with Matt at his luxurious hotel. Dangerous. But only if she allowed it to be.

''In that case, okay, Matt. I'll meet you here in fifteen minutes.''

Another shaft of lightning almost blinded her. And immediately after, a gigantic rumble, and the downpour intensified. It wasn't a night to be going out. It was a night to stay home. She didn't want to stay home.

Storms had always excited Blair. Something about seeing nature's power on the loose exhilarated her.

But tonight, a different kind of excitement set her pulses throbbing, her senses vibrating. It was wrong, she knew, to feel this way, to feel this elation, this thrill, this delicious anticipation. Matt was married, and forbidden to her.

She knew it. Her mind knew it. Her soul knew it. They were all bombarding her with dark warnings.

So why wouldn't her heart listen?

MEREDITH WAS WATCHING from her bedroom window as the Jaguar pulled away.

Blair chanced to look up and saw her through the rain-blurred glass. The blonde's face looked pale, pinched.

Frightened.

Frightened? Why should she look frightened?

Matt put the Jag in gear and moved the vehicle smoothly onto the drive. Meredith was lost to sight.

Shoving her ghostlike image to the back of her mind, Blair smoothed the skirt of her red-and-white silk dress and sank back in her seat.

"Seat belt fastened?" Matt asked.

"Yes."

"Roads aren't good," Matt murmured when they wheeled from the drive to the paved highway. "Got to watch for hydroplaning when it's like this." They splashed through a vast sheet of water. As they started uphill, he picked up speed.

"We should be at the hotel by seven," he said, and added, with a wry smile, "God willing and weather permitting."

Within minutes, they crested the hill and started down the other side, a short but very steep slope with a grassy bank on one side and a hazardous drop on the other.

"Like some music?" Matt asked.

"Sure. What have you got?"

The hill had steepened, and a sharp curve was coming up.

"Classical or—"

He broke off abruptly, and Blair swung her gaze from the curve to the man beside her as she felt the snap of tension in his manner.

"What's wrong?" she asked, but even as she spoke, she felt a chill of apprehension.

Matt was jamming his foot on the brake, over and over. Slamming it hard, right to the boards.

He swore harshly. His thigh muscles bulged against the fabric of his trousers as he used all his force, again and again, on the brake.

"Matt—"

"I'm going to steer it up the bank! Hang on, this is going to be—"

The Jaguar hit the bank and skidded sickeningly as rocks and earth and roots refused to budge under the vehicle's massive weight. Matt wrenched the steering wheel and attempted to climb the bank again. This time it threw him back across the road.

They had reached the curve. Matt shouted again. "Hold on, Blair, we're going over."

They were the last words she heard as the Jaguar roared over the edge. If he uttered any others, her scream of pure terror drowned them out.

The last thing she felt, as they sailed into space, was his arm coming around her and desperately pulling her close.

And the last thing she tasted was fear.

Chapter Eight

"Blair," Matt's voice was hoarse after countless desperate efforts to get a response from her. "Can you hear me?"

No answer.

If only he could see, but it was so dark. Dark as the grave, and surely just as cold. He gathered Blair's unconscious figure more tightly against his numb body. She needed to be warm, urgently needed to be warm. He could do nothing for her. He was trapped. His leg was trapped, somehow, between the steering wheel and the seat.

The leg wasn't broken, at least, he didn't think so. But it would be badly bruised.

That was the least of his worries.

His main worry was Blair. She must have hurt her head. How bad was it? Was she in a coma? He had to get her to a hospital. His uselessness, his sense of utter frustration, was driving him crazy.

When was someone going to find them? No one at the hotel was expecting them. And Meredith would be in bed, sound asleep after dosing herself with pills. She wouldn't miss them until morning.

He whispered into Blair's hair. As he inhaled, he

smelled vanilla and violets. He closed his eyes, his
throat threatening to close as a wave of yearning seized
the muscles, yearning so intense and so hopeless it almost made him weep.

Dark. Rain. Pain.

Trees.

The trees had saved their lives.

As Blair had screamed and dug her face against his
shoulder, he'd seen through the gray sheet of rain that
they were going to crash onto a dense stand of rugged
pines.

Ten feet to the left and the Jaguar would have hurtled
down the gorge.

Death, not life, had flashed before his eyes.

The crash was a nightmare he didn't want to dwell
on. His thoughts veered to the rain that hammered on
the roof like a deluge of metal nails. The downpour
hadn't stopped for a second during the long hours
they'd been trapped here and darkness had fallen.

Water. He couldn't see it, but he could hear it sluic-
ing in a never-ending flood down the windscreen.

Water. The water on the road. That gigantic puddle
he'd swooshed through just after they left High Meadows.

It must have gotten into the brakes. He should have
pumped them right away, several times, to—

Guilt ripped through him. If she was badly injured,
he'd never forgive himself.

He tried to discern the outline of her face, but the
night was too dark. She was breathing, though, and her
breathing was steady.

Dark. Rain. Pain.

The words circled his brain like vultures. He tried to
focus, but it was impossible. The hellish jolt when

they'd smashed down on the trees had jarred every cell in his body, and had jarred his thoughts, too. They kept bouncing in every direction in no proper sequence.

"Blair," he whispered in anguish, but he had almost given up hope of getting an answer.

He was wedged in hard against the door, which seemed to be staved in. His left hip was without feeling. He tried to move it, to make himself more comfortable, but as he did, a hot poker of pain shot up his arm.

He felt sweat pop out all over his body.

Gritting his teeth, he tried again, but he felt himself begin to pass out. He froze. He must stay conscious, must be conscious for Blair when she came to.

She'd clung to him, right up to the moment of the crash. Clung in absolute terror. And at the very last, as they'd crashed onto the trees, she'd called out his name.

He'd been able to do nothing to cushion the blow—

"Matt?"

Her voice was just a thread of sound. It was a wonder he heard it over the battering rain. He wanted to shout for joy.

Instead, he whispered, "Blair? Thank God, I was afraid you—"

"Matt, are you all right?" It sounded as if she was talking from some faraway place.

He brushed a kiss over her brow, his heart chilling as his lips met icy, clammy skin. "I'm fine, just jammed in here, dammit—can't get my leg out. My cell phone's in the back seat and—"

She tried to sit up. He heard her stifle a moan.

"Blair—"

"Just my head, it hurts like the devil." She sounded vague, disoriented. "Must have bumped it. But I can wriggle my toes and everything else seems to be okay."

Matt felt relief wash over him like a blessing. "Thank God. Oh, thank God for that."

"Matt?"

"Yeah?"

"I'm going to look for the phone."

"Are you up to it?"

"Won't know till I try!" Her words cracked in the middle.

"It was on your side, right behind you—I tossed it into the corner after I got that last phone call. Lord knows where it might be now."

"Dammit," she muttered, "I can't get my seat belt unfastened."

"Here, let me see if…"

She slumped as he reached with his right hand. After some fumbling, he managed to release the buckle.

"That's it," he said. "Look, are you sure you're going to manage?"

"Half a sec." He heard her shifting. "First of all, I have to get turned. There. And now I'm going to kneel on my seat and—" She broke off with a cry.

"Blair! What is it?"

"My head." The words caught on a sob. "Oh, Matt, the pain, it suddenly—it just got so bad."

She fell sideways against him, and he put his arm around her and held her tight.

"Oh, baby," he murmured, "oh, baby, I'm so sorry."

"Not your fault. Better now anyway."

Her perfume was in him again, in his head. Making him dizzy. Drawing him. Irresistibly. He pressed his lips to her hair, lingered there, exquisite sensations rippling through him. He pressed his lips to her brow, then to her cold cheek…and oh, God, if she hadn't wanted him to claim her lips, would she have tilted her face so he could find her mouth so easily?

Her lips were cold, but the fever burning between them was hot. He kissed her as if he was dying and there was no tomorrow. She was eager, and as desperate as he. Her chilled fingers were pressed to his cheeks, the tips lost in his hair. She felt so light, so fragile…and he wanted her so badly he trembled.

He could feel the swell of her breasts against his chest. It felt like heaven. This was heaven. A few minutes ago, when he'd been so afraid for her, afraid she would never regain consciousness, he'd thought he was in hell. Now, in his arms, he had everything he wanted in life.

And he would have her, make her his. He would. But he wasn't yet free to do so. One day, though…

Her lips clung to his, and it was sheer torture dragging his face away.

He still had his arm around her. He held her close, felt the flesh of her upper arm under his fingers. "I shouldn't have done that." Tenderness spilled from his heart into his voice. "I'm sorry."

Her quivering sigh almost undid him, but somehow he managed to keep from losing control, from giving in to his desire and plundering her mouth the way he desperately wanted to.

"Don't be sorry, Matt." The drumming rain almost blotted out the words he strained to hear. "I'm not."

AND SHE WASN'T.

Blair knew she should feel shame, regret, remorse. She didn't. What she did feel was honest. She had let Matt know how she felt about him at last. And she wasn't sorry. His life was a mess, and if she could give him some shred of comfort, she would do so, and damn the consequences.

She hadn't expected him to kiss her, but then she hadn't expected the sudden, poleaxing pain that had shafted through her head, playing havoc with her balance and sending her tumbling against him.

The pain was gone, at least the devastating agony was gone, but it had left behind a dull throbbing. It was bearable. Anything was bearable now, she thought, glad of the dark so Matt couldn't see the tears in her eyes. Matt had kissed her. The kiss had been the sweetest thing she'd ever known. She would treasure it forever.

"Okay," she said huskily, "let's get at that cell phone. I hope I can make it, Matt."

She was so weak and her balance still so off-kilter that an exercise that might normally have taken her five seconds took five minutes, but in the end, she made it.

Awkwardly, in the dark, she handed him the cell phone.

By the time she'd slumped in her seat again, he'd made his call.

"Twenty minutes, tops, and they'll be with us," he said, and she heard him put the cell phone on the dash. "Come over here and I'll keep you warm."

Gladly, feeling as if she were going home, she moved into his embrace. He enfolded her with his right arm, and she nestled her head against his chest.

"You did a great job climbing for the phone," he said softly. "How's the head?"

"Somebody's in there with a road drill, trying to find his way out. And I wish I could stop this silly shivering. But we were lucky—how come we were so lucky? I thought for sure we were goners."

"We hit some trees, they stopped us short."

"What happened to the brakes, Matt?"

"Water, I guess."

"Bummer."

Blair's voice trailed away.

Matt felt a jolt of alarm. "Blair, you're not going to pass out on me again, are you?"

He heard the faint reverberation of a chuckle from her chest. "Wouldn't dare."

But she did sound woozy, drifting. He should try to keep her awake. "Blair, tell me what happened with you after we lost contact. You'd applied to go to journalism school in Ontario. Were you accepted?"

"Mmm. There for three years. Then I came back to Vancouver and did a final year, just like you, Matt. Remember when you came to stay with us?" Her sigh seemed to come from the depths of her soul. "I'd never met anybody like you before."

Anxiety tightened his chest. She was beginning to ramble. It scared him. Keep her awake. He must keep her awake. Desperately he tried to come up with things to say.

"You were a quiet one, weren't you?" He spoke over the sound of the drumming rain. "Always reading, as I remember, or writing, or studying…when you weren't editing the school newspaper, that is, or doing volunteer work at your dad's medical clinic—Blair, are you listening?"

"Listening?" She sounded drowsier than ever. "Listening to you is such a joy. I've always loved listening to you, Matt. Except for that once."

An ineffable sadness had crept into her voice.

He felt an odd prickle at his nape. "When was that, Blair?"

"When you tol' me you'd fallen in love with Meredith. When you tol' me you were going to marry her. That's when. I wanted to die.'' Her breathing caught on a despairing little sob. ''She was my bes' friend, she knew how I felt about you…I'd written her a ton of letters about you. But she wen' after you anyway. You didn't have a chance…and you broke my heart. Matt, you never knew it, but you broke my heart.''

Matt realized, by the sudden heaviness of her body against his, that she'd passed out again. He shook her, roughly enough that if she'd been lingering in a twilight state, he might have brought her back.

Her only response was a sigh.

All he could do was hold her close, pray for her and pray that an ambulance would come quickly.

He'd never known, never guessed she'd once been in love with him.

Nostalgia squeezed his heart as a sudden rush of memories swept him to those long-ago days when he'd boarded with her family during his final year of college.

When he'd met Blair, she'd been eighteen, in her last year of high school. Her father was a gynecologist with irregular hours, her mother a mystery writer to whom time meant nothing. As a result, Blair and Matt, by dint of living in the same house, were thrown together. From the beginning, Matt had recognized a kindred spirit, and it hadn't taken long for him to develop a real affection for the Straiths' sweet and intelligent daughter. She had an openness and a sense of integrity that had appealed deeply to him.

Over the months, their friendship evolved. Blair would cheer him on during his football games, and he'd give her moral support when she was taking part in one of her school debates. They liked to go to controversial movies together, then sit up late, arguing heatedly about various points they felt strongly about.

His attitude toward Blair had been affectionate, gently teasing, protective. He'd felt like a big brother.

And that's how he'd believed she thought of him.

He'd treasured their friendship.

But everything had changed when Meredith came back from Europe.

She'd been away on a one-year art scholarship, so although she was Blair's best friend, he'd never met her. She returned two months before he was due to graduate. And the moment she saw him, she set her sights on him.

He was an easy target.

She was beautiful, sexy, vivacious, fun. He hadn't known Meredith was poaching, ruthlessly poaching, on what she believed to be Blair's territory. An unforgivable betrayal.

He tensed as he felt Blair's body twitch. "Blair?"

He waited, not breathing.

But there was no answer.

And still there was no answer when, after what seemed like an eternity, Matt heard the welcome wail of sirens.

"WE NEED your wife's medical card, Mr. Straith."

Matt dragged his thoughts from Blair and pushed himself from his leaning position against the waiting room wall as he looked up and saw the nurse in the doorway. She was holding out a crimson leather bag. Blair's bag.

She's not my wife, he could have said, but he wanted her to be, so he didn't correct the nurse.

He limped across and took the bag with his right

hand. The left was in a sling. Bruised all to hell, the ER tech had told him, but no broken bones.

"Just like your leg," she'd added cheerily. "You're a walking miracle—I heard your car's a write-off."

She'd gone on to offer painkillers, but Matt had refused. He wanted nothing to dull the agony he was feeling. He couldn't get the memory of Blair's ashen face from his mind. She'd regained consciousness on the way to the hospital, and the doctor had done a neurological check, then had her whisked to radiology. Matt shuddered as he tried to keep his fear at bay. They were taking a long time.

"Bring the card to the information desk," the nurse said on her way out of the waiting room.

Matt leaned against the wall again and took the weight off his left leg. With the strap of the bag over his shoulder, he lifted the flap and peered inside.

Her medical card would be in her wallet, or it might be with her credit cards in her checkbook folder. He extricated the leather folder and saw a sheet of paper tucked inside it.

He nipped it up with his teeth, intending to keep it there while he riffled through her cards, but it slipped free and drifted to the carpet.

It fluttered open as it fell, and as he scooped it up, his glance fell casually over the contents.

It was a short note, written in beautiful copperplate with an artistic flourish. Familiar handwriting.

He recognized it immediately as Meredith's.

Odd. Why would Blair have a letter from Meredith in her bag? He'd have to ask her about it later.

About to fold the note, he paused as a word leaped out at him.

Kill.

Kill? He did a double take.

Someone is trying to kill me.

His stunned gaze skimmed over the rest of the words, words his wife had apparently written the day before she'd gone missing. The letter was dated March 9.

Matt sank on the nearest chair. Meredith had believed herself in danger. Why had she kept that from him?

And Blair had lied to him.

Dammit, the woman had lied to him!

She hadn't come to High Meadows of her own volition, she'd come in response to Meredith's desperate plea.

Whatever was going on, Blair was playing a secret part, a part she'd kept hidden from him.

He felt as if an invisible hand was screwing his heart into a knot. Blair's honesty was the thing he valued about her the most. Her integrity. Her trustworthiness.

She'd fooled him. Played him for a sucker.

What was her game?

The depth of his disappointment was nothing compared with the profound intensity of his anger. Anger aimed mostly at himself. He'd had his fill of deceit. Meredith's betrayal had shattered him. Now this.

It was insupportable.

He jammed the letter into the bag, found the medical card, got up from the chair, limped to the door.

He'd hang around until he found out from the doctor what Blair's prognosis was. If it was good, he was going home.

If she was well enough to talk with him in the morning, he'd come and confront her with what he'd found out.

It was close to one-thirty before Blair's doctor came looking for Matt.

He was in the waiting room, eyes closed, half-asleep, when the brisk middle-aged woman tapped him on the shoulder.

"Miss Enderby's going to be fine." She slipped her hands into the pockets of her white jacket as Matt, blinking blearily, uncoiled himself from his chair and got to his feet. "She has a whopper of a headache, but she's quite lucid. I want her to stay here overnight so we can keep an eye on her, but everything looks good, no bleeding, no fractures—"

"Well, that's one huge relief." Matt raked a weary hand through his disheveled hair.

"You're a lucky pair, Mr. Straith." She walked him out of the waiting room. "I'll take you along to see her now, but don't stay more than a few minutes."

"Ah…that's okay," Matt said. "I'll…let her rest. I'll see her in the morning."

The doctor raised her brows.

He thanked her, said good-night…and sensed her watching him curiously as he limped away.

He could understand her surprise, but what he had to say to Blair could wait until tomorrow. It would be better if it did.

She'd be in no state tonight to hear what he had to say, and he hoped that by morning he'd have himself sufficiently under control so that when he did talk to her, he'd manage to show no sign of the resentful anger and tremendous disappointment he felt over her duplicity.

THE SILVER digital clock on Meredith's bedside table said 2:34 a.m.

The blonde stared at it as she dialed the number she knew by heart.

When she heard the familiar voice at the other end of the line, she said, in an urgent, gritty whisper, "He's back—it all went wrong—"

A searing curse burned the line, and she dug her teeth into her lip.

"Spit it out!" he hissed.

She gulped. "Just like you said it would, the car went over at the curve. But it landed on some trees—"

"How do you know?"

"I heard him come in. I went downstairs, pretended I still had a headache and was looking for my pills—"

"And?"

"They're keeping her in hospital overnight—"

"And him?"

"He's okay. What…are we going to do now?"

There was a taut silence, and through it she could hear his mind working. "Right," he said finally. "Here's what we'll do. His birthday's tomorrow—today, now, actually—and the portrait's finished. What a perfect excuse to throw his lordship a surprise party tonight." His chuckle held no humor. "After it's over—it'll be over. For him."

"But what about her? I don't want her around, poking her nose where it shouldn't be. She's beginning to suspect something, I'm sure of it."

"I'll get her out of the way, just leave her to me. All you have to do is organize the party. Oh, one other thing."

"What?"

"Before your friend leaves, I want you to tell her your memory has come back. And here's what I want you to say…"

BLAIR WIPED the back of her hand shakily over her eyes and felt the spill of burning hot tears.

God, what a pitiful creature she was, crying her heart out because Matt had gone home without coming in to see her.

It was her own fault. He must despise her, for kissing him the way she had. Just as she despised herself.

Idiot! Damned idiot! And not only had she kissed him, she'd gone on to tell him he'd broken her heart when he'd fallen in love with Meredith.

There was no excuse for laying that on him. Oh, sure, she'd been half out of it and rambling, but she was well aware that a very sane part of her mind had known exactly what she was doing. She'd wanted him to know how she felt about him.

And she'd been proud of herself, happy she'd confessed her deepest, most guarded secret.

Now she was sunk in a black hole of shame.

She'd ruined any chance of rebuilding a friendship with Matt. Instead, she'd sent him scurrying for cover.

Tears filled her eyes again, and she squeezed the lids shut. The tears rolled sideways, into her hair. She felt a sob rising in her throat. She swallowed it. She'd never felt more miserable. Not even on that day Matt had told her he was in love with Meredith, and she'd felt so unutterably betrayed by her best friend, who had then had the gall to ask her to be bridesmaid at their wedding. Oh, she'd gone through with it, head held high, and kept her resentment and unhappiness to herself. But once they were married she'd cut Meredith out of her life.

In doing so, she'd closed the door on Matt's friendship—

She heard the faint click of the door opening.

Matt! He'd come back. After all, he'd come back.

She tried to raise her head from the pillow, but pain zigzagged through her skull, and with a groan she sank down again. The room was in darkness, but she could hear the faint tread of feet on the tiled floor.

"Matt?" she whispered, trying to see.

But all she could make out was a shadowy figure approaching the bed. It seemed to be a man's figure, not the feminine shape of the nurse. As it came close, a foreign scent encroached on the room's antiseptic hospital smell, the sweet and pungent fragrance of cigar smoke.

He moved so fast he took her completely by surprise. One minute she was lying there, peering up, confused, wondering about that distinctive tobacco fragrance. The next, the intruder had wrenched the downy pillow from under her head and was pressing it onto her face.

She cried, but the sound was muffled. She kicked, but her legs were bound in by the sheet. She tried to tear the pillow away but didn't have the strength. She clawed at the attacker's arms, dug her nails in, but he was wearing a jacket, and she knew he wouldn't even feel them. She grabbed his hands, but they were like steel. She yelled for help until her throat was raw, but no sound came.

She was already weak. She became weaker as she struggled, her attempts to free herself more futile by the second.

And then everything became distant. Everything started to fade. Her mind spiraled in ever diminishing circles. Into space. Out to forever. And she knew nothing more.

Nothing but emptiness.

HE WAITED until she was limp, but not too limp.

He didn't want her to die.

He needed another dead body like he needed a hole in the head.

But he did want to frighten her. Frighten her away.

Swiftly he lifted her skull and replaced her pillow.

He leaned over, put his ear to her mouth and after satisfying himself she was still breathing, he slipped away.

IMPOSSIBLE TO SLEEP.

Matt limped to his bedroom window and looked out. At last the rain was diminishing. It was now a light drizzle. But the night was still dark.

What was that by the gazebo? Looked like the glow of a cigarette.

Not Richard Hunter. The man didn't smoke.

Then who? Who was lurking there at this time of night?

Grimly, Matt dragged on a pair of jeans, pulled on a shirt and made his way quietly downstairs where he took a flashlight from the hall closet.

He exited by the front door and without using the flashlight made his way to the back. Keeping well away from the pool and its muted light, he crept across the lawn. He could no longer see any glow in the gazebo.

That didn't mean the trespasser had gone.

Cautiously, he moved forward. The rain was cold against his face, and his bruised leg felt as if somebody was driving stakes into it with every step.

He circled the summer house, every muscle tense, every cell on red alert, but sensed that he was alone.

He stepped into the gazebo, and the moment he was

out of the rain, he smelled it. The pungent aroma of a cigar.

Who in the name of God had been standing here smoking a cigar in the dark?

Frowning, he flicked on his flashlight and played it across the white-painted duckboard.

And that's when he saw it. On one of the smooth slats. The stub of a cheroot. He picked it up and stared at it.

He recognized it immediately as an exotic brand that had to be imported by special order from a company in Cuba.

And he knew only one person who smoked this brand.

Jason Thorne.

Chapter Nine

The storm had raged itself out by dawn, giving way to a sunny, rainwashed morning.

Blair lay in her bed, staring blindly at the ceiling. Her thoughts kept trembling to the terror she'd felt at the hands of her attacker, and then to the incredible relief that had poured through her when she'd come to and found him gone. With a sob, she'd flung her pillow off the bed, loathing the tobacco scent that still clung to it.

She hadn't slept a wink after that. Memories of the attack had pounded her, the lingering remnants of her terror pressing down on her as relentlessly as the pillow had.

She'd gotten up to go to the bathroom around six, and when she'd looked in the mirror and had seen her gray pallor, she'd shuddered. In bed again, she tried to close her mind to what had happened, but it wasn't easy.

And when she succeeded, her thoughts switched to Matt, and those thoughts were, if anything, even more depressing. It hurt unbearably that he hadn't visited her before he'd gone home. She dreaded seeing him, but she knew she'd have to before she left for Vancouver.

She had to tell him about the attack. She didn't want

to alarm him, though, so she'd make it clear the man hadn't intended to kill her. The intruder could have done that easily, if he'd wanted to. He'd only meant to frighten her. And he surely had!

She'd been so shattered when she'd come around she hadn't even been able to ring the bell and call a nurse. Then, when she did get her breath back, she decided to keep quiet. She didn't feel up to having a horde of Mounties galloping to her bedside and asking her questions.

Questions she wasn't sure how to answer. If she were to be truly helpful, she'd have to tell them every detail she remembered, and that meant telling them about the smell of cigar smoke lingering around her attacker.

And wouldn't she feel bound to tell them that Jason Thorne smoked cheroots that had exactly the same fragrance?

Jason was Matt's friend. Why would he want to harm her? Heavens, she'd only met the man once! It made no sense whatsoever.

In the end, she'd decided she'd fill Matt in on what had happened and let him decide what the police should know.

AFTER SHE'D EATEN breakfast, the doctor came around, examined her carefully and pronounced her free to leave.

"You're going to feel groggy for a day or two, so take it easy. And don't do any driving until you're feeling better."

Blair wondered unhappily if she'd ever feel better again, at least as far as Matt was concerned, but she said, "Fine...and thanks for everything you've done. I appreciate it."

As soon as she was alone again, she placed a call to High Meadows. When Aileen answered the phone, Blair asked if she could speak to Meredith.

"She's gone out. Mr. Straith's here, though. Just a moment—"

Blair didn't want to talk to Matt. At least, not about the purpose of this call. But Aileen had put down the phone, and a minute later Matt came on the line.

Remembering their steamy kiss and her confession of love, Blair felt her cheeks turn pink. "Hi, Matt—"

"How are you feeling?" His tone was abrupt.

"I'm fine. I can leave any time. But the clothes I was wearing last night are filthy. I wanted to talk to Meredith, ask her to—"

"She's out. What do you want? I'll bring it in."

Just what she'd wanted to avoid—Matt among her undies. "Panties and a bra." She felt her pink cheeks become scarlet. "You'll find them in the dresser. And in the closet, grab a pair of shorts and a top."

"Anything else? Toiletries?"

"No, I've had a shower. They've supplied me with shampoo and stuff. Just the clothes."

"Hairbrush? Toothbrush?"

"Uh-uh. They gave me a toothbrush, and I have a hairbrush in my bag."

"I'm on my way, then."

"Just a sec! How are you?"

"Oh, just fine. Everything's A-okay."

Blair heard hard irony in his tone, and though she guessed only too well how he felt, it still rocked her. He despised her, probably didn't even want to talk to her.

"I'm glad you're okay." She cleared her throat. "Matt—" her voice was husky "—we...have to talk."

"Damned right we do!"

"I have to tell you about—"

But he'd slammed down the phone.

Blair sank onto her bedside chair, grimacing wanly as she tucked her hospital gown around her knees.

Matt was going to lash out at her for the way she'd behaved in the car. He'd made that quite clear.

She felt like a naughty child, about to be scolded for daring to put her hand in the cookie jar.

MATT SENT HER CLOTHES to her room via a nurse, who told Blair he was going to wait for her in the reception area.

When she was wheeled to join him ten minutes later, she saw him before he saw her.

He was standing by a window, looking out. In a white shirt and dark shorts, with his black hair glinting in a stray ray of sunshine, he was a bone-melting sight.

But when he turned at the sound of the wheelchair, he was frowning, and his eyes were ominously dark.

He greeted her with a terse hi, and she noticed, as he crossed to take the parcel of dirty clothes from her, that he had a limp.

"Does your leg hurt?" she asked.

"I'll live." Those dark eyes searched her face as if looking for scars. "It's you we've been worried about."

"I feel just a bit shaky. Otherwise I'm really okay."

He made a sound that resembled a grunt, then brusquely he ushered her outside to a navy car.

So much for small talk! Blair mused wryly as he opened her door. She slipped into the seat, dropped her bag on the floor and waited until he was in the driver's seat beside her before asking brightly, "Whose car?"

"Belongs to the hotel."

His tone was short to the point of being rude.

Blair felt a spark of defiance. Maybe she *had* encouraged his kiss, but as far as she remembered, he hadn't needed much encouragement! In fact, he'd seemed to downright enjoy the experience, kissing her with a passion that had curled her toes.

Hmph! No way would she try to draw him into conversation again!

Her vow to remain silent lasted for five minutes, until he turned off the highway that would have taken them to High Meadows and wheeled onto a side road.

"Where are we going?" she asked.

"A quiet spot where we can talk without being interrupted." It was a terse response.

The road wound among scattered houses, then left the houses behind to end up in a small parking area amid towering trees. Theirs was the only car.

They got out, and Blair drank deeply of the crystal air. It was a glorious day—blue skies, singing birds and a rich, loamy smell coming from the undergrowth. As she walked with Matt toward a narrow bridge leading over a creek, she sent up a silent prayer of thanks that they were both still alive.

They followed a path through a stand of trees and came to a small lake with a sickle of white beach and not a soul in sight. Across the lake cottages peeked at them, and on the water several boats bobbed lazily.

Matt led her across the smooth sand to a cedar picnic table. He swiped some leaves and grit off the bench facing the water and said, "Have a seat."

She set her bag on the table, swung her legs over the bench, sat down and tucked her feet under the bench.

Matt didn't sit. He started limping back and forth, six steps this way, six steps that, over and over, until she wanted to scream at him to get on with it. His hands were jammed into his pockets, his face set in a brooding scowl.

Blair had known he was upset, but she hadn't expected him to be this distraught. Good lord, he looked positively haggard. Surely just one kiss hadn't been such a dreadful sin? But maybe in his eyes it was.

She dug her teeth into her lower lip. Was it a sin to feel the yearning she felt now? Was it a sin to notice and admire the set of his wide shoulders under the cotton fabric of his white shirt, the perfection of his tanned features, the crisp, dark hair sprinkling his arms and legs?

She'd always thought he had the most fantastic legs—long, lean, powerfully muscled. An athlete's legs.

Legs that were going to take him away from her once again.

Friendship lost because love got in the way.

She blinked as tears misted her eyes.

When she looked at him again, he'd stopped pacing and was staring at her.

She felt a jolt of apprehension when she saw his taut expression.

"Blair," he said, "you have to leave."

"It's all right, Matt. I'd already decided to go back. I should have gone yesterday." Her voice caught. "I'm sorry. I'm so ashamed of the way I've behaved—"

"As well you might be," he said grimly. "But we'll get to that in a minute. First, there's something you should know. I had a mechanic look at my car. He found that somebody had tampered with the brakes."

For a moment, Blair could hardly take in what he'd said. But when she did, she felt chilled. "Who on earth could have done such a thing?'' Her voice sounded choked.

''Whoever phoned the other day, I have to assume.''

A motorboat shrieked across the lake. Blair waited until the noise had faded before she spoke.

''So—'' she took in a deep breath ''—the kidnapper did mean business. Matt, don't you think you should tell the police what he said about ransom notes? They're going to need every clue they can lay their hands on.''

''I've already done that. On my way to pick you up.''

''Oh, Matt.'' Blair scrambled to her feet and walked to him. ''What are we going to do?''

''Not *we,* Blair. You have nothing to do with this. No part in it whatsoever. You weren't even supposed to be in the car last night.''

''So you're saying that whoever did it knew you were planning to go to Vancouver alone,'' Blair said slowly. ''Matt, who knew about that...besides Meredith and Aileen?''

''Hunter knew. Nobody else except for the guys I was supposed to meet—a group of Japanese hoteliers. Oh, and Jason Thorne. I mentioned it to him when I called to tell him we'd be taking you to Thornebank for dinner. But hey, you can count Jason out—I've known the guy for years, and I'd trust him with—''

Your life? Blair thought Matt had sounded defensive, almost as if he himself wasn't convinced of Jason's trustworthiness but was too loyal to admit it. Her pulse had picked up speed. ''Matt, I've got something to tell you. Last night someone snuck into my hospital room in the dark and tried to suffocate me with my pillow.''

''What?''

''It's all right—oh, don't get so upset!'' She felt a stab of alarm when she saw the wild look in his eyes.

"He didn't mean to kill me—he could have, but he only wanted to frighten me."

Matt grasped her upper arms as her words poured out. "Tell me everything," he demanded harshly. "To the last detail. What did the police do about it? Why the hell didn't you phone me, tell me right away? I'd have come straight to the hospital."

"Huh! You couldn't get rid of me fast enough last night!" She hadn't meant to say it. The words had spurted out on their own. But may as well be hung for a sheep as a lamb. "You left," she accused bitterly, "without even coming in to say goodbye!"

"Because I was so mad at you for not telling me about the letter!"

Matt was incensed. He'd also never been so disgusted with himself in his life. Blair had just told him somebody had tried to kill her, and instead of showing her sympathy, compassion, he was blazing out at her because she'd—

"Letter? How did you find out about the letter?" A look of comprehension dawned in her eyes, and her expression became fierce. "Were you poking around in my purse when I was with the doctor? Well, of all the sneaky—"

"The nurse told me to look for your medical card."

Matt heaved out a frustrated breath. This was going wrong. All wrong. He'd meant to tell her she had to leave because of this lunatic on the loose, and then he'd meant to inform her, with a suitably shriveling glare, that he'd discovered her deception regarding Meredith's letter. Instead, here they were shouting insults at each other, and he wasn't sure which of them was more out of control.

"That's why you were so mad at me?" she asked

incredulously. "Because I didn't tell you about the letter? I couldn't! When I showed it to the police, back in March, they said I wasn't to show it to anybody!" She glared at him. "Particularly you, since you were their prime suspect!"

"Oh, Lord." Matt rotated his neck, but stress had knotted his muscles beyond relief. "I apologize for jumping to conclusions. I should have known you had a good reason for not showing me the letter."

Blair hated to see him so totally dejected. She wanted to reach out to him but managed to restrain herself. "Apology accepted," she said with a sigh. "I wish I could have shown you the letter, Matt. I felt badly about not—"

"Meredith trusted you. She apparently didn't trust me. I can't understand that. I've never given her any reason to doubt me."

Until last night, he thought. But though he knew he should feel burdened by guilt, he could not. What had happened between him and Blair had seemed the most right thing he'd ever done.

His anger had dissipated. All he felt was anxiety, anxiety for Blair.

"Let's talk everything over calmly," he said. "At least, as calmly as we can, given the circumstances. Tell me about this attack on you, the guy with the pillow."

Blair sank down on the bench, facing out, leaning back against the table, and told Matt everything. She didn't stumble until she came to the part about the cigar smell.

"It was so strong," she said, "and I recognized it. It was clinging to his clothes, but he must have been smoking before he came into the hospital. It wasn't a stale smell.'' She shut her eyes. ''It was the same smell as from Jason Thorne's cheroots.''

''Dammit, I just can't believe he'd be involved in any of this.'' But despite his sturdy tone, Matt felt his heart sink as he recalled the early hours of that morning, when he'd found the cheroot stub in the gazebo.

''There's something you're not telling me.'' Blair regarded him through narrowed eyes. ''What is it?''

He hesitated, reluctant to cast more suspicion on Jason. But Blair had been upfront with him, so—hating every word he was saying—he filled her in.

Her eyes widened with shock. ''You don't think—''

''I'm trying not to,'' he said. ''Trying not to jump to conclusions again. Here's what I'm going to do. I'm going to take you to High Meadows and arrange for someone to drive you to Vancouver. Then I'll go to Thornebank. I'll play it cool, but I'll find out if Jason has an alibi for last night.''

''I'm coming with you.''

''No way! You've had three near misses—first the gunshots, then the car crash, then this business with the pillow.''

''Matt, we've agreed that my being in the crash was pure chance. Whoever this man is, he doesn't want me dead. He could easily have killed me on two occasions. He didn't. He wanted only to frighten me.''

''You're not coming to Thornebank.''

''I have a right to confront Jason! I want to check out the expression in his eyes when he sees me. I'll know if he was the one in my hospital room last night. Woman's intuition, call it what you will. I'll just know.''

Maybe, just maybe, she had a point. Surely it was

her right to confront this man if he'd terrified her. And Jason might make some little slip.

He couldn't believe he'd just thought that! Jason a killer? The idea was absurd.

But he did need to go to Thornebank to put his mind at rest. And if Blair felt that need, too, he could hardly deny her the opportunity to satisfy it. But immediately after that, she was on her way. He didn't want her at High Meadows a second longer than necessary.

He wanted her out of danger.

IT WASN'T UNTIL they were on the road to Thornebank that he remembered how apologetic she'd been when they started talking…and how easily she'd agreed to go to Vancouver. He'd expected an argument, same as the first time he'd asked her to leave. But this time, she'd said she'd already made up her mind to go. Why the change in attitude?

And what had she been apologizing for? For hiding the letter and its contents? No, at that point, she hadn't known he'd read the letter.

He glanced at her, intending to ask her what she'd been apologizing for, but she was lying back, and her eyes were closed. He frowned when he saw how pale she was.

Lord, she was a spunky one. Tenderness spilled over him as he looked at her. Not only spunky, but beautiful. And passionate.

He felt a tightening in his groin as he recalled their kiss. It had haunted his dreams during his fitful sleep.

No, he wouldn't ask her why she'd apologized. Not now. Whatever it had been, it was something that had upset her deeply. He'd seen the tears misting her eyes when she'd whispered that she was sorry.

He wouldn't mention it at all.

Unless she happened to bring it up.

There was silence in the car until he turned into the Thornes' driveway.

"We're here," he said in a low voice.

She opened her eyes and sat up straight. "I'm not looking forward to this," she said.

"Don't worry," he replied. "Neither am I."

POPPY ANSWERED the door.

Blair thought the other woman looked tired, but her smile was welcoming.

"Well, this is a nice surprise!" she said. "Come in. Let's go into the den. Jason's there."

Blair felt Matt's hand in the small of her back as they followed Poppy along the hallway. Her tension increased, but added to it was tension of a different kind. She ached to turn, put her arms around Matt's waist and have him fold her in a tight embrace. In his arms was the only place she felt really safe. And if it turned out that Jason had no alibi for last night... She shuddered.

"You okay?" Matt's lips brushed her hair as he whispered the question.

She nodded.

He ran his hand lightly up her back, let it rest at her nape. His fingertips seared the sensitive skin just below her ear, setting her nerves aquiver.

Desire sizzled through her, making her dizzy. *Don't do that,* she wanted to beg. *You're driving me crazy.*

She closed her eyes as he dropped his hand.

They followed Poppy into the den, where they found Jason lying back in a brown leather recliner. The first thing Blair noticed was that he was smoking. The smell of his cheroot scented the air.

The second thing she noticed was that his right arm was in a cast.

"What the hell happened to you?" Matt said.

"He broke his wrist," Poppy said. "That's what happened. Damned fool."

"Don't get much sympathy around here." Jason's deep-set eyes twinkled. "But maybe I don't deserve any."

"No maybe about it!" Poppy said. "Any man who can't change a light bulb without breaking his bones—"

"You fell off a chair?" Matt asked.

"A ladder. The light had burned out in the upstairs landing," Poppy explained. "The man should have asked me to change it, or Brandon. He's never had a head for heights!"

"So when did it happen, Jason?" Blair asked, and her heart skipped a beat as she waited for his answer.

"When I got back from Vancouver yesterday afternoon. *Early* yesterday afternoon." His smile was teasing. "So if you're wondering if maybe I'd had too much brandy—"

"No, no, of course I wasn't!"

"Good, because I was, unfortunately, stone-cold sober. Had I been drunk, the whole thing might not have felt so bloody excruciatingly painful!"

"So you can't drive?" Matt's question came out casually. "Can't even open a beer can?"

"That's right," Poppy answered for her husband. "And he's making the most of being hors de combat. Had me up all night, wanting the painkiller the doctor prescribed or a glass of water or a back rub or another cheroot—"

"Yeah, I guess what they say about men is true—

they make poor patients. Poppy got no sleep, and it certainly hasn't improved her temper!''

Poppy made a playful swipe at him, and he ducked.

"So—" he grinned "—enough about me! To what do we owe this visit?''

Blair knew, by the way Matt's eyes had darkened, that he felt a real lowlife for even for a moment suspecting his friend of wanting to hurt him. But she saw him fake a cheery grin.

"Hey, we came around here looking for a bit of sympathy! You're not the only one who's had an accident. Hell of a thing happened to Blair and myself last night, on our way to the village for dinner. Brakes failed, and the car went off the road. Blair was in hospital overnight—"

"Blair?" Poppy's expression was aghast. "Are you all right?"

"How about you put on a pot of coffee for these good folks?" Jason's concerned gaze skimmed from Blair to Matt, and then to Blair again. "It did occur to me that you look like death warmed up, Blair."

"Thanks, Jason, that sure makes me feel a whole lot better!" Blair said with a chuckle, though the last thing she felt like doing was laughing. Death warmed up. Yes, that was exactly how she felt.

"You come to the kitchen with me, love," Poppy said, putting a comforting arm around Blair. "And fill me in. Matt can stay here and give Jason all the details."

Matt gave Blair a warning look, a look that said, "Not *all* the details." She answered with an almost imperceptible nod. She had no intention of telling Poppy anything but the barest outline of what had happened.

She would say nothing of the mechanic's report about the brakes, and the attack on her in the hospital.

With a broken wrist, Jason couldn't possibly have been the one who crept up on her and pressed the pillow to her face, and if Poppy had been up with him all night, he couldn't have been the person smoking a cheroot in the gazebo. And until they knew who the guilty party was, the fewer people who knew what had happened, the better.

In the kitchen, as Poppy made coffee, Blair told her the bare details of the accident. Poppy asked a few questions Blair could answer, but she wanted to cut Poppy off from asking any she didn't feel she could.

Walking to the window, she smiled at Poppy and said, "Do you mind if we don't talk about it any more? It's such a lovely day, I just want to enjoy it."

"Can't blame you for that. And let's hope this change in the weather lasts."

Brandon appeared outside. He must have come out a side door. Absently, Blair watched him as he slouched over the forecourt, juggling a couple of stones.

He threw them at one of the cans strung from a nearby tree, and both times hit his target. His aim was remarkably accurate. Then he crossed to a red Honda sitting in the forecourt, leaned against it, struck a match and lit a cigarette.

As he took a drag, Blair felt her heart give a gigantic lurch. She thought it was going to stop altogether.

Even from here, she could tell that what Brandon was smoking was not a cigarette.

It was a cheroot.

Chapter Ten

Matt eased the car from the driveway onto the road.

"Well," he said, "we sure were going up a dead-end alley. And thank God for that!"

Blair turned in her seat and looked at him. The lines fanning from his eyes looked deeper than they had before. "I know it was hard for you, Matt, thinking Jason might have been involved, and I'm glad for your sake that he wasn't. But I'm afraid there's a possibility Poppy's son might be the guilty party."

Matt jerked his head round and frowned. "Brandon? Oh, I doubt it, Blair."

"Matt, he was outside the kitchen window, and when Poppy and I were talking, I saw him smoking."

"I know he smokes. He has for years. Nothing Poppy can do about it."

"A cheroot, Matt. He was smoking a cheroot."

"Oh, no!"

"Poppy noticed and yelled out the window that he was going to get in trouble for stealing Jason's cigars. Apparently, it's not the first time, and though Jason's pretty generous about it, Poppy said he's been grumbling at the number missing recently."

For a long moment Matt didn't speak, and then he

said, "Could Brandon have been the one in your hospital room?"

Blair stared through the windshield as she tried to fit the youth into the picture. "I don't know. Whoever it was, he was very strong. I tried to push him away, but it was like trying to shove aside a steel beam."

"Brandon's strong."

"Yes, you said he pumps iron. But somehow I got the impression that my attacker was...older. Oh, that's stupid, I know—I didn't even see him! Yet..."

"Impressions can be important. Intangible as they are, they can leave a solid imprint on the mind."

Matt seemed abstracted as he drove on. After a while he said, "If Brandon was the one lurking in the gazebo last night, perhaps it wasn't the first time. I noticed last Christmas he developed a crush on Meredith. If he's lovesick, maybe he was hanging around hoping to catch a glimpse of her." His mouth thinned. "I don't like it. She's been through enough without having to worry about somebody spying on her."

"Matt, what time was it last night when you saw the glow of light in the gazebo?"

"Let's see—I got back here around two, talked with Meredith for a while—"

"So she knows about the accident?"

"Oh, yeah. I told her. She happened to come downstairs looking for her pills just after I got home. Then I went upstairs. Couldn't get to sleep, though. I believe it was probably around three-fifteen when I noticed somebody outside."

"How accurate would that be?"

"Pretty accurate. A few minutes either way. Why?"

"Because the intruder came to my room just after three. I remember because I'd been looking at my watch a few moments before. There's no way the man could have gotten out of the hospital, driven to High Meadows and be casually smoking a cheroot in the gazebo when you looked out. Not within that time frame.''

''So that counts Brandon out,'' Matt said slowly. ''Either of being in the hospital room or of being in the gazebo. He couldn't be in both places at once, but—''

Tires squealed as he pressed hard on the brakes and made a U-turn.

Blair gasped. ''Wow, you could've warned me!''

''We're going back. We'll have to tell the cops about the assault last night, but first I want to talk with Brandon. Let him clear himself if he can. Then we won't have to pass his name to the RCMP.''

WHEN THEY WERE halfway up the long driveway leading to Thornebank, they saw Brandon's red Honda coming toward them. Matt pulled up, got out. He waved Brandon down, and the Honda stopped a few feet from where Matt was waiting.

Blair opened her car window, hoping to hear what was going on, but the breeze blew Matt's words away. A few moments later, however, she saw the youth emerge from his car. His expression was a study of sullen resentment.

He stood there with his muscular arms folded over his chest and watched as Matt crossed to Blair. Leaning down, Matt said quietly through the open window, ''Sit tight. I hope this won't take long.''

Blair watched as he gestured to Brandon with a nod. The two walked together into the woods, Matt limping, Brandon kicking irritably at the odd twig.

She followed their departure until she could see them no more, then let her head fall back against the seat.

Her mind was a turmoil of disturbing questions.

Was it possible that Brandon was behind all the bad stuff that had been going on? Was he the one who had kidnapped Meredith? The one who had stuffed the pillow over Blair's face and taken potshots at her? Was he the one who had tampered with the brakes of Matt's car? The one who had made the phone call threatening to kill Matt?

If so—Blair's heart gave a lurch—Matt might be in terrible danger at this moment. Alone in the forest with a lunatic.

Ignoring his order to sit tight, Blair pushed her door open, got out and crossed to the forest.

It was dark and cool amid the towering trees, green and earthy. And peaceful, until she heard the voices ahead. Voices rising. Matt's harsh, demanding. Brandon's resentful, hostile.

She moved forward and saw a small clearing. Right in the middle the two males stood, glaring at each other like stags about to embark on a fight to the death.

She stayed in the shadows, feeling the sickness that always churned her stomach when she saw people fighting.

Matt's hands were clenched into fists at his side, and she knew by that and the jut of his jaw that he was barely managing to contain himself.

"If you weren't in Whistler last night," he was saying, rage vibrating in his words, "then where the hell were you?"

"None of your business!"

"I'm making it my business. But hey, maybe you'd prefer to be questioned by the cops. We're talking attempted murder here, and if you have no alibi for— Your mother and Jason were up all night. They're the ones I should be talking to. They'll know if you went out.''

Even from her position twenty feet away, Blair could see the flicker of alarm in the youth's expression. ''So what if I went out? There's no law against that, is there? I have nothing to hide.''

''Fine. Then you'll have no problem talking to the cops. And if you were with friends, you'll have an alibi. I'm glad to hear it. I wouldn't want to see you locked up in some stinking jail, because I don't want to see Poppy hurt. So who were you with?''

''I never said I was with anybody.''

''So you were out, but you were alone.'' Matt made to turn away. ''That does it, Brand—''

Brandon said roughly, ''Hang on.''

Matt faced him again. ''Yeah?''

Brandon muttered something under his breath.

Matt snapped, ''Speak up!''

''I said you saw me last night.''

''Where?''

''In that house next the woods.''

''The gazebo?''

''Whatever. I was just having a smoke. You came out and I took off. I went home.''

Blair briefly closed her eyes as she felt a sagging relief. If Brandon had been in the gazebo, then he couldn't possibly have attacked her.

''What the hell were you doing in the gazebo in the first place?'' Matt rasped. ''Were you spying on my wife? Goddammit, Brand, I never figured you for a Peeping Tom.''

''Maybe you should do a bit of peeping yourself, man!'' Brandon's tone was defensive, but it was also shaded with scorn. ''Your wife's not the little angel you think she is. There's things going on at High Meadows that—''

''What kind of things?''

Brandon shrugged. ''Why don't you make it your business to find out? Seems like you're good at doing that. You've got what you wanted to know from me— like I said, I wasn't in Whistler last night so you can just—''

He'd wheeled as he was speaking, and as he did, he saw Blair.

Their eyes locked. She knew he'd been on the point of using a four-letter word, but he stopped short.

Dull color surged into his face, and he stuck his hands into his pockets.

He had to walk by her to get out of the clearing, but he kept his gaze averted. As he slouched past her, she smelled the cigar smoke clinging to his clothes—and remembering last night, she shuddered.

Matt's expression was grim as he limped to her. ''You're as white as a ghost. What the heck are you doing here? I thought I told you to stay in the car!''

''You did,'' she retorted, ''but I don't have to do everything I'm told.''

A door slammed, and a moment later they heard the Honda taking off.

''Well,'' Blair said, ''you've cleared that up.''

''At least we know he wasn't the one who attacked you. We're no further along, though, in finding out who did.''

She wondered what he thought of Brandon's remark about Meredith. She wasn't about to ask him, and it soon became obvious he wasn't about to tell her.

Matt said, ''We'll have to tell the police about the attack.'' He glanced at his watch. ''Oh, damn.''

"What's the matter?" Blair asked.

"I have a meeting at the WhitePeak in half an hour. With all that's going on, I'd forgotten about it. The businessmen I was supposed to meet in Vancouver last night—we're having the meeting up here this morning instead. But I want to get you to High Meadows."

"You're going to be late if you do that, Matt." They started toward the car. "Tell you what, why don't I come with you to Whistler? You drop me off at the police station, and I'll meet up with you at the hotel later. How long do you expect your meeting to last?"

"A couple of hours."

"Then after I've given the police my report, I'll browse around in the shops in the village, meet up with you when you're done."

"Okay. But then we'll go to High Meadows and you'll pick up your things and leave."

"Right," Blair said, resigned.

"But I'm not letting you drive. I'll have somebody chauffeur you home in one of the hotel cars and have your Camry delivered tomorrow."

"I'm perfectly capable of driving."

"Blair, trust me on this, you're in no state to make that long drive. You look as if a puff of wind would blow you into the sky like dandelion down. I'll take your keys off you by bodily force if I have to."

Blair felt her cheeks turn pink at the prospect of tussling with Matt. The idea held a certain charm.

"All right," she said, "you win."

Her voice had been husky, and he looked at her. His gaze flickered to her flushed cheeks, and she wondered if he had read her thoughts.

When she saw his hands tighten on the steering wheel, she knew beyond a shadow of a doubt that he had.

MATT'S MEETING went on for more than three hours.

After he'd finally seen the four Japanese businessmen off, he crossed the WhitePeak's luxuriously appointed foyer to the reception desk.

He'd dropped Blair off at the police station on his way to the hotel, but not before giving her a key to his private suite. He'd told her to make herself at home there if she got tired of browsing in the village. He hadn't expected to be delayed.

"Clarice." He addressed the receptionist. "I was expecting a guest. Do you know if she's arrived?"

"Yes, Mr. Straith. Miss Enderby went up to your suite a couple of hours ago—she phoned the desk and had coffee sent up shortly after she got here."

"Great."

Matt took the elevator and strode along the plush-carpeted corridor to the door at the far end marked Private.

He unlocked the door and went in.

"Blair?"

He expected her to meet him, but when she didn't, he felt his nerves flare with apprehension.

"Blair?" With swift limping strides, he moved from the entry along the short corridor into the living room.

She wasn't there, nor was she in the kitchen or the bathroom. Alarm coursed through him—alarm that intensified when he went into the living room and noticed her crimson bag on one of the sofas.

Something had happened to her.

He felt as if a powerful fist had hit him in the gut.

Had the attacker followed her here? Had he—

Pulses hammering, he wrenched open the bedroom door. His heart stopped when he saw her lying lifelessly on her back on the bed.

She murmured and turned on her side. Curling a hand above her head, she settled into a more comfortable position and expelled a deep breath.

She was sleeping.

And his opening the bedroom door must have disturbed her but not wakened her.

Matt leaned against the wall, feeling as if he'd been to hell and back in the space of three seconds. He dragged a hand over his eyes, then dropped it to his side. His gaze flicked to the bedside table, where he saw a tray with a tall silver coffeepot, half a lemon Danish, a pretty mug, a silver sugar bowl and cream jug.

By her hip, on the duvet, was a glossy magazine.

She looked so right, lying there in his bed.

Slowly, his steps silent on the carpet, he moved across the room and rounded the bed.

Her glossy brown hair was spread like hanks of silk over the white pillow. Her breathing was soft and rhythmic, her pink lips parted, her dark lashes a smudged shadow over her pale cheeks.

The raising of her hand above her head had caused her blouse to gape slightly at the neck, and he could see the edge of her lace-trimmed bra, ecru and delicate. He could see a pulse beat in the hollow of her shoulder.

He wanted to kiss it.

But knew he mustn't.

His eyes clouded. His heart ached.

He should leave, let her get some sleep. She badly needed it, after what she'd gone through the night before.

"Matt?" Her voice, drowsy as the summer day and just as warm, brought him to reality. She stretched, lazily.

"Sorry, Blair." Did she realize what she was doing to him, stretching her arms like that? Did she know the collar of her blouse had fallen away, revealing the swell of her breasts, making them pout at him as if they were begging for attention? His throat muscles tightened. "I didn't mean to wake you."

"I'm the one who should be sorry." She wrinkled her nose as she smiled at him. "Falling asleep in your bed like Goldilocks! I wanted to take off my sandals and put my feet up while I was having my coffee, and when I poked my nose in here, it just looked so darned inviting. But I'd hardly started my coffee when I got sleepy. I thought I'd put my head down for a minute, and—"

"No apologies necessary. You're welcome in my bed any time—" He broke off. Now *that* could have been better phrased.

She must have thought so, too. Her features tightened, and she sat up quickly. In doing so, she dislodged the glossy magazine, and it fell off the bed onto the floor.

Matt bent to pick it up, but at the same time, she leaned over, and their heads collided with a crack.

She winced and sat abruptly, her eyes closed, her hands pressed to her temples.

He found himself sitting on the edge of the bed, his hands gently circling her wrists.

"Blair?" Dammit, how could he have been so clumsy? "I'm sorry, I should have—"

"No." Her hair was over her face, and she peeked

at him through the strands like a gray-eyed kitten. "It was as much my fault as yours. It was an accident."

"Like we need another of those!"

"Oh, don't look so worried, Matt. I'm fine, really. I've got a hard head."

"Yeah, sure." But in his relief, he found himself grinning.

"It's so good to see you smile again," Blair said, and she meant it, but she wished, at the same time, that he would get off the bed. She felt like swooning, and it had nothing to do with the bump on her head. It was his closeness, the male scent of him, his sexual magnetism.

"You feel better after your nap?" he asked.

"Like a new woman!"

His gaze drifted over her face, her hair, her hands—which she'd clasped together to keep from reaching out and pulling him to her—and back to her face. Her skin tingled as his gaze lingered passionately on her mouth.

"We should be going," he murmured.

"Mmm." She'd never in her life felt less like moving.

"Blair, I'm curious about something."

"What?"

"This morning, you apologized, or started to, but I stopped you, told you we'd get to it later. We never did. And I hadn't meant to bring it up, because talking about it seemed to upset you. But I'd really like to know, if you want to tell me."

"Oh." Her lashes dropped, hid her eyes. "That."

"The last thing I want is to cause you distress," he said softly. "If you'd rather not say—"

She raised her eyes to his, met his steady gaze. "You were so cold to me when you picked me up at the hospital. I thought it was because I'd invited you to kiss me in the car when I came to after the crash—''

She broke off when she saw his stunned expression.

''You thought—good God.'' He shook his head. ''As I remember it, I was the one who did the kissing.''

''I didn't try to stop you.'' Her cheeks were on fire again. ''I should have.''

''Because—''

''You're married.''

''Would that have been the only reason?''

For a long, long moment, the only sound in the room was their breathing. And then, at last, she whispered, ''Yes.''

He groaned. ''Come here.'' He put his arms around her and drew her against his chest. ''Blair.'' His words were muffled in her hair. ''I'm not free to say the things I want to say to you. And won't be, until Meredith regains her memory. I can tell you, though, that our marriage was over before she disappeared. I can't bring up the subject of divorce while she's the way she is— God knows what it might do to her fragile mind. But if the day comes when she does get better, I'll be on your doorstep asking you for a hell of a lot more than friend- ship.''

Blair felt tears spring to her eyes, felt them spill over to wet her cheeks. Her joy at knowing Matt wanted more than friendship from her was almost wiped out by the despair that overwhelmed her as she thought of Mer- edith's amnesia.

Would the blonde regain her memory one day?

Or would she remain in limbo forever, trapping Matt, that most honorable of men, in a loveless marriage?

''And you've made me very happy,'' he said, as he drew her to her feet, ''by agreeing to go to Vancouver.

The most important thing in the world—my world—is knowing you're safe."

WHEN THEY GOT to High Meadows, Aileen met them in the foyer and told them Mrs. Straith was lying down. Her headache had apparently returned, and according to the housekeeper, she'd gone up to her room midmorning.

She'd left orders she wasn't to be disturbed.

"And how are you feeling, Miss Enderby, after that awful accident?"

"I'm fine now, thanks," Blair said. "But it was a close one."

"If you weren't so keen on old cars," the housekeeper said to Matt, with just the faintest hint of reproach, "you would have had a state-of-the-art car with airbags, and then Miss Enderby might not have ended up in the hospital at all!" She sailed away, having said her piece, which she'd quite obviously been hoarding up for just the right moment.

Matt raised his brows and grinned at Blair. "Never thought she had it in her!" he whispered. "Talk about still waters!"

Blair wasn't in the mood for humor at the moment.

"I'm going to pack my bag," she said quietly. "When should I expect the driver?"

"In about half an hour, okay?"

"I'll say goodbye, then, Matt. You'll be in touch?" Her voice was thick with contained emotion. "Let me know how everything goes?"

"You bet."

Blair turned to leave, but she heard him make a small sound, and as she hesitated, he grabbed her shoulders, hauled her to him and claimed her lips in a kiss so passionate it sent her heart into orbit.

When finally he released her, his eyes were burning.

He touched his fingertip to her lips, let it brush the slightly swollen flesh for one quick, tense moment.

Then he dropped his hand.

"I know I shouldn't have done that," he said huskily, "but I wanted to make sure you wouldn't forget me."

Before she could regain control of her ragged breathing, far less come up with some coherent reply, he was limping toward the door.

He slammed it behind him, and the noise of the crash drowned out her aching response.

"Forget you?" she murmured in anguish. "As if I ever could."

IT TOOK HER only fifteen minutes to pack.

She then went down and set her bag by the front door, then went to the kitchen to say goodbye to Aileen. She caught her just as she was leaving. She'd been given the rest of the day off, she told Blair happily, and was going to stay overnight with her sister in Squamish.

After she left, Blair started toward the front door. She was crossing the foyer, when she heard the clatter of footsteps.

She turned and saw Meredith running down the stairs.

"Where's Matt?" The blonde's voice was shrill, her face pale, and an odd light glowed from her eyes.

"He's gone to the hotel. He has some business to—"

"Oh, thank God!" Meredith clasped the newel post at the foot of the stairs. "Oh, thank God he's not here. I don't know what I'd have—"

"Meredith?" Blair walked to her. "What on earth's

wrong? Why are you glad Matt's not here? I don't understand.''

''No,'' Meredith cried, ''you don't understand. How could you?'' Like an animal caged, she started walking this way and that, long fingers raking through her cropped hair, full pink lips trembling.

Finally, just when Blair was about to ask again what was wrong, Meredith came to a stop in front of her.

Her eyes were wild.

''I've remembered, you see, what happened to me.'' Her sapphire ring sparkled as she clutched her thin throat. ''My memory has come back, Blair! I know where I was for those three months I was missing. I know who kidnapped me. And oh, God, oh, God, how I wish I didn't.'' She began to weep, tears swimming in her eyes and running like opalescent pearls down her cheeks.

Blair stared at her. ''Your memory has come back? But who—''

''Matt.'' Meredith fell to her knees on the carpet and dug knuckled hands into her eyes. ''Matt was the one,'' she sobbed. ''My husband was the one who wanted me dead.''

Chapter Eleven

Blair stared in disbelief. "Matt?"

A sob catching in her throat, Meredith raised her head. Her eyes were swimming with misery and reproach.

"Oh, I knew you wouldn't believe me! You just can't see past him, that's been plain from the word go."

"I don't know what to say, Meredith! You've obviously had a shock, and maybe you've gotten mixed up. You had a headache, and you fell asleep. Maybe you had a nightmare and—"

With an outraged cry, Meredith stormed to her feet. "Don't you think I know the difference between dreams and reality? Between nightmares and reality? I tell you, my memory has come back."

"Look, why don't we calm down, talk this over rationally."

"I remember *everything!* From the very beginning! How can I convince you?" She threw one arm out in an angry slicing gesture. "I can remember our first day at school, when we both wore blue dresses. I remember the trips we used to take to Stanley Park with your mother, and the special cakes my mother always made for our birthdays. I can remember being nervous of your father when I was little, because he used to swing me up on his shoulders, and I was scared I'd fall. I remember that double date we had with Judd Morton and his brother when we were sixteen, and we were both sick after because we'd never had wine before and we swore each other to secrecy forever.''

''My God.'' Blair ran a trembling hand through her hair. ''You do remember. This is incredible.''

And it was. Most of the things Meredith had spoken of, Blair had forgotten. They'd been in some cobwebby corner of her mind, but now they were in the light of day again, as clear and bright as if they had happened yesterday.

Stunned, she watched as Meredith walked to the window and stood looking out. The blonde's slender shoulders were slumped, as if she could hardly bear the burden of her memories.

''It was Matt.'' She was trying to keep her voice steady, but without success. ''He kidnapped me in March. He came up to Blackcomb looking for me. We'd fought the night before—you must have heard that— anyway, he told me we had to talk, we had to get away where we could be on our own, he wanted to make up.'' She inhaled a shuddering breath. ''We went in his car, he said he'd drive me back later for mine. Only—'' her voice cracked ''—there was no later.''

Blair felt dazed, as if she had lost her connection with the world around her. ''What happened?''

''He drove me to a mountain—I didn't know then that it was Cougar Mountain—and he made me hike up an old logging trail and through deep forest to a cabin. Miles from anywhere. He told me no one ever came there anymore, hadn't for years. I kept saying I wanted to go back. He wouldn't let me.'' She brushed a hand over her eyes. "And once we got to the cabin, he locked me in, and left me there."

"How did you get away?" Blair forced out the words.

"One day I found the door open!" A tear slithered down Meredith's pale cheek. "He came up once or twice a week with food, and he always locked it after he left. I don't even know why I bothered to try it that day, but I did, hours after he'd gone, and it was open. On the way down the mountain, I was terrified he'd come back. I ran, I fell…I think that's when I hurt my head, lost my memory—"

The shrill ring of the phone interrupted Meredith's words. She made no move to pick it up, and after a brief hesitation, Blair answered.

The call was for her. It was her father's doctor phoning from the nursing home.

"Blair, I have to tell you your father has taken a bad turn. We feel it might be best if you get down here as soon as possible."

Blair gripped the phone tightly. "Is he—"

"He's very weak. We think he may not last the night."

After he had hung up, Blair put down the phone and gripped the edge of the table.

"What is it?" asked Meredith.

"My father. He's had a bad turn." Blair fought hard to keep control of herself. "I have to go." Agitated, she hurried to the narrow window at one side of the front door. "Matt said he'd send a car for me."

A black sedan was pulling up in the forecourt.

"Oh, there it is." As she grabbed her bag, she felt absolutely torn in two. She wanted to stay at Whistler and get in touch with Matt, let him know what was going on. Meredith was so convincing. She *had* regained her memory. What she had recalled of her childhood was ample proof of that. But her implication of Matt in her kidnapping—never, ever would she be able to make Blair believe he had anything to do with it.

The doorbell rang. She paused.

"Meredith, are you going to go to the police—tell them your memory has come back?" Her nerves strummed with tension.

Meredith twisted her hands, her expression anguished. "Not yet," she said. "I'm going to have to think things over, decide how to keep myself safe. Come on, I'll see you to the car."

They went outside together, and just before Blair slipped into her seat, Meredith put her arms around her and hugged her tightly.

"We were such friends once," she whispered, and ran a hand down Blair's back. "I'm so sorry things have turned out like this. Don't worry about me. I'm going to talk things over with Matt tonight. I'll give him whatever he wants, and then maybe we can put all this behind us."

She stood there as the car pulled away.

And watched and waited until it passed out of sight.

As soon as it had gone, she walked with quick steps into the house.

She picked up the phone, still warm from Blair's fingers. She dialed the number she knew by heart.

When she heard the voice on the other end, she said triumphantly, "She's gone! I did as you said. Oh, she seemed not to believe me, but after tonight, well, when she has to talk with the police in the next day or two, she'll have to tell them what I said."

"Good. You've given the housekeeper the night off?"

"She's gone to Squamish to stay with her sister. She won't be back till morning."

"Great. Double-check with the caterers, make sure they're going to arrive by seven and be gone by ten." His laugh was hard. "You're looking forward to tonight?"

Her answering laugh was shrill. "It's going to be the best party I ever threw," she retorted. "I can't wait for it to be over."

DURING THE ALMOST two-hour drive, Meredith's accusations regarding Matt sent Blair's mind into a state of turbulence, a state intensified by anxiety about her father.

She had the driver drop her off at the nursing home, and though he offered to hang around until she came out, she swiftly sent him on his way after tipping him generously.

Though the day had started off sunny, heavy lowering clouds loomed over the North Shore mountains, and as Blair threw a glance over her shoulder, she saw that the waters of English Bay were gunmetal gray. A rising wind, warm but strong, gusted leaves around her ankles as she ran up the front steps. It was going to be a nasty night.

Not a night to be out.

The first person she bumped into when she entered the nursing home was Amery Gill. Middle-aged, with thinning black hair and tidy features, her father's doctor had an unassuming manner and eyes that missed nothing.

He caught her arm to steady her.

"Whoa, there!" His smile was warm. "The news is good, Blair. Your father rallied some time ago, and his condition's stable again. If I could've contacted you I would, but I knew you'd already be on the road."

Blair was glad for his supporting hand. All of a sudden, everything was catching up with her, and she felt dizzy. "He's better? Oh, thank heavens." She grimaced. "With Mom out of the country, I feel so responsible for him. I was dreading the thought of having to phone her, give her bad news when she's so far away."

"I'll take you to see him now. You can stay awhile?" he asked as they started along the tiled corridor together. "You don't have to go back to Whistler tonight?"

"No, I don't have to go back." Yet now that her father was out of danger, she desperately wished she could be with Matt.

He didn't want her there, though. He'd wanted her safe. A corner of her heart glowed as she recalled how he'd held her when he'd told her that.

But was he safe? Now that Meredith had regained her memory, would she incriminate Matt? Blair couldn't bear to think about that.

"I'll stay with my father for a while, talk to him— though I know what I say won't register."

"We never know just what does or doesn't. But we do hope there's a connection, though we may not be aware of it."

He opened the door to her father's room.

"Have a good visit," he said. "I'm leaving. I'll see you next time."

"Next time." She slipped into the room. With her eyes on her father, she closed the door behind her and leaned exhaustedly against it.

Alex Enderby was lying in bed, his eyes closed. The curtains were open, and gray light cast shadows over his lined face. Blair felt a sting of tears as she looked at him. How she wished her mother were here.

Blinking back the tears, she moved to sit on the chair by the bed. Taking in a deep breath, she leaned forward and clasped the hand lying on the cover. Her father's long-fingered hand, the beautiful, elegant hand of a once highly skilled surgeon, now a useless tool.

"Daddy?" she whispered. "I'm here. It's me, Blair." No response.

Her heart aching, she let her gaze dwell on his kindly face. "I'm so glad you're better. You gave me quite a scare today. I was up in Whistler when Dr. Gill called me. I was staying at a house called High Meadows..."

This was what she always did. She talked, telling him everything she'd been doing, what story she'd been working on, which friends she'd been seeing. Sometimes she thought she detected an answering light in his eyes, sometimes a quiver of response in his hand. Usually, afterward, she decided she had only imagined these things.

It didn't matter. She needed the contact, needed to tell him what was in her heart, as she'd done since she was a child. He had always been more than a father to her. He'd also been a friend.

"Do you remember Matt Straith?" She smoothed stray strands of her father's silver hair, then took his hand in hers again. "Matt stayed with us when I was eighteen. You and his father had been friends years before, and you offered Matt room and board." Memories rushed in, and Blair swallowed to relieve the lump in her throat. "He married Meredith. You remember her,

Daddy, and her mother, Jane? Jane Grigor? She was our housekeeper—''

Her father's hand jerked convulsively. Startled, Blair stared at him. As she looked into his face, the skin at her nape prickled. He was no longer asleep, and his eyes were fixed on her with an intensity, a ferocity that shook her to the core.

''Anne.'' His voice was rusty. His shoulders shook as he tried to sit up. ''Sister Anne. Tell Meredith. Have to tell Meredith. Let her know…'' He slumped on his pillows, and his voice trailed away.

Not wanting to lose this unexpected contact, this rare lucidity, Blair said eagerly, ''A nun, Daddy? Tell Meredith about a nun—someone called Anne? But Jane wasn't a Catholic. I don't understand.'' Confused, she tightened her grip, willed him to stay awake. To say more.

''Meredith,'' he muttered. ''Mother. Sister Anne. Tell her. It's important. Nobody knew. Secret.''

''Daddy, go on!'' He looked as if he was dropping off again, and she felt a stab of panic. ''Daddy, what do you mean? Was she a nun? Who was a nun? Who is this Anne?''

But it was no use.

She knew it was no use. His features were flaccid. His mouth fell open. His snoring was deep and steady, his hand in hers limp.

Blair's breath rushed out in a heavy sigh of defeat. Of despair.

She looked blankly around the room as if she could somehow find an answer in the white walls.

But there was no answer.

Whatever it was her father had tried to tell her was going to remain a mystery.

Just one more mystery, she thought miserably, to add to the many mysteries already seething around in her head.

"GOING HOME NOW?" the receptionist said sympathetically to Blair when she walked to the front desk an hour later.

"Mmm." Blair threw her a tired smile. "Is there a phone I can use? I need to make a couple of calls."

"I have to go to the ladies' room. Why don't you use my phone here at the desk and cover for me till I get back?"

"Sure. Thanks."

Blair called for a taxi, then, after a moment's hesitation, placed a call to the Whistler WhitePeak.

"Front desk. Good evening, Clarice speaking."

"Clarice, this is Blair Enderby. I was at the hotel with Mr. Straith this morning."

"Oh, yes, Miss Enderby. How may I help you?"

"Can you put me through to Mr. Straith?"

"Oh, I'm sorry, but he's gone for the evening. He left some time ago. His wife called me." She'd lowered her voice, as if she didn't want anyone else to hear. "It's Mr. Straith's birthday, and she's throwing a surprise party for him. He knew nothing about it, but I had to give him a message, tell him he had to be home by seven. He seemed puzzled, but he did leave just as she'd asked. I can patch you through to his office at High Meadows if you—"

"What time did his wife phone?"

"Oh, it must have been around six. Are you sure you don't want me to connect you with—"

"No, thanks." Blair tried to get her thoughts in order. "It wasn't important."

"Okay then. You have a good night, now."

Blair had just replaced the handset in the cradle when the receptionist ambled back from the ladies' room.

"Are you feeling okay?" Frowning, she scrutinized Blair's face. "You don't look so good, Miss Enderby. Did you just hear some bad news?"

"Heavens, no," Blair said, "no bad news." She turned and saw the flash of headlights at the front entrance. "Well, there's my cab. That was quick."

"Take my advice, go straight home and stay there. It's not a night to be on the road."

THE RECEPTIONIST'S words of advice echoed in Blair's head a couple of hours later as she drove from Vancouver to Whistler in her mother's red sports car.

It was certainly not a night to be on the road.

She'd never seen rain like it. Even with the wipers set at high speed, their frantic swishing could scarcely keep up with the downpour, and her efforts to see were hampered by periods of intense blackness interspersed with the frequent blinding glare of oncoming headlights.

And through it all the desperate message pounded in her brain. *You have to get to High Meadows and find out what's going on!*

In an effort to distract herself, she turned on the radio. She was about to switch it off because of static when she heard the name Quentin Kingsley. It seemed familiar, and in a moment she recalled a conversation at Thornebank the night of the party when Larry asked Matt about the original owner of High Meadows.

Quentin Kingsley had been the man, an abrasive politician, an opponent of nuclear testing and the bomb.

Glaring headlights seared Blair's eyes, and she gripped the steering wheel tightly as an enormous truck barreled past, sending a sheet of water over her windshield. For several seconds she couldn't see where she was going. By the time she did, she realized she was steering straight for the cliff face. With a cry of dismay, she wrenched the wheel and got on course.

"Kingsley tried to get a bill passed whereby government grants would be made available to families who wanted to build nuclear shelters. There was little support for the idea…"

Static crackled. Blair fiddled with the dial, but she'd lost the station. She switched off the radio and resigned herself to driving with only herself for company.

Interesting, though, that bit about nuclear shelters. Perhaps there was something there she could use in her story about Matt. A connection between High Meadows and Quentin Kingsley.

If the politician had been such a passionate proponent of nuclear shelters for the masses, wasn't it likely he would have built one for his family?

At High Meadows?

Where would he have constructed it? Close to the house, but not too close, yet easily accessible.

Just as the gazebo was.

Excitement rising, she played the favorite game of every writer. The what-if game.

What if there was indeed an underground shelter?

And what if Richard Hunter found the entrance to the old bunker when he'd been digging that flower bed Meredith wanted?

And what if he'd decided to build the gazebo over the shelter so he could use it for his own nefarious purposes! What might he be involved in? Gun smuggling? Fencing stolen goods? Drug trafficking? The possibilities were endless. And horrific.

And would go a long way to explaining why he had been so possessive about the gazebo, why he'd even gone so far as to paint the duckboards in an attempt to keep her out.

The strident blare of a horn made Blair jump. She glanced in her rearview mirror and realized that while she'd been so engrossed in her thoughts, she'd let the car slow down. A stream of headlights warned her that a dozen drivers behind her were probably cursing her driving skills.

She realized she was trembling. Gripping the wheel firmly, she pressed her foot down on the accelerator. Her speed picked up, and she didn't let it falter again.

Only when she saw the lights of Whistler did she slacken speed to turn off the highway.

She wanted to talk to Matt alone. She didn't want to take the risk of spilling out all she knew when she reached High Meadows. Instead, she'd find a pay phone in the village and call him.

She no longer trusted Meredith.

And she had never, from the second she'd laid eyes on him, trusted Richard Hunter.

"BLAIR? Is that you?"

Blair had expected Aileen to answer the phone, but even as she heard Poppy Thorne's voice on the other end of the line, she remembered the housekeeper had the evening off. Dark dread gripped Blair's heart. Why would Meredith have given Aileen time off when she'd been planning a party? Because she didn't want her around later?

"Blair?" Poppy sounded anxious.

"Yes—Poppy. Is Matt there?"

"Speak up, love, I can't hear you over all the noise."

There was certainly a din coming over the phone. Stereo thumping, voices, laughter, general hubbub. Blair leaned against the cold wall of the phone booth. "Matt. Is he there?"

"Oh, sure! I'll get him."

It seemed like forever before he came to the phone, but it could only have been a couple of minutes.

"Blair?"

She closed her eyes. Love flowed through her like the sweetest honey, trickling to every corner of her heart and filling it. "Matt."

"Hang on." He'd raised his voice. "I'm going to give the phone to Poppy and take it in the office."

She waited another minute, then she heard a click followed by Matt saying, "Got it, Poppy." And another click as Poppy hung up.

"Blair." She imagined him hitching his hip on the edge of his desk. "It's good to hear you. Listen, I've got something to tell you, something important—" He broke off, then whispered, "Somebody's coming. Talk to me."

So he was as nervous as she was, or it sounded that way. At least, he was being cautious. "Matt, about Quentin Kingsley, do you know if he ever built an underground shelter at High Meadows?"

"Sure he did."

Blair heard the sound of a man's voice, then heard Matt say, "It's okay, Jason, no problem. Yeah, I'll be with you in a minute. Mind shutting the door?"

"Where is it, Matt?" Blair asked.

"Where's what?"

"The shelter."

"Oh. I think close by the woods. My father turfed it over when he bought High Meadows. It's somewhere around where the gazebo is, if memory serves me right.'' His voice regained its intensity. ''That was Jason. He's gone. Listen, you left your tape recorder here. When I was dressing for this damned party, I ran over the interview we had, meaning to add some more stuff for you, and when I got to the end of our talk, I heard you and Meredith arguing.''

''I was going to edit it out, Matt.''

''No, you don't understand. The earrings—''

''What about the earrings?''

''On the tape, Meredith said she'd told me last fall she'd lost one. That was a lie. She never did. And her second lie was that she had lost one in the first place. She hadn't. At least, not then. Blair, she was wearing the set the day she disappeared.''

''Are you sure?''

''Sure as I've ever been of anything in my life. I remember looking at them that morning when she came down for breakfast and thinking of the day I'd given them to her—''

''Your wedding day.''

''Yeah, and thinking how things had changed since then.''

For a moment there was silence, then Blair said, ''Do you think Hunter has both earrings now?''

''I looked in Meredith's jewelry box. They're not there, nor is the amethyst and gold ring she claimed to have had made. I doubt there is one. I'm betting Hunter has both earrings. And I'm betting he has them stashed away in his cottage.''

Blair's mind had skipped to the things her father had said and other questions she wanted to ask Matt.

''Matt—'' she winced as thunder cracked ''—did Meredith ever say anything to you about a nun?'' She blinked as lightning flashed across the black sky. "Sister Anne?"

Static crackled on the line. "Sorry." Matt's voice seemed to be coming from a thousand miles away. "Didn't catch that. You were suggesting Meredith had a sister?"

A tremendous crash of thunder rocked the phone booth. Blair dropped the handset, and by the time she'd recovered it, her nerves were frayed to breaking point.

When she held the phone to her ear, the line was dead.

As was her mind.

Or so it seemed.

"Matt?" she begged.

No answer.

The connection was severed.

With a sinking heart, she replaced the receiver.

Matt had misunderstood her. He'd thought she'd said something about Meredith having a sister.

As thunder reverberated across the heavens, Blair sagged against the door of the booth as a thought hit her out of the blue.

Was it possible? Did Meredith have a sister? A sister by the name of Anne?

And if this woman did exist, did she go by the name of Annie?

And was she Annie Hunter, married to Richard Hunter?

It wasn't until Blair was in the hardware store down the street, five minutes later, buying a heavy metal flashlight, that she realized Matt didn't know she was in the area.

Her mind had been too busy thinking of other things, skimming ahead to what she planned to do next.

She was going to sneak into the gazebo, under cover of dark and the storm, and search for the underground shelter.

Chapter Twelve

Matt shot back the cuff of his shirt, looked at his watch and stifled an oath. His impatient glance flitted around the living room and from there out the uncurtained window to the patio, where Richard Hunter was acting as barman for those who'd wanted a smoke after dinner.

Half an hour had elapsed since Blair's call, and he'd wanted ever since to take off for the gardener's cottage. Once there, he planned to search not only for the earrings, which must be hidden there, but also for some evidence to confirm the suspicion Blair had unknowingly planted.

The suspicion that Hunter's wife, Annie, might be connected with Meredith.

"Darling?"

Think of the devil, and the devil was by his side. Meredith, paler than usual but looking sleek and sophisticated in an ankle-length white satin dress, had her fingers on his arm, her cornflower blue eyes on his.

"Yeah?" He'd never seen her as uptight as she was tonight, and her brittle tension made him apprehensive. What was she up to? It was like waiting for a bomb to go off. Thank God Blair wasn't here, but safe in Vancouver.

Meredith gestured toward the oil painting above the marble mantelpiece. "So. Do you like your birthday gift?"

Matt wondered if his brain was going to explode with the frustration that was pounding savagely through him. He wanted to tell her he hated the damned painting, but guests were watching, waiting for his response.

"Jason's done a wonderful job," he said. "And you both played your parts in keeping it a secret. Well done."

He let his gaze shift to the painting, but as he looked at it, his blood was ice-cold. It was a faithful rendition of Meredith. The new Meredith. He'd have known, even if Jason hadn't told him, that the portrait had been completed since her return. The eyes were different. Oh, they were still wide and beautiful, but there was a layer of underlying cunning that hadn't existed before.

The kidnapper had experimented with Meredith's mind. Brainwashed her. Hypnotized her. Terrorized her. Matt was convinced of it.

He dragged his gaze from the disturbing portrait as Poppy joined them.

"Matt, Meredith, Jason's wrist is bothering him and he's forgotten his pills. You won't mind if we leave now?"

"Of course not," Matt said, and his words were echoed by Meredith's.

For the next minute or two, there was a flurry of goodbyes as the Thornes took their leave of Meredith and the other guests, and after getting the couple's coats, Matt scooped a black umbrella from the stand in the entryway.

As they stepped into the night, the sensor light above

the front door clicked on. Matt held the umbrella over Poppy as he accompanied the couple to their car.

The rain was still lashing down, thunder cracking, the odd shaft of lightning piercing the murky sky. Jason opened the driver's door. "In you go, Poppy."

"Of course, you can't drive with that cast," Matt remarked.

"Besides, I had more than a few brandies," Jason retorted. "To ease the pain, of course!"

He stood to let Poppy pass, but instead of slipping into the car out of the rain, his wife hesitated.

"Matt." The light from the front door slanted over her face, and he detected apprehension in her eyes. "I'm really worried about Meredith. Since she's come back, her auras are so different. It's as if—"

"Yeah." Matt knew Poppy claimed to see auras. He believed nothing of the kind. But he had to agree with her that Meredith was different. "She's going to get help—she's made an appointment to see a neurosurgeon."

It occurred to him that he'd never checked with her on that; he made a mental note to do so at the first opportunity.

"I'm glad to hear it," Poppy said. "But, Matt, be careful. I got such bad vibes tonight. Your barman, the gardener—"

"Honey—" Jason sounded impatient "—can we get going? My arm's hurting like hell."

"We'll talk, Poppy," Matt said. "I'll give you a call tomorrow." But he wasn't about to discuss Hunter with her or with anyone else. He'd keep his suspicions to himself until he ascertained that they had a solid foundation.

Jason helped his wife into the car and shut the door.

Umbrella aloft, Matt walked Jason to the passenger side.

"The painting," he began, only to have Jason cut him off.

"It was a good idea that went wrong," Jason said grimly. "It's not Meredith, not the Meredith I knew. But I had to finish it—can't leave things half done. I only wish I'd completed it before she disappeared. I look into those cornflower blue eyes of hers now and I see—"

"What do you see, Jase?"

"Old buddy—" to Matt's astonishment, the artist looped his good arm around him and embraced him in a quick, fierce hug "—you sure as hell don't want to know what I see."

He released Matt abruptly and got into the car without another word. Poppy revved the engine, and a moment later they took off along the drive.

Matt was shocked by the powerful emotion he'd sensed in his old friend. Jason Thorne was a man who felt things deeply but he normally kept his emotions rigidly locked up.

Frowning, Matt turned toward the house, but before he'd taken a step, the automatic light above the front door clicked off.

Barely aware that he still held the umbrella, or that the lashing rain was tap-dancing like mad on the taut black fabric, he made a decision.

He would check Hunter's cottage. The opportunity was one not to be missed. The gardener was busy dispensing drinks. The guests would assume he was still talking with the Thornes.

As fast as his painful leg would allow, he rounded

the house to the path that led to the gardener's cottage in a small clearing in the forest.

His nerves were on edge, but he felt excitement rise in him like the churning waters of the nearby river. It was possible the gardener had played some part in the disturbing incidents of the last few months. If so, Matt might find some clue to all the mysteries surrounding High Meadows and its inhabitants.

As he approached the cottage, he fingered the key chain in his pocket. On it was the master key for the small house. He'd never used it, not since Hunter had moved in.

He brought out the key chain, isolated the key he wanted and slid it into the front door's lock.

It gave silently.

Folding the umbrella, he tossed it behind a nearby magnolia tree.

And after wiping his feet free of mud on the doormat, he slipped like a shadow inside.

BLAIR PARKED her mother's car halfway up the drive, pulling to the side under the trees.

Heart hammering like mad, she climbed out and pulled up the hood of her raincoat. Damned rain! But at least the night was warm.

The lashing downpour, coupled with the darkness, at least afforded her concealment. She made her way cautiously up the drive, heavy metal flashlight clutched in one hand, but switched off.

The forecourt was in darkness, but she could hear the drumming of rain on car roofs, and she reckoned there were about a dozen vehicles. She maneuvered among them, intent on reaching the lawn. Once there, it would be relatively easy to attain the gazebo unseen.

But she was still in the parking area when the front light flashed on unexpectedly. She huddled behind the nearest vehicle and froze. Narrow escape! Five seconds later and she'd have been out in the open, in plain view of whoever was coming out.

It was Matt—her pulse leaped—but he wasn't alone. Needles of rain stabbed her face as she peered around the car. He was dressed in a dark suit and white shirt, and he was holding a huge black umbrella over somebody.

Poppy.

And just behind Poppy was her husband.

Blair pressed closer to the vehicle concealing her and watched the threesome walk down the front steps. She sent up a prayer she wasn't behind Jason's car. She wanted to talk to Matt but she didn't want to become involved with the Thornes.

Not right now.

Jason's car chanced to be the one nearest the house, and Blair blew out a sigh of relief. Shuddering in the shadows, she watched, too far away to hear anything that was said. After a while, Poppy slipped into the car. Then Matt and Jason rounded it together.

Go! she urged Jason silently. *For pity's sake, go!*

But he seemed in no hurry, and just as she thought he was at last about to leave, to her absolute astonishment, she saw him put his left arm around Matt and grip him in a powerful embrace. What on earth was that all about?

She was still reeling from the sight when the car spun off. She was so busy pondering upon it that by the time she gathered her thoughts together and got to her feet, the light at the front door had clicked off.

And Matt was lost to her view.

She called out, but her voice was lost in an angry roll of thunder.

She started toward the front steps, cursing in the dark as she bumped into a car. She expected the automatic front door light to come on again any second as Matt mounted the steps, but it didn't. Too late, she realized Matt hadn't gone into the house.

Where had he gone, then?

She hesitated and decided to follow the path leading to the kitchen.

If he'd gone that way, she might catch up; he'd been limping and wouldn't be able to move very fast.

But when she got to the side of the house, she didn't see him. She stood on the path, peering into the dark. And felt her heartbeats jar together when lightning illuminated the world for just long enough to let her see the reflection of Matt's black umbrella before he disappeared into the forest.

Where was he going? She hurried after him.

In the forest, it was blacker than sin.

She switched on her flashlight, kept it directed right in front of her feet as she trod with wary steps along the narrow path. Then daringly, once she was in the thick of the trees, she flashed the light ahead.

Her breath caught as the beam played on the walls of a cottage—a small cottage with curtained windows, a magnolia bush by the path and a front door trellised with roses.

And walking through that doorway into the cottage was a tall, dark figure she recognized only too well.

She saw him freeze in the doorway as the beam of the flashlight caught him from behind.

"Matt," she called after him, "wait up!"

HE'D THOUGHT the worst when the light had flashed past him. He'd thought Richard Hunter had followed him. His heart had almost stopped.

But when he heard her voice, he knew this was worse. Worse than having the gardener find him trespassing. This was a nightmare come true. He wanted her safe. He had thought she was safe.

He spun, anger raging in his voice as he greeted her. "What the hell are you doing here? And how in God's name could you be here already when you phoned me from Vancouver less than half an hour ago?"

Breathlessly, Blair stopped in front of him. The beam from the flashlight swung as her arm fell to her side. "I was phoning from Whistler," she said, gasping, "I didn't have time to tell you."

Lightning flashed, and with a sharp curse he grabbed her and pulled her inside. He kicked the door shut and heard the Yale lock click in place.

"Matt, is this Richard Hunter's cott—"

"Why are you here?"

He felt her wince from the harsh demand in his tone.

"I phoned the WhitePeak from Vancouver," she said, "to talk to you about something, but Clarice told me Meredith was throwing a party for you."

"You came all the way up here for a damned party?"

"No, I didn't come all the way up here for your damned party! If you'd just let me finish—"

"Okay, so finish!"

"I couldn't understand why Meredith would be throwing a party for you when her memory's back and she's accusing you of being the one who kidnapped her, so I—"

"Back up!" Good grief, what was she saying? "She

remembers? She actually remembers? And she's blaming me?''

''You don't know anything about it, do you?'' Blair's voice was laced with horror. ''Oh, Matt—after you left she came downstairs. She said her memory had come back—she said you were the one who kidnapped her, the one who locked her in a cabin on Cougar Mountain, the one who... Oh, Matt, why is she lying?''

RICHARD HUNTER wiped the cocktail trolley and glanced through the slashing rain at the gazebo. Triumph welled inside him, triumph and a gloating delight.

He'd planned the perfect crime, and he was going to get away with it. His single regret was that he could share his genius with only one person. The whole world deserved to know of his cleverness. And tonight was the climax. Anticipation of Straith's death thrilled through him, ripping at his heart like the serrated edge of a knife.

His glance fell to his watch. It was ten minutes since Jason Thorne had left, but under the awning the scent of his tobacco still lingered. It hung over the cheroot stubs squashed on the ceramic ashtray.

His mouth twisted in a smug smile. This morning, when he'd snuck into the hospital, it had been a master stroke to detour into the men's room and smoke one of Thorne's cheroots before he attacked. Blair couldn't have failed to inhale the tobacco fragrance before he rammed the pillow over her face. She was a journalist, after all. Even in her terror she'd have noted it, and filed the fact in her mind to regurgitate for the police.

So many red herrings.

The Mounties were going to be completely bamboozled. This was one case where they were definitely not going to get their man.

"How about a Drambuie, Richard?"

He looked up from the trolley and saw that smarmy Larry the lawyer.

"Right away, sir."

He poured the drink, handed it over.

The lawyer drifted to the small group he'd been standing with outside the dining room door.

"I'm going in now." His voice came to Hunter. "How about you?"

They opened the sliding door and ambled inside.

The gardener waited until they were gone.

And then he grabbed his rain jacket from the back of a chair and shrugged it on.

The party wouldn't go on much longer. The Thornes had gone. That would set the signal for the others to leave. Soon they'd all be gone.

He had to get the gun. Have it ready.

With stealthy steps, he hurried around the side of the house.

And as he went, he dug into the hip pocket of his black pants and pulled out the key of the cottage.

"I HAVEN'T the first clue as to why Meredith's lying about the kidnapping," Matt growled, "but I sure as hell am glad you didn't take her words at face value."

"As if I would!" Blair retorted. "Matt, doesn't this make you believe more than ever that the kidnapper hypnotized her? She truly seemed to believe what she was saying—I've never seen anyone so distraught."

She heard a fumbling of fabric.

"You can switch the flashlight on," Matt said. "He's got the curtains drawn. Blair, God knows what's going on—whoever we're dealing with has a mind so twisted it's impossible to get a make on what he's going to do next. With that threatening phone call…''

"When he said he was going to kill you?" Blair skimmed the flashlight around the room and saw a leather lounger in front of a large TV set. On the coffee table were empty beer cans. She played the light on a bookcase crammed with paperbacks. Stephen King. Truman Capote. Dean Koontz. Raymond Chandler. Arranged neatly on a nearby shelf was an assortment of videotapes, immaculately labeled. Mrs. Straith gardening, skiing, in her studio.

"Look at this," she murmured. "Videos of Meredith."

"Yeah." Matt's tone was abstracted. "Blair, I've been thinking. When the kidnapper made that threat, the implication was that Meredith was no longer in danger. Now I'm beginning to wonder if she's still a target and he's got some Machiavellian plan to get rid of both of us."

"But why, Matt?"

Wood scraped as Matt tugged open the top drawer of a desk. "If Richard Hunter's behind all this… Blair, when you talked on the phone about Meredith having a sister—"

"No, what I said was, did Meredith ever talk to you about a nun, Sister Anne. I visited Daddy when I was in Vancouver, and for a few moments he got very lucid, quite fierce, in fact, and told me I had to tell Meredith about Jane Grigor's secret. Sister Anne."

"But he could have been telling you Meredith had a sister. Anne. And if she—"

"Meredith was an only child, Matt. Jane was forty when she had her baby. She used to tell us she'd resigned herself to dying childless until she found herself pregnant with Meredith. She'd never have lied. She was true-blue honest. And why would she have lied about something like that?''

"Jane Grigor's secret," Matt said slowly. "Just for argument's sake, let's suppose that—oh, perhaps several years before she moved to Vancouver—Jane had another child. A daughter. And her name was Anne. Isn't it possible that she could be Hunter's Annie?''

"Oh, anything's possible." Blair watched as Matt quickly searched every nook and cranny in the desk and came away with nothing. "But I don't see what—"

"If I was killed—" Matt closed the hinged desk "—Meredith would inherit everything. High Meadows, the WhitePeak chain, all our other assets. Then if after a while Meredith died, too, Hunter's wife could come forward as next of kin and lay claim to everything!''

"Well, yes, that's logical enough, but where does Meredith's kidnapping fit in?"

"Let's suppose he's building up a complex and bizarre scenario intended to completely throw the Mounties off the trail. Let's go right back to square one. Let's suppose he kidnaps Meredith in order to hypnotize her into killing me.''

"But wouldn't she then be the prime suspect?"

"Oh, no, our man's far too clever for that." He took her arm. "Kitchen."

"Okay, let's suppose she's in the clear. How's he going to get her out of the picture?"

"You've got me there. At any rate, her amnesia must have thrown a wrench in his plans, because until she regained her memory, she wouldn't be able to carry out his orders.''

"But now she says she's got her memory back."

Blair's mind flicked to the scene with Meredith, when the distraught blonde had spilled all.

The kitchen was barely big enough to swing a new-born kitten. It took only a couple of minutes to ascertain that the earring wasn't hidden there. Nor was any other evidence of wrongdoing.

They moved to the bathroom. Found nothing untoward.

"Right," Matt muttered. "The bedroom. The bastard's got to have slipped up some way. There's no such thing as the perfect crime."

"We have to go to the police."

"And tell them what?"

"Well, tell them…" Blair's voice trailed away.

"We don't have one shred of solid evidence against the man."

"But they could check out his wife in Ontario, find out if his Annie is Meredith's sister or possibly a half-sister." Blair's eagerness faded. "We'd still have no evidence Hunter was involved in Meredith's kidnapping."

"Blair, bring that flashlight over here."

Blair crossed to join him beside the bed as he lifted a framed photograph from the bedside table. She shone the beam on the picture and saw it was a portrait of Richard Hunter on his wedding day. His bride's hair was red, her cheeks plump, her expression cheery. Her eyes, Blair noticed, were hazel and round and rather small.

"She doesn't look in the least like Meredith." Blair wasn't sure if this was a good thing, or bad. She was so befuddled she couldn't remember the hypothesis she and Matt had come up with minutes before.

He replaced the photo. "She could be a half-sister."

The front door slammed.

Meredith jumped.

Matt swore.

''Switch off that flashlight,'' he whispered, but she'd automatically done so. ''The closet—come on!''

Fortunately Matt knew the layout of the room. He hauled her across to the built-in wall closet. And fortunately the rain against the roof and the window muffled the squeak of the folding door as he dragged it open and shuffled her inside. Her heart lurched as she dislodged an empty hanger and it tumbled to her feet.

''Move back,'' Matt whispered in her ear. His voice had been hoarse, but the arms he'd enfolded her with were firm. Powerful. Reassuring.

Limply she collapsed against him.

And a moment later, through the narrow slats of the door, she saw the bedroom light flick on.

A shiver of fear raked through her. Matt must have felt it. His embrace tightened convulsively. His hand cupped her head, nestled it close against his chest. The musk-male scent of him filled her head, made her knees even weaker than they already were. She slid her hands under his jacket, around his waist, clutched his shirt, desperately clutched his shirt.

Was he as terrified as she? Against her cheek she could feel his heart beating. The rhythm was strong and steady but surely faster than normal. Hardly daring to breathe, she tried to check what was happening, but Matt had her clamped to him, and she could see nothing.

She could hear the gardener, though. He was humming. ''Rich Girl.'' It wasn't the first time she'd heard him humming that melody, but the possibility that it had a dark and hideous meaning for him made her heart sink with dread.

Meredith Straith was a very rich girl, indeed, or would be, if anything happened to Matt.

Was Richard Hunter prepared to commit murder—twice—to get his hands on the Straith fortune?

Chapter Thirteen

"Rich Girl." Humming under his breath, he crossed to the dresser.

He stared at his reflection in the mirror. His eyes had a feverish glitter, and his color was high. He snapped open the can of pop in his hand. It was still cold from the fridge. He'd have preferred a beer—he *needed* a beer. But tonight—his lips thinned in a cruel smile—he needed a clear head more.

Turning away, he gulped from the can, then set it on the bedside table beside his wedding photo. He got down on his haunches, slid his hand under the mattress...

And brought out the gun.

He stroked it lovingly, tenderly, as if it was a naked woman. "Tonight," he whispered, "you'll come through for me, baby. You'll come through for me tonight."

He got to his feet, flapped open his jacket and slid the weapon into the inside pocket, then let the jacket fall into place.

He turned, looked at the closet and frowned.

The earring.

Dammit, he'd wanted to sell it. It was worth a small

fortune. But tomorrow the Mounties would be all over every corner of the High Meadows estate. He'd have to get rid of the earring. The risk wasn't worth it.

Anyway, the kind of money he could get for that small item of jewelry would soon be peanuts to him.

To him. And to Annie.

He clenched his fists as his thoughts veered to his wife. Annie. She deserved everything she was going to get and more.

She'd waited long enough for her share of the good things in life. And after the kind of upbringing she'd had, with those stinking foster parents—

Rage and savage resentment at the world's unfairness roared in his ears, along with blinding hatred. Viciously, he shoved the closet door back and reached to the shelf.

The shoe box was right where he'd left it. He pulled it down and poked among the bits and pieces—receipts, string, loose change—until he found the earring.

''Gotcha!''

He extricated it from a tangle of rubber bands and tucked it into his hip pocket. On the way to the house, he'd go by the river and hurl the earring into the rising water. It would sink to the bottom without a trace. As for its mate— He laughed, and the evil sound echoed at him from the bedroom's bare walls. It was in a place nobody would ever find it.

Still chuckling, he shoved the box onto the shelf.

The door clattered as he flung it closed.

He paused, frowning. He thought he'd heard something. It had sounded like a squeak.

Head tilted, he listened, but heard nothing except the sounds of the storm.

He shrugged. It had probably been a mouse. It

wouldn't be the first time one of the little bastards had snuck in here looking for crumbs.

Better get moving, get back to the party before he was missed.

He grabbed his can of pop, hurried out of the room and across the small entry.

When he got outside, he pulled the door shut behind him and heard the Yale lock click firmly into place.

Thunder rolled across the sky, and the reverberations rang over and over in his ears as he headed for the river.

"LET'S GET OUT of here!" The words exploded from Matt.

Blair expelled her breath in a hiss. She grabbed Matt's shirt tighter as he fumbled out from behind the rack of clothes. "I thought—oh Matt, when he shoved open the closet door, I thought he was going to—"

"He got the earring." Matt slid his hand down her arm, found her hand. "I saw him take it from that shoe box. But I don't think that's what he came back here for."

"What then? Ouch!"

"You okay?"

"Bumped my knee against something. I've got the flashlight, but I'm afraid to put it on."

He put an arm around her and drew her close. "Through the doorway here, out into the hall...and here's the door."

He fiddled with the lock and opened the door.

The storm swept in on them, the force of the gale smacking the breath back into Blair's lungs. She huddled against Matt as he wrestled the door shut again.

"What did he come back for, if not the earring?"

She bent her head against the strong wind as he helped her along the dark path.

"Something under the mattress."

"What?"

"No idea. He had his back to the closet."

"Damn. Matt, what are we going to do now?"

They'd come to the end of the forest path. Ahead of them, obliterated by the rain, was the stretch of lawn leading to the house. Blair tugged her hood over her head, but it was too late. Her hair was already sodden, and rainwater was running down her face.

"What *you* are going to do—" Matt's tone was grim "—is leave."

"Matt, that's the third time you've tried to get rid of me!" She tried for a chuckle, but it sounded forced. "Are you trying to tell me something? Do I have bad—"

He grabbed her by the shoulders and shoved her backward. She felt her spine come up against the solid trunk of a tree. A large tree. They were sheltered from the rain, but it pelted down all around them, cocooning them.

"What I am trying to tell you—" his face was so close to hers she could feel his breath whip her mouth "—is that I want you out of here. I want you safe."

"I want to be with you," she cried, unable to contain her anguish. "I'm not about to run away and leave you to—"

His mouth stopped her words with a desperation that set her pulses off in a race to nowhere. His hands framed her face, capturing it. His lower body was sloped aggressively against hers, trapping her in place, and her heartbeats jammed as she became aware of her vulnerability.

He lifted his lips the barest fraction.

"And I want to be with you." Intense emotion rasped in his voice. "But more than that, I want you to be safe."

He groaned and claimed her lips again. This time his kiss was so hungry desire flared through her in urgent response with a power that made her tremble.

She heard him murmur her name like the most intimate caress, and it stimulated a mewing animal sound in her throat. He pressed closer to her until she felt the muscled ridge of him through the lightweight linen of her pants. Sexual excitement drummed through her veins, making her wanton and joyous and Gypsy wild.

Fiercely she slid her arms around his neck, and the wet strands of his hair clung to her fingers. He dragged his mouth from hers and planted frantic kisses along the curve of her jaw. With a moan, she arched her head back, only half-aware that she was blatantly inviting access to her neck, the base of her throat and beyond.

His kisses followed the path. He nudged his way inside the open neck of her blouse. His lips flirted shamelessly with the upper swell of her breasts.

"I want you to be safe." Passion made his voice rough. His hands were inside her jacket. He ran them up and down her ribs, his breathing heavy. He spanned her waist with outstretched fingers. Impatiently, he moved his hands upward. Her breath caught on a whispered sigh as his thumb pads grazed over the peaks of her breasts. In an instant the silky tips pearled. She shivered as coiling sensations ribboned from the tautened buds to her core, to her most sensitive feminine flesh, where she was aching, painfully aching for—

She gasped as his fingertips teased her nipples. Gasped and felt her legs sag. She'd never felt like this before. But even as she reeled from the endlessly dazzling rapture, he unhooked the front clasp of her bra. Her breasts bounced free, and she almost swooned when he cupped them—tenderly, possessively, as if they'd been formed for his enjoyment alone, and for him alone to treasure.

"Oh, God, Blair." Pain was in his voice, pain mingled with ecstasy. She wondered if she could stand much more of this blinding pleasure, and her body convulsed as his lips locked over one beaded tip. She felt his tongue run over it again and again. Felt his lips move in urgent rhythm, sucking, licking, arousing.

He glided his hands around her waist, dipped them down and splayed his fingers over her buttocks. Molded them. Took them. Pulled her hard against him.

Thunder rolled. For a second she thought her heartbeats had crashed. But then lightning strobed. And for the most fleeting of seconds, it illuminated their private shelter.

Matt had lifted his head, and their eyes locked. His were glazed with wanting, his face strained, his lips parted. Somewhere inside her, she felt a clenching of muscle, a drenching of tissue.

And pounding through her, the inexorable primal drive to mate.

Black night again followed the light.

They sank together on the dry-needled earth under the branches of the gigantic tree.

"ARE YOU SURE, Blair?" he whispered. But he'd already taken off his jacket and was spreading it to make a silk-lined bed for her back, her head. She twisted, and he realized she was shrugging off her wet jacket.

The night was warm, steamy warm. The forest floor

under the sheltering tree was baked dry. But all around, the rain was releasing the dank, musty smell of wet soil, the earthy scent mingling with the festive fragrance of green pine and the tang of mint from plants growing wild. And above it all, and sweeter than all, was the vanilla-violet scent of her perfume.

But even that took second place to the honeyed delicacy of her breath, which he inhaled as he covered her body with his, supporting himself with his hands set on either side of her head. Then the flavor of her breath was in his mouth as he claimed her lips in a ravenous kiss.

She responded with a fervor that made his head spin. Her arms were linked tightly around his neck, and her fingers delved deeply into his hair. Her lips parted feverishly as his tongue probed its way to the inner moistness of her mouth. She met its aggressive thrust with a seductive invitation. The coiling of her firm, wet flesh in his mouth made him hard as granite, and he knew that nothing short of death could make him turn back now.

"Hold me." A groan resonated in his voice. He lay back, pulled her so she was almost lying over him. He couldn't see her in the dark, but he could feel the damp strands of her hair tickle his cheek. "Hold me." He took her hand, felt it tremble. Guided it to where he throbbed for her touch.

BLAIR'S BREATH caught in her throat when he whispered his plea. As he pressed his hand to the swollen bulge between them, blood rushed in a voluptuous swell to her breasts. His hand slid under hers for a moment, and her mouth went dry as she heard the rasp of a zipper.

A dark, hot pulse of excitement raked through her, excitement underlaid by the dragging delirium of lust. His hand was again on hers, coaxing, cajoling, begging. She closed her eyes, gave in to sensation. She slipped her fingers inside. She felt the teeth of the zipper scratch her knuckle. She covered the jut of him as it strained against the confinement of his cotton briefs.

A whimper choked from her throat as she felt the hard shaft quiver in response to her caress. Her most tender flesh had become heavy, wet. And as wave after wave of desire hammered through her, the intensity of it almost sucked the breath from her lungs, and she knew nothing would stop her now. Nothing short of death.

He tangled long fingers in her hair, using the rain-soaked tassel as a rope to bring her face to his. His kiss was slack and moist, his skin burning, his scent the essence of musk and man. An aphrodisiac of the most powerful kind. An aphrodisiac that sang like fine champagne through her veins and dulled her brain until nothing existed for her but the man under her.

"I want you." He breathed the words against her lips. She felt his mouth move against hers, felt the tip of his tongue slide sensually over her lower lip. "I want you."

And oh, how she wanted him.

And would do anything, anything he asked her to.

She slipped her fingers inside his briefs, heard the sharp, swift hitch in his breath. Boldly she closed her hand around his shaft and heard him moan. Wickedly she moved her curved palm, playing him, drawing him, squeezing him, tormenting him and teasing the satin-smooth tip until it wept and her fingers became moist and slippery. She heard his breathing become more and more harsh, as he became more and more aroused. The harsh, fast breathing of a man at her mercy. As a woman, she gloried in her power.

"Blair, stop, you're going to—"

He groaned again, grasped her wrist, threw her hand against the dry-needled earth. And with a low growl he prepared her for a determined torture of his own. She didn't resist as he dragged off her slacks and sandals, nor did she fight when her bikini panties followed.

Only when he slipped a hand between her thighs, an intrusion of the most intimate kind, did she gasp and flinch.

"Blair? Do you want me to stop?"

"No, no..." The smallest of sobs escaped her. He immediately drowned it out with a desperate kiss. But even as she felt herself become limp, utterly drained by a fresh flood of desire, his fingers trespassed again beyond her triangle of silky brown curls, and she shuddered. "Matt—"

"Hush," he whispered. "Hush, my darling, and let me love you."

Her head arched back as she felt his fingers unfold the most delicate of petals in search of his goal. Her lungs closed, she froze, she waited...and when he touched her, she closed her eyes and moaned. This was ecstasy. Ecstasy peaking. Nothing existed but that pouting, responsive bud. Full and moist, it reached to him as it blossomed, welcomed his fervent caress and quivered for more.

Within moments, she was panting, giddy, pleading. But he showed her no mercy. He teased her as she had teased him. He brought her higher and higher until her body was rigid and her breath short and shallow and rough. How much more of this could she take? How much more of this carnal rapture? Had he felt like this, spun mindlessly heavenward, when she had worshiped him in just such a way?

At some point—she was so delirious she didn't know when—he moved his lips from her mouth to her breasts. He kissed and sucked until she was almost out of her mind. She arched her hips, rotating against him, wanting, wanting.

His breath was hot on her belly as he kissed a fiery path to meet her arching demand. It tangled with her curls as he brushed his mouth across the dark, damp silk. It was wild and wonderful and incredible and impossible as his lips found the rosy nub throbbing exquisitely for his touch. He kissed her where no man had ever kissed before.

Her throat was so tight she could hardly swallow. Desire so intense it felt like pain. Pleasure so keen it was unbearable. And when she thought she was ready to die, he rose over her again, claimed her mouth with the taste of her still lingering on his lips and drove into her with a savagery that made her cry out.

Thunder roared, and lightning arced the heavens, and the rain drummed down all around them.

But as she matched him thrust for thrust, and they rode the galaxies together, the only storm they were aware of was their own.

WHEN IT WAS OVER, they lay side by side, drained, satiated.

Matt tightened his arms around Blair and held her as if he never wanted to let her go.

At last he expelled a reluctant sigh. "We'll have to get going," he murmured, layering kisses on her brow.

"Everybody's going to wonder where the hell I've been."

"And when they see your crumpled jacket—" Blair's voice wasn't quite steady "—what the hell you were doing!"

"I'll have to run upstairs and change. And you, my darling, will get back in your car—" He broke off. "But your car's still here, been here all day. How did you get here from Vancouver?"

"After I left my father, I took a cab to Mom's place. Borrowed her car. I'm parked halfway down the drive out of sight among the trees. But Matt, I'm not going back in the car. I'm not going anywhere."

With a frustrated mutter he got to his feet and hauled her up beside him. "Here, let's get ourselves tidied— *then* we'll fight."

She fastened her bra and blouse and got dressed. Then she put on the black jacket, twitching her shoulders irritably as rain dripped from it down the neck of her shirt. "Okay," she said, "I'm decent."

So was he. She heard the rasp of his zipper as he tugged it up, heard the rustle of fabric as he shrugged on his jacket.

"Damn!" he said. "I had an umbrella. Left it at the cottage, at the front door. Do you have your flashlight?"

"Oh." Blair fumbled on the ground, and when she found it, she scooped it up and gave it to him.

"Wait here," he said, and took off along the path.

Blair leaned against the tree.

"Wow!" she whispered. "Wow and double wow!"

For the first time in her life, she knew what it was to experience total fulfillment. The experience was one she would never forget, and she was astonished at how un-repentant she felt at having made love with a married man. She didn't feel guilty. Why should she? She'd seen Meredith being sexually provocative with the gardener, and she'd not seen one glint of affection in the blonde's eyes when she looked at Matt. All she had seen was contempt.

Matt deserved better.

And if he wanted her to be part of his future, she'd take him on any terms.

She heard his steps thumping along the path. He switched the flashlight off as he came up to her, and she felt him thrust it into her hand.

"You take it," he said. "You'll need it, to get back to the car. Blair, I want you to drive to Whistler, go to the WhitePeak. I'll give you a key to my suite. Don't answer the door for anybody but me, and I'll come to you as soon as I can." He overrode her attempts to protest. "Will you do this, please, for me?"

Oh, God. How could she not? For him, she'd do anything.

"All right, I'll go." But she let him know, by the flatness of her tone, that she was obeying him under duress.

They walked without speaking to the edge of the forest. Ahead, in the dark, lay the lawn. To the left lay the house and the river. To the right the drive and the road to Whistler.

They paused, and the wind whipped off Blair's black hood, letting the rain lash sideways against her head, soaking her hair. She paid it no heed.

He gave her the key, then gave her a brief hug. "Go now, and drive carefully."

"Matt." She placed a chilled hand on his wet cheek. "I wish you…"

"Yes, Blair—you wish…?"

She could hear a faint thread of impatience in his tone. He wanted to go, to get back before he was missed.

She bit back the words she so desperately wanted to say. *I wish you would come with me. I wish we could spend the rest of this night making love in your beautiful suite at the WhitePeak.*

Instead, she reached up, and pressed a tender kiss to his mouth. Her soul shivered as she tasted the lingering flavor of sex on his lips.

"I wish you…a happy birthday," she whispered.

And before he could respond, she sped away. Before he could hear the sobs that had broken through and were choking noisily in her throat.

SHE MEANT to do as Matt asked. She really meant to go.

But as she switched on the ignition in her mother's car, it came to her in a flash that she'd forgotten to tell him her suspicions regarding the gazebo.

She switched off the engine. Fell back in her seat.

Matt had refused to go to the police because they had no hard evidence to incriminate Richard Hunter. But suppose the gardener had come upon the shelter and was using it for illegal purposes? They would have all the hard evidence necessary to get a conviction.

And once incarcerated, he might break down and confess to all the bad stuff that had been going on here. His involvement with Meredith, for one thing, and his redheaded wife's connections to her. Connections he had concealed if they did, indeed, exist.

She couldn't drag Matt from his party, but neither did she want to wait until the party was over before having a look at the gazebo.

What was to stop her running her own investigation? Nothing.

She had her flashlight, and when she'd thrown her travel bag into the trunk, she'd seen a tire iron.

She hesitated for one more second, then gritted her teeth, opened the car door and jumped out.

THE FRENZY of the storm continued unabated.

From the gazebo, she should have been able to see the house. As she peered through the slanting downpour, all she could see was the patio. It was lit up for the party.

The lights in the pool had been shut off. The only illumination came from the huge round globe above the dining room door, under the awning.

She was far from its soft white glow.

But she was taking no chances.

With her heartbeats skittering like frightened jackrabbits, she took off her jacket and used it as a shroud to contain the beam of the flashlight. She switched it on.

MATT SLIPPED into the house by the side door and like a shadow moved up the back stairs and headed for his bedroom.

When he came out four minutes later, he was wearing a different suit, one that was almost identical to the one he'd been wearing earlier.

He ran down the stairs, weaving a tidying hand through his hair. His eyelids flickered when a pine needle came away in his fingers.

What had happened out there tonight…he'd never meant it to happen. But when he and Blair had been stuck in that closet together, with her breasts pressed to his chest and that perfume filling his head, he'd been so aroused he could have taken her there and then without a qualm. The danger presented by the man just inches away had served to heighten his awareness of her, stimulate him further.

She'd been terrified. He heard her squeak as Hunter had slammed the door shut. He thought they were done for. He stared though the slats. He could have sworn the gardener had stared right at him.

But he'd been wrong.

Hunter had muttered something about mice and had taken off.

But behind him he'd left, in his bedroom closet, a man engulfed with desire.

And in that man's arms the sweetest and most desirable woman on earth.

It had turned out to be an explosive mixture.

He glanced at his watch. Blair would be several miles away by now. And thank God for that.

He shrugged, adjusting his suit jacket. The pine needle was still in his hand.

He slid it into the jacket pocket, a smile playing along his mouth.

When he got to the foot of the stairs, the smile wanted to fade. He forced himself to keep it there as he crossed with purposeful steps to the living room.

Somebody had rolled back the carpet, the stereo was playing again, and people were dancing. He cast a purposely casual glance around, but his mind had never been more alert. Hunter was nowhere to be seen. Neither was Meredith.

Where the hell could they be?

Were they together?

THANK HEAVENS for thunder!

Blair waited with bated breath for the next deafening

peal, and when it came she crashed the tire iron on the padlock of the trapdoor she'd found beneath the duckboard, concealed by a layer of bark mulch.

When she'd seen it, her nerves had tightened until she'd thought they might snap. So she'd been right. The shelter was under the gazebo. And judging by the way Richard Hunter had tried to keep her out, he had secrets here.

She shone the flashlight into the cavernous interior. It looked like a deep well. As she played the light along the bricked walls, she saw metal rungs running down one side.

Blood roared in her ears, pounding out a message of warning. *Leave!* it said. *Go! There can be nothing down there but danger!*

She switched off the flashlight. She put on her black jacket. Kneeling with her back to the well, she edged a foot down, groping blindly for the first rung.

She hated the dark. She hated wells. Always had.

She felt sweat prick every inch of her skin, felt her heart beat like an anvil against her ribs.

She had to go down.

Slowly, carefully, she descended, her terror of the black a monster waiting to spring. On the tip of her tongue was a piercing scream, ready to rend the night at the first hint of danger.

She reached the bottom safely, felt her sandals hit the ground. Cement, by the feel of it.

Letting her breath out with a loud hiss, she leaned against the wall. The air was dank, and it ran a smothering hand over her face, almost making her cry out.

The flashlight. It should be safe to shine it here. She looked up the well, but she could see nothing, hear nothing—except the rain smashing against the gazebo roof.

She held the flashlight forward, and her shaking hand made the light waver. The place was empty. No tables, no chairs, no furniture of any kind. No guns, no stolen goods, just a big empty space, with empty shelves lining the walls. She shone the light to the ceiling. It was bare.

She'd been wrong about Richard Hunter, wrong to suspect him of using the shelter for nefarious purposes.

She'd better get out of there, close the place again. Weakly, she pushed herself from the wall.

And as she did, the light flashed to the floor in the far corner.

Something was there.

A bundle of rags, it looked like.

Unafraid, danger past, Blair moved to the corner.

She shone the flashlight directly on the—

Bile surged and burned her throat. No pile of rags, but a rumple of clothes. And wearing those clothes, a body. The small body of an Asian woman. Her round face was pale in death, her eyes open and staring. Staring at nothing.

"No!" Blair bent double as sickness churned in her stomach. It couldn't be, could it? The body of Jeannie Chang, Matt's housekeeper? Sagging against the wall, she at last managed to open her eyes and confront the horror. The horror of murder.

Oh, God, no, no, no...

She wheeled from the body, the ray of the flashlight swinging over the floor. And as it did, she saw something else.

Someone else.

The slender bulk, close by, of another body.

She stumbled forward. Her hand was so wet with

sweat the flashlight threatened to slip from her grip. She tightened her hold and with sobs heaving in her chest, forced herself to look at the second victim.

It's a nightmare, she thought. *Got to be a nightmare. I'll wake up any minute, drenched in sweat but delirious with relief to realize I fell into a bad dream.*

She closed her eyes tight, held them that way, then slowly, very slowly, opened them. And screamed. A shrill, piercing scream that should've wakened the dead—but didn't.

She recognized that face, that pale, oval face, recognized the cornflower blue eyes, the full lips, the amethyst and gold earring glinting from one small ear.

Her legs started to give way. She started to crumple to the ground. She heard her voice, thin with horror, spiraling away from her in ever-diminishing circles.

Meredith.

And her last thought, before she faded to oblivion, was that while she and Matt had been making love—adulterous love—Richard Hunter had taken Matt's wife down here, to this shelter under the gazebo, and killed her.

Chapter Fourteen

"Another Scotch?"

"Sure." Matt's voice was slurred. "Why not?" Stumbling, he crossed the patio and held his empty glass out to Richard Hunter, who was tidying the cocktail trolley, sliding stoppers into heavy crystal decanters, putting lids on bottles, emptying ashtrays into a metal bucket. "Was a great party, mmm?"

"One of the best." The gardener filled the glass, but when he proffered it, Matt waved it aside.

"Hell, give me the bottle. And have a drink yourself, why don't you?" he added as he took possession of the Scotch bottle.

"Not when I'm working, sir."

Matt shrugged. "Whatever."

He raised the bottle to his mouth and gulped a small mouthful of whiskey. It hit his gut like a ball of fire. His first drink of the night. It had been easy to keep getting his glass filled and then move out of Hunter's view, easy to dispose of the alcohol in other ways than drinking it, easy to delude the gardener into believing he was drunk.

It was imperative his mind be absolutely clear. He didn't know what was going to happen, but the tension he'd felt emanating from Hunter after he'd come from the cottage had sent him a deadly warning.

The last of the guests had left some time ago. Lord knew where Meredith had gotten to. He hadn't seen her since she'd said her goodbyes to the Thornes. Had she gone to bed? Given her newly acquired dislike for socializing, it wouldn't have surprised him. What had surprised him had been the party. He'd forgotten it was his birthday.

He leaned against the wall, eyelids drooping, and pulled his tie loose. From under his lashes, he looked with fake bleariness at the gardener and felt his heart give a rough thud. The man's eyes were aglitter with hatred, his body taut as if ready to spring.

He was going to make his move.

The air trembled with malevolent intent.

Matt let the bottle slip out of his hand and pretended a startled jump when it crashed to the brick surface and shattered.

"Damn!" He bent, gripped the broken bottle by the neck. The perfect weapon. "My drink. I los' my drink." Every cell in his body was ready to defend or attack.

But when he uncoiled himself and straightened, wobbling convincingly, he was unprepared for the sight facing him.

Richard Hunter had come out from behind the drinks trolley. He was standing with his back to it, with his back to the gazebo and to the heavy mist that had fallen over the valley after the storm passed.

And in his hand, pointed steadily at Matt, was a gun.

"OH, GOD...OH, GOD, let me out of here!"

Out of here... Blair's voice was thrown at her from the walls of the bunker, hollow, mocking as she scram-

bled across the floor in a hysterical flight from the dead
bodies she'd found.

Found *when?*

She pushed the flashlight into her pocket and started
climbing. Fingers like thin claws around each rung, one
at a time.

A hoarse gasp as she slipped, a rush of strangled
breath as she regained her footing. Hours ago. It was
hours since she'd passed out. She'd needed only a fleeting, horrified glance at her illuminated watch face to
tell her that. She'd been lying on that foul floor—with
two corpses a hand sweep away—for several hours. The
guests would be gone, and Matt would be alone with a
murderer.

It seemed to take forever to reach the top, and when
she at last scrambled into the gazebo, it took a moment
for her to realize that something had changed.

The rain had stopped. That was it. The wind had
ceased, and the storm was over. But in its place was
fog. Fog so thick she could see nothing. Her flashlight
was useless. It would never penetrate this suffocating
blanket.

She stood, trying to listen, but her breath kept catching on ragged, tearing sobs. This was terror. Absolute
terror. The terror of not knowing.

Richard Hunter had killed twice. He was ruthless. He
would be prepared to kill again.

If Matt was already dead, was the gardener at this
very moment dragging his lifeless body across the lawn
to bury it with his other victims in this perfect hiding
place?

The thought spurred her to action.

As she crept from the gazebo onto the lawn and

started in the direction of the patio, she told herself she
had to keep faith that Matt was still alive.

Did he know Meredith was dead?

Was he—as she was—racked with guilt because
while they'd been making love, such beautiful love,
Richard Hunter was murdering Matt's beautiful blond
wife?

After creeping forward for what seemed like forever,
she heard the crunch of gravel under her sandals and
realized she'd lost her way and was in the forecourt.

It took her a few minutes to ascertain that the vehicles
remaining belonged there. She'd been right, then. The
party was over.

She'd never known such stillness. And in that stillness, she smelled evil. It drifted to her nostrils with the
fog, the tendrils of it making her feel sick.

Sick, and with the nausea churning in her stomach, a
frenzy of fear twisted in her brain.

She had to get to Matt. Had to tell him about the
bodies. Had to warn him.

But she must be quiet, and she must try to be calm.

She took five or six steadying breaths, then, on tip-
toes, keeping her steps as light as she could, she found
the wall of the house. Touching it with her fingertips,
she felt her way along until she rounded the building to
the back.

The fog was thick. Like charcoal cotton wool, but
wet on her skin.

Heart in her mouth, she moved forward, and at the
sound of voices ahead, loud voices, she froze.

And listened. With every cell desperately strained,
she listened.

Matt's voice. She identified it first. Relief swept over

her like a blessing. Thank you, God, oh, thank you, God.

But who was he talking to?

The other voice came to her, harsh, contemptuous and oh, so familiar. She clenched a fist over her mouth to crush her cry of dismay. The other voice was that of Richard Hunter.

Head tilted, eyes closed, she stood and listened for another minute. But though she couldn't make out what was being said, she heard no other voices. As she'd feared, Matt was alone with the murderer.

And though their voices could be heard only faintly, the tone was clear. Richard Hunter had the upper hand.

Tears clogged her throat as anxiety ripped through her. She moved forward an inch at a time, hardly daring to breathe. And at last, through the tattered edges of the fog, she saw the patio. She stepped sideways behind a tall shrub.

The gardener was standing with his back to her. He was in front of the drinks trolley, and he was facing Matt. Matt was leaning against the wall, a broken whiskey bottle in his hand. His face was white, brightly illuminated by a round globe of light from above. His hair was disheveled, his tie awry—

He was drunk! Good lord…Matt was drunk!

But as the gardener gestured arrogantly with his right hand, Blair felt a scream of terror in her soul.

Richard Hunter was wielding a gun.

And he had it pointed straight at Matt.

"SO YOU SEE—" the gardener sneered "—you've reached the end of the road, Straith. I'm going to shoot you in the head, then I'm going to plant the gun in your hand. Everyone's going to believe you've killed yourself.''

"Not logical…least, not from where I'm standin'.'' Matt blinked and scratched his head. "See, if a guy kills himself, he's gotta have a motive. And I sure as hell can't figure out what motive I'd—''

"No, you don't see it, do you? Okay, here's how the story's gonna go. Mrs. Straith—'' his tone held ironic amusement "—got her memory back this morning, and she told your little sweetie pie from Vancouver that you were the one who kidnapped her. Now, thing is, Mrs. Straith was planning to go to the police with her story tomorrow, but she made the mistake of warning you first, and you knew the game was up, so you decided to call it quits and kill yourself.''

"Yeah," Matt said slowly, so slowly he sounded as if he was on the point of dropping off to sleep, "yeah, but—''

He threw himself sideways, and at the same time hurled the broken bottle at the gardener.

It might have worked had it not been for the spilled whiskey. He skidded on it and lost his balance, ruining his aim. But it also threw off the gardener's aim, and his shot went wide, ricocheting against the wall.

Matt scrambled to his feet, but Hunter already had the gun fixed on him again.

"Freeze!''

Matt froze.

"So,'' Hunter said musingly, "not so drunk, after all. You're cleverer than I thought, Straith, but still not quite clever enough. Now—'' his laugh was hard "—if you're a praying man, it's time to say a word, one last word, to the man in the sky. And then you're history.''

BLAIR HAD taken advantage of all the noise to creep around the patio, concealed by the fog.

She wasn't sure what she was going to do. All she knew was she had to distract the gardener. And do it now.

Her arms were twined around her in a vain effort to keep her shudders under control. She winced as the flashlight in her pocket pressed painfully against her breast.

And that was when her idea came.

Pulse accelerating erratically, she pulled the flashlight out.

And using every iota of strength at her disposal, she hurled the heavy metal flashlight at the huge picture window. With an explosion so loud it almost stopped her heart, it crashed through the glass.

Hunter whirled toward the window at the sound and fired straight at the spot where the flashlight had gone through.

Blair wanted to shout, "Get him, Matt!" But no sound came from her throat.

It would have been unnecessary anyway. Matt needed no urging. He lunged at the gardener, tackled him with all the brutality and finesse of a professional rugby star, and brought him to the ground. The gun went flying.

But even as Blair felt the beginnings of a trembling relief and was about to move forward and retrieve the gun, she was stopped by the sound of a blood-curdling scream coming from the dark interior of the room behind the broken window.

She stared, incredulously, as a pale figure walked with the jerky steps of a robot toward the enormous opening in the glass.

Meredith, clothed in white satin with bright red blood

seeping through her dress in the shape of a bedraggled crimson blossom.

Directly over her heart.

I'm losing my mind. Blair fell to her knees. *I'm losing my mind. I've just seen Meredith. Meredith's dead. Already dead. And under the gazebo.*

The tableau could have been fashioned of stone. For an endless moment, nothing moved. No sound was made. Then as the copiously bleeding figure took two staggering steps toward them and pitched facedown to her death on the lethally jagged glass, Richard Hunter gave an enraged howl.

"Annie!"

Annie? Blair did a double take. What? She could tell Matt was equally stunned, but her bewilderment was immediately overtaken by dismay when she saw that Matt's shock kept him off guard. He momentarily loosened his hold on the other man.

The gardener took full advantage. In one violent movement, he shoved Matt off him and surged to his feet. Matt scrambled up, too, but he wasn't quick enough.

Hunter snatched up his gun and trained it on his opponent.

His back was to Blair.

Neither of the men had seen her yet.

And neither seemed to have connected the shattered window with an outside force.

Blair felt a terrible, icy-cold rage at Hunter swell inside her as, showing all the signs of a mind gone mad, he jeered at Matt.

"You thought she was your wife, didn't you! All along, you thought she was your wife. She wasn't your

wife. She was your wife's twin sister! My wife! Annie—''

Matt's eyes were stark, his expression haunted.
''What the hell have you done with Meredith, you bastard?''

''Dead. Long dead. And buried.'' The gardener's
cackle made Blair's hair stand on end. ''And don't tell
me you're sorry. I heard the pair of you fighting that
night after you went upstairs—oh, you didn't know that,
did you! I was on the balcony. I heard her shouting at
you, telling you how you weren't so smart, after all,
finding out she'd been having an affair. She'd had dozens. And then she went on to rub your face in it—told
you that all these years when you'd been trying so hard
to start a family, the family you wanted so bad, she was
playing you for a fool. She'd never wanted a kid, and
she had her tubes tied the week before you got married—''

''Where is she, you filthy creep?''

Blair's head was spinning. She could hardly believe
what she'd heard. So that's why Matt had wanted to
divorce Meredith.

''Where is she?'' Hunter sneered. ''I'll tell you where
she is. She's with that nosy old lady, Jeannie Chang.''

''Where, damn you?''

Hunter paused melodramatically. And then he said,
in a voice that was corroded with hate, ''Under the gazebo.''

With a steady hand, he aimed the gun.

''Why did Mrs. Chang have to die?''

Matt must be boiling with fury and in total shock,
but he was still endeavoring to play for time. Urgency

twisted a knot in Blair's belly. What could time do for him?

Everything was up to her.

"Mrs. Chang? The old lady had to go because she found out too much! She picked up the phone one day and by chance heard something she shouldn't have heard—"

Hunter's voice followed Blair as she moved like a wraith inside the sheltering cover of the fog. She knew that when she stepped onto the patio, his back would be to her. Matt's wouldn't. He would be facing her.

And he would see her.

Would he be able to keep his astonishment from showing? Or would he start, widen his eyes, utter an involuntary exclamation?

If he did, they were both as good as dead. Hunter would whirl and fire. He would shoot her, then he would shoot Matt.

Their lives depended on Matt's ability to keep his responses under control. Could he do it?

She sent up a silent prayer.

One that might be her last.

"Why did you set Annie loose on Cougar Mountain?" Matt spoke as coolly as if he was involved in party chitchat.

"Because that's where the cabin was, where she'd been staying." The gardener's tone was contemptuous, and Blair realized he felt smugly superior to Matt. "I had to keep her hidden. I knew there'd be pictures of your wife in the media. I couldn't risk someone seeing Annie and—"

"Noticing the resemblance, thinking she was Meredith."

"Okay, Straith, enough."

''Just one more thing. How did you manage to get Meredith off Blackcomb?''

Hunter's laugh set Blair's teeth on edge.

''Your wife,'' he jeered, ''was never on the mountain that day. She was already dead and in the bunker. You played right into my hands when you took off on that fishing trip. I told your sweet wife that I'd found something below the gazebo, and once I got her down there—'' he made a choking sound ''—that was it.''

Blair slipped off her sandals, left them on the wet grass and stepped silently out of the fog. Her heart was hammering so hard she wondered that they didn't hear it. It was the only sound she heard, save for the steady drip of rain from the roof. Hunter had stopped talking. She sensed his tension, knew he was about to make his move.

She knew the exact moment Matt spotted her. Knew it only because his lips parted. Nothing else. And she felt an immense wave of relief sweep over her.

She glided forward until she reached the drinks trolley.

From it, she chose the largest, heaviest crystal decanter, one filled to the stopper with sherry. She lifted it with the utmost care, biting her lip as she concentrated on keeping it away from the other bottles and containers.

When she had it safely in her hands, she gripped the long, narrow neck like a baseball bat. She moved, black as midnight and as silent, until she was three feet from the gardener.

Behind him.

And slightly to his right.

''Okay, Straith.'' Hunter's voice was high with ex-

citement and anticipation. "Enough small talk. Prepare
to die."

Blair braced herself as she'd done before hurling the
flashlight. She heard a faint click. The safety catch on
the gun being released? She swung the decanter back
to gain momentum. And then, taking in a steady breath,
she swung it forward, with all her might, to hit the gardener's skull.

"I THOUGHT—" Matt walked toward her. He appeared
to be moving in slow motion. "I told you to go to the
WhitePeak."

"Oh, Matt," Blair fell into his arms, grabbed tight,
afraid she was going to pass out. "I thought he was
going to kill you. I thought—"

He folded her in a fierce embrace. "Shh," he whispered into her hair. "You were magnificent, absolutely
magnificent. When I saw you come up behind him, I
almost... And was it you who broke the window? You
threw—"

"The flashlight." Tears smarted behind her eyes.
They welled up, rimmed over, started trickling down
her cheeks. "Oh, Matt, I found the shelter. It's under
the gazebo. I went down and found—"

"You went under there?" He took her by the shoulders, held her and looked at her incredulously. "My
God."

"It was awful. A nightmare. Meredith's body, and
Jeannie Chang's." She began to sob convulsively, and
he pulled her into his embrace again, holding her so
close she could hardly breathe. But she needed it,
needed his support. Just a few feet away lay Hunter's
wife, Annie. A shudder scraped through her. And Hunter. Blair felt a tearing pain. She'd killed him!

"It's all over now, Blair." Matt's voice was steady, reassuring, but she knew that he must be just as heart-sore as she was. "It's been a bad nightmare. But very soon now it'll all be over."

But would it? Even as she listened to him trying to comfort her, even as she tried to keep her body from shaking, the horrors crowded down on her. And even as she listened to him, she could smell the blood from Annie's dead body, could smell Hunter's evil lingering in the air, could almost smell the sweet and pungent scent of fresh tobacco from one of Jason's cheroots. The memory of that night in the hospital was so strong, so smotheringly strong—

A scuffling sound came from behind them, and they whirled.

Oh, dear God.

Hunter wasn't dead. She'd just knocked him unconscious. And he'd come to. He was still lying where he fell, but he'd managed to reach his gun, and it was now, albeit waveringly, fixed on Blair.

"Don't move." Blood ran down his skull and dripped on the bricks. "You stupid—you could've been safe if you'd stayed away. Now you're both going to die."

Gun still pointed at her, he started working his way to his feet.

Blair thought she was going out of her mind. Death stared her in the face, but she couldn't focus on any-thing but the scent of tobacco, the scent so thick in her nostrils it seemed real. Seemed not to be a figment of her fevered brain. It was getting stronger by the mo-ment, and she could have sworn it was coming to her through the fog.

The sense of an invisible presence was so intense she braced herself. If he tried to help, she'd be ready.

But the gun. It was fixed on her, waveringly, but still dangerously.

Crash!

Darkness!

As the white globe above the door exploded, she leaped toward Matt, almost bowling him over.

She heard the crack of a gunshot, heard a voice from the mist. ''Run!''

Brandon's voice.

But she and Matt were already running.

They stumbled into the fog, rounded the hedge, Matt's hoarse, breathless voice rasping to her ears.

She could hear Hunter behind them, hear him swearing, but the sounds were soon lost to the violent rush of blood in her head as she and Matt careened on.

It seemed like forever before they reached the greenhouse. Then they were inside. In the pitch dark. The smell of exotic flowers thick in the warm, moist air.

Without a sound, Matt closed the door.

''Let's go to the back,'' he whispered. ''Give us time to catch our breath. He won't come in here. He'll think we'd headed for the house.''

Blair jumped as the door crashed open.

Blinked and cringed backward as the lights came on and flooded the greenhouse with white.

''I know you're in here!'' Hunter yelled. ''And you won't get out alive!''

Blair started to shake. Matt pulled her noiselessly under the long table, behind some empty boxes. Her heart wasn't going to make it, she knew that. Any moment now, terror was going to stop it forever.

She felt Matt's lips at her ear.

''That was Brandon,'' he whispered. ''He must have thrown one of his stones. Brilliant aim.''

''D-do you th-think he g-got away?'' Blair's stuttered words broke off sharply when she heard furtive footsteps. Coming closer…and closer.

She curled up, closed her eyes tight, tried to make herself as small as she could, tried to edge back but found she could go no farther. A low shelf was in her way. Something sharp dug into her neck, and she stifled a cry.

She reached to feel for whatever it was and push it aside, and her pulses gave a dizzy leap when she realized she was holding the vicious-looking curved knife she'd seen the gardener with the day she'd come looking for Meredith.

''I know you're there, though I can't see you…yet!'' Hunter's menacing warning made the hair at her nape rise.

Trembling, she fumbled for Matt's hand. When she found it, he made to grasp it, obviously thinking she wanted comfort, support.

What she wanted was his male strength, and his courage.

''Take this,'' she breathed in his ear.

Matt frowned. *What… My God, it's a knife.* He grasped the warm wooden handle tightly.

And waited.

Listened. Waited. Braced.

The footsteps were so close now, the floor vibrated slightly with each small pressure. And with each vibration, he silently sent up another prayer.

Help me with this. Help me keep her safe.

''I'm coming to get you.'' The gardener's voice had a singsong tone like the voice of a child playing hide and seek. "I'm coming to get you... Here I come, ready or not!" He gave a laugh that was pure evil.

He walked by them, mere inches away. Matt felt the faint draft of air, saw the blur of black trousers.

He waited two seconds, then he slowly, carefully, and without the slightest sound glided sideways from the boxes and uncoiled himself from his crouching position.

He leaped blindly. Grabbed Hunter from behind. Locked him in a savage hold with one arm. Heard him grunt. Felt his unleashed power. The crazed animal power of a madman. A madman who was about to turn his gun on Blair.

With that one thought in mind, Matt threw up a prayer for forgiveness and ripped the knife's sharp blade cleanly across the gardener's throat.

BRANDON STOOD in the open doorway, his brain staggering, his emotions roiling.

He'd already been in the bunker, found the two corpses there. That had been enough shock for one night. Then, when he'd stumbled in the fog to the patio, he'd seen another body lying across the shattered window. And now...

He gawked in disbelief at the scene before him.

The Straiths' houseguest was crouched by a long table, crying hysterically.

Richard Hunter, the High Meadows gardener, was lying dead on the planked floor. His neck had been slashed. Blood was everywhere.

Straith was leaning against the table, a crimson-stained knife in his hand, and he looked as if he was going to throw up at any moment.

Brandon said awkwardly, "Must have been a hell of a party."

Chapter Fifteen

Meredith's memorial service was held in the Kitsilano church she'd attended as a child. The service was private, and following it, her coffin was laid to rest alongside Jane Grigor's in a nearby graveyard.

When the small group of mourners emerged from the cemetery, Matt, Blair and her mother were immediately surrounded by members of the media who blocked their way as they tried to get to Matt's car.

Blair clung weakly to one of Matt's arms, Sara Enderby to the other, as reporters rammed mikes in their faces and hurled questions at them.

"How come your wife never knew she had a twin sister, Mr. Straith?"

"Blair?" Blair recognized Lee Po, a reporter from the *Vancouver Sun.* "Where do you fit into the picture?"

"Is it true you've been involved in an affair with Matt Straith?"

"Mrs. Enderby—" a bulky middle-aged journalist obstructed Blair's mother "—your husband was Jane Grigor's gynecologist. Did he deliver both twins? Is this a grim example of the good twin, evil twin syndrome? How much—"

"Give us a break, fellas." Matt shouldered the reporters aside and somehow managed to make a path through the jostling journalists and camera people. "You'll get your answers in good time. Right now, we need some space."

Cameras whirred. Flashbulbs exploded. Someone's equipment jolted Blair's hip. She clutched Matt's arm more tightly. Felt his muscles bunch under his black suit jacket. She was thankful for his protection. She knew she could trust him to get them safely out of this.

He did. Finally, they made it to the car. Matt bundled Blair and her mother into the front seat, slammed the door, then he fought his way around the hood. After tussling briefly with one particularly aggressive cameraman, he managed to open his door and get inside.

He ignored the faces, the cameras pressing against the car windows, and took off along the street, slowly at first and then gathering speed. Within minutes they'd left the media behind.

Blair felt her mother's arm go around her.

"Are you all right, baby?" she asked softly.

Blair slumped. "That was ghastly, wasn't it? But it's over now. And thank heavens for that."

It was over, but she still felt stunned. So stunned, she couldn't think, couldn't get her mind to work. The only thing working was her stomach. It had started to heave when the reporters had stuck the mikes in her face, and it was still heaving. She pressed a hand to it. She didn't feel well, didn't feel well at all.

"Matt, let's go to my place, it's closer than Blair's." Her mother's voice floated dimly over her head. "It will be better. Some of the reporters will be on their way right now to Blair's building, hoping to catch her as she goes in."

"Yeah." Matt's voice seemed to come from a distance, "That might be a good idea. What's the address?"

Nausea swam through Blair, ebbing and flowing like a tide. Her head was spinning, as was the world around her. Vaguely she heard her mother giving Matt directions.

"We're going to find dust everywhere," Sara went on. "My plane was late leaving Heathrow and by the time the cab got me from the airport to the condo this morning, I just had time to splash my face and change my clothes before I took off again. The cabbie got me to the church with seconds to spare."

"I'm glad you could make it. Blair needs you. She's been through hell." Matt's fingers tightened on the steering wheel. "She was the one who found the bodies."

With a panicky sob, Blair tried to swallow the bitter bile rising in her throat. "Matt." She clutched his arm as the heaving waves became more forceful. "Pull over. Quick. I'm going to be sick."

THE BEDROOM was shadowed, her mother's palm on her brow cool.

"How are you feeling now, baby?"

Blair tried to focus as her mother turned on the bedside lamp. A pink glow lit up the room. She'd just wakened, and the moment she stirred, she sensed someone close by. She saw her mother sitting on a chair, her cap of brown curls disheveled, her eyes dark with anxiety.

"Mom?"

"Yes, baby?"

"What time is it?"

"Late. It's almost midnight."

"Good Lord, I've slept almost around the clock." Blair pushed herself groggily on her elbow. "Where's Matt?"

"In the living room. He's been beside himself with worry. Blair—" She broke off, but her voice had held a tentative question.

Blair sank back on her pillows and sighed. "I love him, Mom." Her smile was wistful. "I've loved him since I was eighteen. There'll never be anyone else for me."

A sound at the door made her glance over, and her heart missed a beat when she saw Matt standing there.

"So," he said quietly, "how's the invalid?"

She wasn't sure if he'd heard her or not. She wasn't sure she cared. He already knew how she felt about him.

He'd never said he loved her, although he had promised her that if Meredith regained her memory, he'd be on her doorstep wanting much more than friendship.

He was free now. But would he want to become involved with another woman after everything that had happened? He'd seen so much betrayal, treachery, evil.

"I'm fine," she said, glad the light was subdued so he wouldn't see the yearning in her eyes. She plucked at the high neck of her nightgown, a beribboned cotton affair her mother had loaned her after she'd bathed. "Embarrassed, though. It couldn't have been a pretty sight, to see me throwing up in the gutter of one of Kitsilano's classiest streets!"

"Not a pretty sight, but a welcome one," he said as he came to stand over her. "Only living, breathing people can throw up, and you, thank God, are alive."

She'd never seen him look so intense, so strained. With a gesture, she invited him to sit down, and the mattress dipped as he took a seat at the end of the bed.

"There's so much I still don't understand," she murmured. "I always believed Meredith was an only child. Jane Grigor was under Daddy's care for several weeks before she delivered—"

"Annie wasn't born here," Sara said. "She was born more than two months before Meredith, in a Toronto hospital. And if I'd known how important that information would have been to you, if I'd known it might have saved you from danger, I'd have revealed Jane's secret without a qualm."

"Daddy told you?" Blair asked.

"Yes, but no one else. Jane had made him promise."

"Why did she give up one twin for adoption but not the other?" Blair asked. "It doesn't make sense."

"It does when you know the whole story."

"Tell us," Matt said. "The truth can harm no one now."

Sara's wedding ring caught the light as she clasped her hands together on her lap. "Jane Grigor was a single woman of thirty-nine when she met—well, let's call him Mr. Smith. I don't recall his name, and it's not important. This Mr. Smith took over the company where she worked, and she became his private secretary. He was very wealthy and successful and had a high profile in the Toronto business world. He was also married. And fifteen years older than Jane."

"She fell in love with him?" Blair suggested.

"Mm. They had an affair. I think he loved her, too, but everything came crashing down when Jane discovered she was pregnant. She didn't believe in abortion, so he gave her an ultimatum—give up the child for adoption at birth, or the relationship's over. Now this is where things take a bizarre twist. Can you guess what happened next?"

"She loved him," Blair said, "so she wouldn't want to lose him. She agreed to go along with his demand."

"Right," Sara said. "And then?"

"Did she know she was expecting twins?" Matt asked.

"Yes, she knew."

Matt scraped a hand over his jaw. "Then I'd say she went into labor early, and the first baby was born. But the doctors managed to stop the other birth."

"Right. And a short time after signing that baby away, she realized she'd made a mistake. She wanted a child even more than she wanted Mr. Smith. So she stayed in the hospital just long enough to regain her strength, and then, without letting her lover know what she was planning, she snuck out of the hospital, took a cab to the airport and flew to Vancouver."

"To a new life." Blair's eyes were wide. "Wow!"

"She picked your father's name out of the Yellow Pages, they clicked, and she trusted him with her secret."

"Whoever would have thought, knowing Jane Grigor, that she had such a secret in her past?" Matt's eyes met Blair's. "She was always so open, honest."

"She must have regretted, to her dying day, giving up that first twin," Blair said. "It must have broken her heart. But Annie, Richard Hunter's wife...she had me completely fooled. In looks she was identical to Meredith, and she walked like Meredith, with that sexy little wiggle, and talked like Meredith, same husky mocking voice."

"All that's quite understandable in identical twins, baby."

"I know, Mom. But when she told me she'd gotten her memory back, she reeled off a whole lot of stuff about the past that I don't see how she could possibly have known. She knew the color of the dresses Meredith and I wore the first day at school.''

"She could have seen photos," Sara murmured.

"All right, but she talked about the way Daddy used to hoist Meredith up on his shoulders. She even knew about a double date Meredith and I went on at sixteen, when we both had too much wine and got sick and we swore we'd never tell anyone in the world about that! How on earth did Annie—"

"I can answer that, Blair," Matt said soberly. "Do you remember those illustrated journals Meredith kept from the time she was quite small? Her diaries? She kept them all, and Annie had access to them. The police found them in Hunter's cottage, along with the videos."

"Those innocent-seeming videos Hunter shot of Meredith, they were for Annie to study so she could do all the things Meredith could do?"

"Except—" Matt's mouth thinned "—the pottery. She couldn't do that. She didn't have the skill. So she smashed Meredith's work to give the impression she was no longer interested in carrying on with her career."

"Their plan was so cold-blooded." Blair shuddered. "So evil."

"Richard Hunter was at the root of it," Matt said.

"But his wife played right along," Sara added.

"The police have discovered that Annie was his second wife," Matt said. "That photo by his bedside, Blair? He must have planted it there, I guess for the very purpose it eventually served. It threw us completely off the track."

"What happened to the first wife?" Sara asked.

"Killed by a drunk driver, apparently," Matt said.

"A guy who could afford a high-priced lawyer to buy himself off. There's no doubt Hunter felt as bitter as Annie did, and resentful of people with money. Annie did have a rough time as a child."

"How so?" Sara asked.

"Police have checked into records from the social services, and apparently the couple who adopted her were decent. But when Annie was three, her adoptive father died, and the mother got involved with an abusive alcoholic who didn't want a child around. Annie ended up in a foster home, where she had some horrific experiences. It seems that after she and Hunter got married two years ago, they set out to track down her birth mother. They not only succeeded, they found out Annie had an identical twin. We can assume that when Annie learned that her twin had not only had an idyllic childhood but was now married to somebody with lots of money, she was consumed by jealousy."

"And she and Hunter decided to get a share of the pot," Blair murmured.

"Not a share," Matt said. "They wanted it all. And their plan, what we've patched together, was diabolical. Hunter was to come out here and get a job, then watch Meredith, tape her, record her, so he could groom Annie to take her place. Police have photos of Annie from before, and they've deduced that Meredith's three-month 'disappearance' was to help account for the change in Meredith's weight. Annie had been much thinner. Hunter had to hack off Annie's hair because, though it had been long like Meredith's, unlike Meredith's, Annie's had been wrecked after years of bleaching and perming."

"And the amnesia ploy would have been to cover up Annie's ignorance of things past. Camouflage any mis-

takes she might make.'' Blair sighed. ''It was all there
for us to see, only we couldn't see it. Jason came clos-
est. He kept saying the eyes were different.''

''And Poppy,'' Matt said. ''She did tell me that Meredith's auras had changed. I paid no heed.''

''So if Hunter had killed you, and assuming everyone
believed you'd committed suicide, what next?'' Sara
asked.

''I guess he and Annie would eventually have married, once all the interest had died down.''

''What about the bruises, Annie's bruises?''

''I was hoping you wouldn't ask that.'' Matt looked
grimly at Blair. ''Turns out Hunter was a wife beater.
Annie had laid charges against him on a couple of occasions but had dropped them both times. He was a
cruel man as well as a ruthless one.''

Silence filled the room for a long moment, except for
the tick of the bedside clock.

It was Sara who eventually broke it.

''I still don't understand how he could have gotten
Meredith from Blackcomb without anyone seeing
them.''

''He told us Meredith was never up the mountain that
day,'' Matt said. ''Annie took her place.''

''Yes, but that doesn't answer the question of how
she managed to slip away—oh!'' Blair put a hand to
her mouth. ''Matt, remember the day the three of us
went up to the hut? And Meredith—Annie—went to the
washroom but took off her bright blue jacket and put
on a floppy taupe sunhat before she came back? I didn't
even notice her, she looked so nondescript, all in taupe.
Do you think that's what she did on that other occasion?
Changed from her fuchsia outfit into something drab?''

''And then with her face hidden by her wraparound

glasses, she could sneak away without attracting the attention of one single soul. Yeah.'' Matt nodded. ''That would explain it. And from there, she could walk into the village and—to all intents and purposes—disappear.''

''The mind,'' Sara said wearily, ''boggles.''

She got to her feet and stretched.

''Well, folks, I'm going to call it a night.'' She bent and kissed Blair's cheek. ''Sleep tight, baby, and I'll see you in the morning.'' She straightened. ''Matt, I can't tell you how good it is to have you with us again.''

She yawned daintily as she made for the door.

When she reached it, she paused and turned.

''Oh, by the way, Matt.'' Her eyes held the faintest twinkle. ''The guest room…it's at the very far end of the hall.''

Matt cleared his throat. ''Right, Mrs. Enderby.'' He'd gotten to his feet when she did. He shuffled like an ill at ease teenager. ''The end. The very far end.''

''Well, good night.''

She went out, but left the door slightly ajar.

Matt chuckled softly, and Blair's heart jolted when he kicked off his shoes and lay on the double bed alongside her. His face was close to hers. His arm came around her.

''She doesn't trust me, does she?'' The edges of his mouth twitched.

''Should she?'' Blair traced a finger lightly over his upper lip.

He gathered her close, and even through the blankets, she could feel the muscled strength of his arms, the firm steadiness of his embrace.

''It's been a hell of a day,'' he murmured. ''All I want to do tonight is lie with you.'' He nuzzled her neck, and she shivered as his breath caressed a sensitive spot. "Okay?"

"Of course."

"But tomorrow—" he kissed her once on the lips and drew in the scent of vanilla and violets "—is another day."

"It is indeed." She returned his kiss with one of her own, one that told him everything that was in her heart.

"We never did finish that interview." His voice was fading, and she realised he must be dropping off. Little wonder. He'd had next to no sleep for the past four days. Besides which, he'd killed a man, and he had just hours ago buried his wife.

"And I don't like to leave things half done." His words were coming out more drowsily by the second. "So what I want to know is, how much time do you reckon we'll need to spend together before you know me well enough to write about the truly private life of Matt Straith?"

"The truly private life of Matt Straith?" Blair drew in a deep breath. Did he mean what she thought he meant? "How much time can you give me?" She felt shy, trembling, uncertain.

"I can give you forever—" his voice was husky "—if that's what you want."

He had opened his eyes. They locked sleepily with hers, and his love enfolded her like the warmth of summer.

"Forever—" she smiled through tears of joy and hugged him tight "—sounds absolutely fine to me."

WHEN SARA ENDERBY came out of her bedroom the next morning, she noticed that Blair's bedroom door was ajar.

She crept to it and peeked in, expecting to find her daughter in bed, asleep, and alone.

She was in bed. And she was asleep.

But she was not alone.

Lying beside her, on the covers, with his arms around her, was Matt.

Sara stood for a long moment drinking in the sight, feeling happiness soar inside her. She had always liked Matt. And so had Alex. In fact, they had shared a secret hope, many years ago, that Matt and Blair would end up together.

Without a sound, Sara softly closed the door.

She would go to the kitchen, brew herself a quick cup of coffee, then drive over to the nursing home.

She couldn't wait to share the news with Alex.

There was going to be a wedding in the family!

SILHOUETTE

INTRIGUE™

COMING NEXT MONTH

UNFORGETTABLE NIGHT Kelsey Roberts

Shadows & Spice

Matt Tanner had a gift for solving mysteries that baffled the experts and DeLancey Jones needed his help. She was haunted by a recurring nightmare which made her too afraid to remember her childhood before the age of fifteen. But would finding her past threaten her chance of a future with Matt?

FRAMED Karen Leabo

Before Detective Kyle Branson met Jess Robinson, he was sure she was involved in her ex-boyfriend's disappearance. She had motive, means *and* opportunity. But once he'd met this beautiful woman, he desperately wanted to believe her story. Was he being played for a fool, or had she really been set up?

A ONE-WOMAN MAN M.L. Gamble

Elizabeth Monette had returned to her home town to find out the truth about her mother's murder. Knowing the killer was still out there, she hired Tommy Lee McCall as protection. This sexy cop could probably stop a bullet with his bare hands, but could she survive his brand of *hands-on* attention?

FUGITIVE FATHER Jean Barrett

Noah Rhyder was a fugitive from justice, accused of a crime he hadn't committed, and his one priority was to find his son. If the only way to do this was to kidnap Ellie Mathieson, the boy's foster mother, he'd do it! He must convince Ellie that she was in danger from the real murderer—and so was his son.

COMING NEXT MONTH FROM

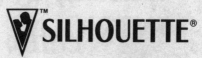

™ SILHOUETTE®

Sensation

A thrilling mix of passion, adventure and drama

ROARKE'S WIFE Beverly Barton
WHILE SHE WAS SLEEPING Diane Pershing
PARTNERS IN PARENTHOOD Raina Lynn
UNDERCOVER COWBOY Beverly Bird

Special Edition

Satisfying romances packed with emotion

OLDER, WISER...PREGNANT Marilyn Pappano
THE MAIL-ORDER MIX-UP Pamela Toth
THE COWBOY'S IDEAL WIFE Victoria Pade
HOT CHOCOLATE HONEYMOON Cathy Gillen Thacker
MEANT TO BE MARRIED Ruth Wind
THE BODYGUARD'S BRIDE Jean Brashear

Desire

Provocative, sensual love stories

THE LIONESS TAMER Rebecca Brandewyne
FIONA AND THE SEXY STRANGER Marie Ferrarella
MILLIONAIRE DAD Leanne Banks
THE COWBOY AND THE CALENDAR GIRL Nancy Martin
THE RANCHER'S SPITTING IMAGE Peggy Moreland
NON-REFUNDABLE GROOM Patty Salier

2 FREE

books and a surprise gift!

We would like to take this opportunity to thank you for reading this Silhouette® book by offering you the chance to take TWO more specially selected titles from the Intrigue™ series absolutely FREE! We're also making this offer to introduce you to the benefits of the Reader Service™—

- ★ FREE home delivery
- ★ FREE gifts and competitions
- ★ FREE monthly Newsletter
- ★ Exclusive Reader Service discounts
- ★ Books available before they're in the shops

Accepting these FREE books and gift places you under no obligation to buy, you may cancel at any time, even after receiving your free shipment. Simply complete your details below and return the entire page to the address below. *You don't even need a stamp!*

YES! Please send me 2 free Intrigue books and a surprise gift. I understand that unless you hear from me, I will receive 4 superb new titles every month for just £2.70 each, postage and packing free. I am under no obligation to purchase any books and may cancel my subscription at any time. The free books and gift will be mine to keep in any case.

I9EA

Ms/Mrs/Miss/Mr ....Initials....................................
BLOCK CAPITALS PLEASE

Surname ....

Address ....

....

....Postcode.............................

Send this whole page to:
THE READER SERVICE, FREEPOST CN81, CROYDON, CR9 3WZ
(Eire readers please send coupon to: P.O. BOX 4546, DUBLIN 24.)